Also by Rin Chupeco

The Girl from the Well
The Suffering
The Sacrifice

THE BONE WITCH TRILOGY
The Bone Witch
The Heart Forger
The Shadowglass

A HUNDRED NAMES FOR MAGIC
Wicked as You Wish
An Unreliable Magic
The World's End

Praise for *The Sacrifice*

★ "Rin Chupeco's newest story is as terrifying as it is riveting, and you will not put the book down until you know each character's fate."

—*Youth Services Book Review*, Starred Review

"Chupeco creates an environment thick with mystery, full of haunting balete trees and eerie ghost sightings coupled with a legend that dates to Spanish colonization of the Philippines."

—*Kirkus Reviews*

"This thriller captures the creepiness of classic slow-burn horror movies... Chupeco is a master."

—*Booklist*

"Chilling horror elements that coalesce into a bittersweet conclusion."

—*Publishers Weekly*

"The blisteringly fast pace and Chupeco's deft use of horror tropes to examine broader social themes means *The Sacrifice* is a horror tale that goes down easy."

—*Paste* Magazine

Praise for *The Girl from the Well*

★ "Chupeco makes a powerful debut with this unsettling ghost story... Told in a marvelously disjointed fashion from Okiku's numbers-obsessed point of view, this story unfolds with creepy imagery and an intimate appreciation for Japanese horror, myth, and legend."

—*Publishers Weekly*, Starred Review

"[A] Stephen King–like horror story… A chilling, bloody ghost story that resonates."

—*Kirkus Reviews*

"A dark novel that will appeal to horror fans, lovers of Elizabeth Scott's *Living Dead Girl.*"

—*School Library Journal*

"There's a superior creep factor that is pervasive in every lyrical word of Chupeco's debut, and it's perfect for teens who enjoy traditional horror movies… The story is solidly scary and well worth the read."

—*Booklist*

"This horror mystery has just the right blend of contemporary teenage life and the fantasy of a ghost story. It is well written and fast paced, and the characters both dead and alive are developed and engaging…well worth having in a teen collection that caters to fantasy and horror lovers."

—*VOYA Magazine*

"The most fascinating scenes contain darkly mesmerizing characters, such as a little girl named Sandra who can see ghosts, a psychopath called the Smiling Man, and the miko of the Chinsei shrine. Chupeco gives her best and most rhythmic passages to them and Okiku, who draws readers into the narrative with the depth of her broken soul and the majesty of her hard-won strength."

—*Boston Globe*

WE'RE NOT SAFE HERE

WE'RE NOT SAFE HERE

NOT

SAFE

HERE

RIN CHUPECO

sourcebooks
fire

Published by Sourcebooks Fire, an imprint of Sourcebooks
1935 Brookdale RD, Naperville, IL 60563-2773
(630) 961-3900
sourcebooks.com

Cataloging-in-Publication Data is on file with the Library of Congress.

Printed and bound in the United States of America.
VP 10 9 8 7 6 5 4 3 2 1

For Zio and Altair,
the backroom aficionados.

[The video begins in darkness. There is nothing but a black screen and a male voice talking rapidly over it.]

Storymancer: Most people know me as Storymancer, and if you are seeing this video, then I might already be dead.

Does that sound dramatic? Sorry. I wish I was kidding. Just trying to inject a little bit of humor in what I feel might be the start of a very downer series for the rest of you. Especially if no one's found me yet.

[A video montage appears onscreen: There is a smiling boy with black hair and brown eyes, talking animatedly in front of an old, abandoned building. It segues into a first-person camera view as he explores caves, and then more old buildings, and then cemeteries. It switches to another scene of the same boy holding a camera where his face is seen. He runs away from something while he is screaming. The video freezes on his panicked face.]

For the most part, I stream a lot of stuff. I usually make videos where I explore abandoned places and try to discover the history behind them. Sometimes for fun, I'll stay a few hours in some of the allegedly haunted buildings and see if anything jumps out at me. I don't have a big following, but I appreciate each and every one of you who subscribe to my channel, which is why I always strive to make my videos as exciting and as interesting as I can.

[The scene fades back to black.]

Beyond that, I guess I'm no one special. I'm seventeen years old, and I've been streaming on this channel since I was fourteen. I live in Wispy Falls, just like the rest of you. Just like everyone else I know. Just like everyone else you know. And that's because there's nothing else outside of Wispy Falls. But that doesn't mean bad things don't happen here.

I bet you folks aren't used to me like this, huh? Normally I'll jump into the fray at the start of my videos and run in with guns blazing, metaphorically speaking. I'd be talking about whatever haunted spot I'm in by now and showing you every creepy nook and cranny I'd found. I've never started a video just rambling like this.

What you're about to watch is the culmination of an investigative project I have been doing the last several months, dealing with the bloodmoon ritual and those who've gone missing in the woods. I was hoping that this series would not be seen by anyone until I had finished my investigation and made a much more polished version of it, but I have a dead man's switch that allows me to manually delay the release of all the videos I have made so far by a week. Sounds a bit dramatic (it's really just a program I set up to post my videos if I don't reply to the program's automated email), but it's what I have to do.

Because I think something's after me.

If you're watching this right now, that means I haven't pushed back that switch another week. Which means I'm missing, or worse.

And if I'm not there to stop these videos from playing, then it means you and everyone else will know about this project.

Here is what we know: We all live in a town called Wispy Falls. I mean this literally. There is no other remaining town that we know of. Outside the woods that surround us, there is nothing beyond but a vast wasteland populated by strange creatures. Something about our woods protects us from them, and this is why people are banned from venturing too far into the trees. Those who have done so have never returned.

[A short montage of various locations within Wispy Falls plays: a downtown district filled with shops and people walking around; a school with children at the playground; people stargazing inside a park, looking up at a very bright, very large full moon overhead.]

Despite the dangers, we have felt safe. The government has taken steps to protect us. To eliminate any threat that creeps out from those woods and into town. In exchange, they ask only a few things from us. To remain inside our homes during the bloodmoon. To never go into the woods. To never question their authority.

But this is a lie. We are not safe.

Doesn't matter that cryptid sightings in town are rare. The latest reports state that the most recent sighting of a cryptid was actually two years ago—but still the government trots out PSAs about them every week like clockwork. And yes—the policies and rules are in place to protect us from whatever the hell is going on outside. But if there haven't been sightings in years, why send them out every week? Well, if there's anything I know about the government, it's that they're always hiding something.

[Official-looking documents fill the screen. Though each is given only a few seconds of screen time, it is clear that these are about creature sightings and reports made over the past several years.]

Isn't that the town motto? "You'll be safe here."

[The video image changes abruptly to a forest. There is a small trail leading into these woods, but the trees appear to grow close together, and nothing else but darkness can be seen beyond the first copse.]

Except they keep telling us not to go into the woods.

Except everyone who went missing in the woods was never found.

Except they have never looked for any of those people, despite all their promises.

You ever wonder how we were the only town to have survived? How the woods around Wispy Falls seem to protect us from the monsters beyond it, yet at the same time it's filled with its own creatures that come out on occasion and try to kill us? And how because we grew up being told all this, we'd just accepted it all as fact without even bothering to question it?

[The video switches to an image of the streamer as a younger kid, twelve or thirteen years old. Beside him is a much younger boy, around six.]

This is my younger brother, Lee. When Lee was only six and a half, he was diagnosed with thymic carcinoma, which spread to his lungs by the time the doctors found it. He was the strongest person I knew. He went through the treatments and the chemo, and we thought he was improving, even though they said the survival rate was lower than most other kinds of cancer.

And then he went missing in the woods on his seventh birthday.

He would have never gone to the forest on his own. Someone must have kidnapped him. But the authorities never followed up on any of our pleas for help. It was the same with every other missing person I've researched over the years. The police wrote them off as lost causes. Even my parents gave up after a while.

[The photograph of both boys fades from view.]

But I'm not giving up.

Recently, there was news of a body in the woods. The one they said was a criminal.

There was never a body in the woods before. Anyone who went missing there was never found.

But if there is a body now, then that means maybe I can find Lee too.

I want to know what happened to him. I *need* to know. And these videos are going to have everything I've ever researched, everything I've uncovered about the woods, and anywhere my investigation has taken me. Everything I've learned so far tells me his disappearance has something to do with the bloodmoon, with the monsters that infiltrate the town, with Wispy Falls—everything.

I have compiled everything I know that is even marginally related to the bloodmoon, the strange circumstances surrounding Ivy Delgado and the Facility, and my own firsthand experiences as I try to discover the many things they have been hiding from us. Some of these videos will include other external videos I deem of relevance, as well as text and email conversations with other people who are also involved, or are at least adjacent to, my investigations. If you see these videos, it is likely they have been posted without their permission (Jelly, forgive me), but again, it had to be done. It had to.

If you are watching this video, then that means I haven't been able to solve the mystery just yet. The first few videos are decent enough, but toward the end there was just so much information coming in I decided to just compile everything and sort it out later. But later, as you now know, hasn't come.

I'm hoping if I show all this to the rest of what's left of the world, then someone out there can finish what I've started. Someone who might have lost a loved one to the woods too, who wants to know just as much as I do. What if they've been lying to us all this time? What if there is something outside the woods they don't want us to see?

Yeah, I'm spitballing here. I have no evidence, nothing to tell me we aren't the only town left on the planet. But that's why I am doing this in the first place. To find out where Lee is. To know what else is out there.

I hope it works. I hope you see this. Please. Find us. We're not safe here.

VIDEO #1

Storymancer Video Blog Entry

LightParticle121 sent me this video shortly after it aired, along with the strange transcript. This is the first video of many that he'd send me over the course of several weeks.

Honestly? I don't know much about LightParticle121. He's obsessed with the news. He likes to go online and warn random people on social media about some of the "coded messages" he'd discovered, which was how I found him. I thought he was just some harmless old dude who'd lost family and friends too, and was trying to cope in his own way, even if he comes off as unhinged.

At least, that's what I thought.

Some background information—I met him at the conspiracy section of the Wispy Falls official message board, but he has a habit of wandering out of that particular cave and heading into the more general sub forums to complain about why no one is paying attention to him, because he's just unlocked the secrets of the known universe, which is why everyone is also out to get him.

[Screenshot #1 appears. It is a comment posted by LightParticle121 on the forums that goes: There are three Hundred twentysix Different TYPES of cryptids that exshist in the world and we know only a tennth of them. Halfp the food you eat Are Crytpids. Lightbulbs can Be Cryptids. Plants are more cryptids than Not. Just because youv never been attackd by Them don't mean they Aren't.]

[Screenshot #2: No YOU Are the Cryptid!! There is Nothing I said that Is a lie, but You Keep Lying, Why is that??? If You Don't Want people Talking about the Truth about the bloodmoon, then why are you here?]

[Screenshot #3: There Are a lot of People Here with Seven Eyes. If you Dont believe me look at your Friends. Are you sure theyr real? Many of them are NOT REAL.]

So, you're probably thinking: This guy sounds like he needs a long-deserved rest in a mental ward. So why aren't you just dismissing the obviously ridiculous things he says and just going about your own business?? I would have—until he posted this.

[Screenshot #4: Look at all the people who went Missing all of them were Sick! That's why they took them Away!]

This gave me pause. My brother had cancer. No one in the news ever mentioned the other people who'd disappeared were sick as well. I think my parents mentioned that my brother had cancer a couple of times to reporters, but I don't think they ever reported that in the news back then.

Maybe that was a coincidence, but what the hell, might as well follow it up, anyway.

Except it's not. A quick look at social media confirms they were all sick. Cancer, MS, acquired hemophilia, Alzheimer's—everyone who was given up for dead in those woods had some terrible disease they were fighting, just like my brother.

Maybe this guy did know something. So, I reached out.

I am attaching the short email exchange we had when he sent me the video, and I think it's relevant enough to document here. I've crossed out the email addresses for privacy reasons.

WISPY FORUMS MESSAGE INBOX

From: Storymancer
To: LightParticle121
Date: 11-32-208 1:41:40 a.m.
Subject: Your thoughts about the Woods

Hello, LightParticle121!

I came across your comment about how everyone was sick before they went missing in the woods, and I was wondering if I could pick your brain about this? I have a brother I lost and I've been trying to investigate his disappearance as well as the disappearances of the others. Could you spare some time to discuss it?

EMAILS

From: xxxxxx@xxxxxx.com

To: xxxxxx@xxxxxx.xxx

Date: 11-32-208 3:25:22 a.m.

Subject: These Are not Mine AND not Yours

I dont know why you want proof I Am just a lawabiding citizen and I will Deny that you asked me anything

I just want to share my work no one ever asks me about my work and I like that you ask me

But I am Lawabiding and there is no evidence I agreed to anything ok

I just like the Poetry of it

I am for the bloodmoon and I am for the Stones no one else can say otherwise

I like Trinity I really do she Smiles at me from inside the television and I know she likes me

Their very nice I talk to her sometimes She is like my daughter I love her very much

How did you find me again

Are you one of them I am a Law Abiding citizen

From: xxxxxx@xxxxxx.xxx

To: xxxxxx@xxxxxx.com

Date: 11-32-208 4:01:23 a.m.

Subject: Re: These Are not Mine AND not Yours

Hello Mr. Light,

Thank you for the email. Did you mean to attach anything to the message? If so, I can't see it.

I didn't exactly find you, but I've heard of you! You are very well known online in your own way.

I also wanted to ask—how did you know that all the people who disappeared into the woods were sick?

Best,

S

From: xxxxxx@xxxxxx.com
To: xxxxxx@xxxxxx.xxx
Date: 11-32-208 5:13:56 a.m.
Subject: Re: Re: These Are not Mine AND not Yours

I don't know you I don't know anyone but I will give you the news

I like giving people the news but no one has asked me about the bloodmoon

I like Trinity she reminds me of my daughter she keeps me company in the house

I will give you the video like you want but their will be nothing else from Me

I will give you my Words I just like the news

They're sick all of them are sick that's who they always target

They will heal they will kneel

11

From: xxxxxx@xxxxxx.xxx

To: xxxxxx@xxxxxx.com

Date: 11-32-208 7:05:19 a.m.

Subject: Re: Re: Re: These Are not Mine AND not Yours

Can you be more specific? Who is targeting the sick people?

    Also letting you know that I received the video, thank you again! And please give my regards to your daughter too!

Best,

S

From: xxxxxx@xxxxxx.com

To: xxxxxx@xxxxxx.xxx

Date: 11-32-208 8:15:36 a.m.

Subject: Re: Re: Re: Re: These Are not Mine AND not Yours

My daughter is dead

Right. On to the video he sent me.

[There is a television in the room. It has always been there. It is tuned to the news channel. No one has turned it on. No one in Wispy Falls ever turns their television on, but it does not matter. The WFTV logo flits across the screen, far too quickly to be more than just a blur, and a gravelly voice begins to speak.]

You are watching WFTV, your number one source for all Wispy Falls news. You are watching WFTV, your only source for all Wispy Falls news.

[The logo flickers for an eighth of a second and disappears to give way to an anchorperson, who shuffles papers on her desk and smiles.]

TV anchorperson, Trinity Vanderlust: Good evening! I am Trinity Vanderlust and here are tonight's top stories. Preparations are currently underway for this year's bloodmoon cycle, when the Earth passes in between the old moon and the sun, producing a rather striking effect on our lunar friend and turning it a beautiful crimson as it often does from September to late December every year. As always, the government would like to remind everyone that after you have all enjoyed yourselves at the community bonfire taking place at the beach at the end of the bloodmoon later this year, immediately return home, lock your doors, shutter your windows, and remain inside for the full night. The government would like to remind you they have protected your family for the better part of a year and you must trust it is only polite to obey them in this instance in the same way that you have obeyed them in everything else. As always, do not look out your windows when you have returned to your homes. Ignore any strange noises that might come from outside. If there is something you think you see out of the corner of your eye...no, you did not. Remain quiet and unassuming and undetectable until the next morning, and only until the sun has risen over the horizon. Do not leave your houses. Do not go into the woods. If any of your loved ones has broken the law and ventured outside, contact the authorities immediately and remain

13

inside your house. There is little hope for them, but there is so much still for you.

In other news, the Wembley family at 137 Chestnut Drive is celebrating Grandpa Abraham Wembley's eighty-sixth birthday two days after his successful historic surgery. We had previously reported on Grandpa Wembley's fatal nox flore disease, a rare condition that causes hallucinations, psychotic breaks, and eventual lung collapse in its patients. But eight months after officially being diagnosed, Grandpa Wembley tells our reporter that he's never been happier, especially now that he is surrounded by his children and grandchildren.

[There is footage of an elderly man on a bed, with an oxygen mask on his mouth. The old man is smiling, if a little blankly. There is something dark wrapped around his neck.]

The family credits his continuing good health to the staff members of the Penumbra Institution, who handled Grandpa Wembley's treatment at no cost.

[A man appears on camera, smiling with teeth. The caption on the lower screen identifies him as Wesley Arciega, with a smaller *Penumbra Spokesperson* designation typed underneath his name.]

Penumbra spokesperson, Wesley Arciega: The procedure took eleven hours, twenty-five minutes, and seven seconds and included seven medical professionals. While there is still no cure for nox flore, we are able to extend our patients' lives for nearly ten years after diagnosis. We at the Penumbra Institution will always prioritize your health first, and everything else second. It will take some time for Mr. Wembley to get back on his feet, but we can guarantee that he will be completely and absolutely sane for the remainder of his life. It's the least we can do.

Trinity Vanderlust: The Penumbra Institution has also just recently announced that all war veterans are eligible for free mental health and emergency medical care at any of the four facilities they have in town. The new policy, which will be rolled out on Monday, will include up to sixty days of inpatient crisis or emergency residential care and up to 180 days of follow-up outpatient care. The package also includes free rides to and from the facility, with Penumbra shouldering all the costs of their medicine.

[The same representative for Penumbra Facility, Wesley Arciega, appears onscreen again, smiling manically. The facility in question now looms behind him, an odd dome-like structure that seems to be made of dense glass, though very little of it is in focus. The camera is fully trained on Wesley Arciega and his wide, smiling face.]

Penumbra spokesperson, Wesley Arciega: Veterans can now receive the world-class free healthcare they deserve without worrying about expenses. While our hospitals are already free for all residents in Wispy Falls, we want to focus on those suffering from emergency crises or who are at risk of harm, because we understand how one's mental well-being is just as important as their physical health. We are doing our best to help save more lives, and nothing could be more important than that.

[The announcer leans forward toward the television screen, as if about to impart some important secret. Her voice drops to a whisper.]

Trinity Vanderlust: Please do not look at the body in the woods today. There are many rumors going around regarding the dead body, and they are all wrong. Dead bodies happen every day. Every. Day. There is nothing special about this dead body. We are already investigating the dead body. Please do not look at the body. Please do not attempt to look at the dead body. We will be doing our best to ensure that everything will be back to the way it was. In the meantime, the authorities have asked for people to remain calm until further details can be provided to the public.

That's all for today. This has been WFTV, your only source for all Wispy Falls news.

[The video ends.]

Yup. Just a little bit creepy, right? Well, here is the problem: This news video doesn't exist.

Or at least, the segment where Trinity Vanderlust talks about the body in the woods. That doesn't exist.

I combed through the news archives that week, and that last part is now completely different.

[Another video is shown of a smiling Trinity Vanderlust. She is dressed in the same clothes as the previous video and her hair is styled the same way, clearly a part of the previous broadcast.]

Trinity Vanderlust: We have just received breaking news. A body has been discovered in the woods. The remains have not yet been identified, and authorities have since closed off Fifth and Twelfth Streets. Local residents are asked to take a different route as heavy traffic will be expected in the area. [She shuffles some papers.] We bring you now to the news conference being held by Chief of Police, Elijah Knight.

[The screen switches to the image of an officer standing in front of a podium surrounded by the flickers of camera flashes. Two other officers stand on either side of him, looking grim.]

Chief of Police, Elijah Knight: Thank you for coming to this conference. As this is an open investigation, I cannot comment yet on the cause of death. I understand this is the first time a body has been found while investigating a disappearance in the forest, and we will be alerting the families of all known missing persons matching this description so that they may come and potentially identify the body.

For now, we are able to release a description of the deceased. This is a Caucasian male, approximately six-foot-two and roughly 220 pounds with black hair and blue eyes. He has no other identifying marks, save that his nose may have been broken at some point in the past and healed incorrectly. He was wearing a black shirt and black pants and has no identification on him. According to our medical personnel on scene, he likely has been dead for close to seventy-two hours.

I want to stress again that this is an ongoing investigation. Please avoid all speculation until this has been concluded. Please call our hotline should you believe you have any information about the deceased. Thank you for your time.

[A flurry of questions comes from the reporters looking on, but the video cuts quickly to Trinity Vanderlust's concerned face.]

Trinity Vanderlust: That's all for today. This has been WFTV, your only source for all Wispy Falls news.

If you're wondering if they called my family, then the answer is no. Obviously, my brother is not a six-foot-two man, so I suppose they decided not to bother. But here lies the question: How did Mr. LightParticle switch out that segment to something so completely different? And why even do that at all?

So naturally, I had to send another email.

From: xxxxxx@xxxxxx.xxx
To: xxxxxx@xxxxxx.com
Date: 2-4-243 7:51:13 a.m.
Subject: Re: Re: Re: These Are not Mine AND not Yours

Hello again, Mr. Light! Just wanted to check—something. This video states that it was aired on January 23 this year, but the video you sent me is very different from what was actually shown on the news. I refer specifically to the part where there was a dead body reported in the woods. Can you just confirm for me where you got this? Or were you the one to have edited that part?

Best,

S

From: xxxxxx@xxxxxx.com

To: xxxxxx@xxxxxx.xxx

Date: 2-4-2243 8:11:19 a.m.

Subject: Re: Re: Re: These Are not Mine AND not Yours

The news the news the news the news

    Who knows the real news

    The body is not who they say it is the body is important

thats why the body is not who they say it's the morissey

So, yeah. Once again, absolute nonsense.

The rest of his emails babble on much like this one, so I decided not to push it for now.

On one hand, I'm almost tempted to wash my hands of him.

On the other, he knew about the sick people, even though I never really got an answer with regard to that.

I had two choices at this point. I could continue to pursue this with an insane man as my only source so far, or back out and keep doing my usual streams of haunted places and cool destinations and shelve the matter entirely.

You can probably make a guess at what my decision was.

This is for you, Lee.

[A video begins, and it shows the timelapse of a forest. The trees above the stationary camera form a canopy overhead with only small gaps in between, the leaves and branches conforming so that they do not overlap each other. Behind them, slates of sunlight shine through that rapidly turn to darkness as night swiftly overtakes day.]

Storymancer's voice: This is the forest. I don't think there ever was a specific name for it. It was always just the Wispy Falls Woods to us. The woods that surround the town. The woods they keep telling us not to go into. You would think it's just a perfectly normal forest. But here's the thing.

[The timelapse continues as night eventually turns once more into day. Beyond that, nothing else within the forest seems to move.]

There are no animals in these woods. I have never seen any there.

I can hear sounds, and some of them definitely sound like they could be animals, but I've never actually met the fauna in question. I haven't heard of anyone in town ever seeing any either. Not even the most adventurous ones who'd been as deep into the woods as they were able to go and survive had recounted ever seeing any. The Backward Lady is the closest people have ever seen inside the forest, but I doubt anyone would consider her a living thing.

[The timelapse stops. Now the forest simply appears motionless before the camera. On occasion, you think you can see some small movements farther in the distance, but it is not easy to say if they were simply leaves rustling against the unseen wind or something else entirely.]

I've been here enough times. Trying to find out where my brother had gone, trying to see if he'd left any clues behind. But far too many people have gone missing, and it's gotten to the point where no one cares where they've gone. Even blamed them for breaking the rules.

[The forest is still silent. Nothing moves here.]

I think I'm going to have to break the rules.

VIDEO #2

The Sprawl: Wispy Falls
Message Board

If LightParticle121 wasn't going to give me any straight answers, then I decided that I would start by looking at his account and trying to see where he'd posted some of his other crackbrain theories and if I could find any clues in some of his comments in the same way I'd found the clue about the victims' illnesses. But after a few hours spent sifting through his work, all I can say is that he makes forty to fifty posts a day, and none of them make any sense. And yet every now and then there are some odd details he reveals that could be important.

I've isolated the ones I feel might be promising and worth another look and took as many screenshots as I could to view later. Some I decided to put up, to add more context to cryptids in general, to the Backward Lady, and to people's overall sentiments when it comes to the creatures that used to plague our town.

[The video begins with a screenshot of askpeople, which Storymancer begins to narrate.]

askpeople/

The place to ask anything you want, but we're not liable for the answers you may get!

everymanoutbreak asks: What is the most frightening experience you've ever had? (serious answers only) (**19634** users liked this)

+ **Serotoningoblin** (3291 users liked this)

I've mentioned this before in another thread, but I'll say it here too. Back when I was around seven or eight years old, my mother was out. Normally we were obedient kids, but something about that day made us antsy for some reason, and we didn't like the idea of staying cooped up at home while our mother was off to (what we thought at that time was) some really cool bonfire party.

We lived maybe three or four blocks away from where the woods begin at the southern part of town, and we'd explored the area enough times that we felt safe.

We hung out for maybe an hour or so, not really doing anything much beyond trying to climb some of the trees and poking around on the ground looking for mushrooms and stuff. One of our neighbors was this old, stoned dude who said he'd pay us twenty bucks by the pound if we could scrounge up some certain mushrooms he was always on the lookout for, so we ventured a lot deeper into the forest than we normally would, because hey, twenty bucks, right?

Looking for psychedelics was what was occupying our attention, so we didn't see her at first. It wasn't until my brother let out this sudden gasp of fear that I finally looked up to see this woman in a brown robe, standing right at the opposite end of the clearing we were in. I didn't know how long she'd been there, just watching us, and the thought that she hadn't moved the whole time we were looking for shrooms made a chill go up my spine. Like she could have just crept up slowly and attacked us, and we wouldn't have known until it was too late.

And I say "watch" loosely, because we didn't actually see her face at all. She had long stringy black hair that I thought at first had fallen over her face to obscure it until I remembered all the descriptions of that ghost who haunts the woods, that she did everything backwards. Which meant that she was actually facing away from us and what we could see of her was her back, except her torso was sort of twisted to look like she was facing us instead. I literally pissed my pants when I realized who—what—she was. I always thought she was some urban legend back then, just something for parents to scare their kids with.

My brother was braver than I. He told me later that he was freaking out but wanted to make sure he could protect me, so he was frantically trying to remember what people said to do when they encountered the Backward Lady, which was to be apologetic and walk away. "We're sorry for trespassing," was what he told her. "We're going back now, and we'll never come out here again."

I still don't know if what he said made her mad or if what everyone said to tell her was wrong, but she started walking toward us. You could see that all her limbs were turned the other way. But she was shuffling forward like it was a natural thing for her. No stumbling or anything. My brother and I came to the same conclusion. We just turned around wordlessly and got the hell out of there as fast as we could. I could have sworn she started chasing us, because we could hear twigs snapping behind us, but we were both too scared to turn around and look.

Eventually we made it out of the woods, but we didn't stop running until we were literally at our doorstep. My brother said he finally turned around then to make sure she wasn't tailing us, and he swore that he saw a dark figure at the farthest end of our block, watching, before turning away and disappearing back into the shadows. We barricaded ourselves inside and huddled under our respective beds until our mom came home.

My brother and I never went back to the woods after that.

+ **schrodingersbeer** (2092 users liked this)

That is honestly frightening and glad you got out of there. Never seen her myself, but have friends who did. I've never heard of anyone ever seeing her face.

+ **garlandgarlic** (1592 users liked this)

Likely anyone who's done so isn't alive to describe her.

+ **Nothoughtsjustvibes** (2982 users liked this)

54m here and lived for most of my life scoffing at the supernatural until ten years ago. My cat got out of the house, and after searching everywhere for her, I concluded that she'd made for the woods, which is only a few blocks away from my house. Ofc I know about how we're all warned to stay away but cat > laws, so screw that, grabbed my gun and headed in anyway. After an hour or so searching heard meowing that I assumed was my cat, immediately headed toward the sound.

Long story short, it wasn't my cat. There was a girl sitting on one of the larger rock outcroppings about twenty feet away. I thought at first that she was lost too. Except I realized a few seconds later that I couldn't see her face—I thought her hair was just covering it at first.

So I, being the idiot that I was, called out to her and asked if she was all right. Nothing. I raised my voice and asked again. Still nada. So naturally I had to stroll toward some strange lady like this was the best thing to do. I don't know what got into me. I remember thinking maybe she was injured or something and couldn't respond.

I was about halfway to her when some instinct told me to stop. She hadn't even turned around the whole time I was making for her, so maybe the oddity of that was what put me on my guard. And then I took another look and realized a few things:

1. Her hands were resting on the stone she was sitting on, and they were pivoted away from me, which meant that she was actually facing away instead of toward me like I had first assumed. Except the front of her brown dress was in my line of sight, which was why I thought she was sitting facing me. So, either she had put on her clothes backward, or she had some condition with her wrists that forced her hands at a 180-degree angle behind her.

2. Same goes for her feet. They were in my line of vision, only they were facing into the rock she was sitting on, which as you all know isn't normal, but I didn't see that until I got close enough.

3. She wasn't there to rest and enjoy the scenery or anything like that. She wasn't looking around at the trees or admiring the view. She was just...there. Not moving, not chilling out, just sitting there.

She didn't move the whole time she was seated on that rock...until what came next.

While I was figuring out what to do, she suddenly stood up without warning and started walking backward toward me, literally. At this point I thought to hell with all of this and turned and sprinted back the way I came from. I could hear rustling behind me, like feet stepping over dry leaves and twigs and stuff, and I made the mistake of turning my head to look back.

She was running. Still backward, but I could make out her hairline on top of her head, the part where her hair stops and the rest of her forehead starts, like if she would bend her head back a little more (forward, from my perspective) I might actually see her eyes. I did not want to see her eyes.

I don't know how I made it back home in one piece, but once I hit the gravel road leading back into the town proper, the sounds behind me faded away. I didn't stop running until I was almost at my front porch. Never again. To top things off, I found my Lucy snoozing away underneath my car, and I could have sworn I checked before I left and she wasn't there. Goddamn cat.

+ **Killtheranger** (1124 users liked this)

The OP who told the story said it happened in the morning, which makes it even more frightening

+ **Girlinthehood** (1100 users liked this)

Genuine curiosity—if you don't believe in ghosts, then what's stopping you from going into the woods at any time?

+ **Jackinthelee** (1165 users liked this)

There are a lot of other things in the forests that can kill you and aren't ghosts. The township forbids everyone from exploring the woods beyond a certain point, so it's not like anyone knows what kinds of animals are actually lurking in there. And given that most of the unnatural deaths in town are due to people disappearing in the woods, there must be something deadly out there. You don't need spirits for that, regardless of what you believe.

+ **Crimsonhunt** (1313 users liked this)

I, for one, believe you. My daughter disappeared in the woods four years ago, and I always believed it was that woman who took her.

+ **Storymancer** (1190 users liked this)

My brother disappeared into the woods when I was younger too. I'm so sorry.

+ **Hallowedgrounds** (583 users liked this)

I'm so sorry as well, for you both. If any of you need someone to talk to...

+ **Crimsonhunt** (458 users liked this)

Thank you, you're very kind. A few buddies and I who've lost family and friends to the woods have taken it upon ourselves the last few years to patrol the area in case anyone does get lost there and needs help.

+ **Meerkatwater** (200 users liked this)

Are you part of that volunteer group who helps with those missing persons cases? The Woodhunters? The one that specifically helps people whose loved ones disappear in the forest? I've heard about you and your friends if so!

+ **Crimsonhunt** (398 users liked this)

Yes. Unfortunately, the cases are still unsolved, but we try our best to be there and help, anyway.

+ **Baconatorfilling** (52 users liked this)

I didn't know that, thank you for your service!

+ **Leavenworth25** (88 users liked this)

Some more info about the Woodhunters: http://wispy-falls.com/news/tag/hunters

They're basically badass people who lost family and friends in the woods and are doing their best to warn other people or help in searches for anyone else who gets lost. People criticize them for being unlicensed paramilitary, but they're real heroes to me imo

+ **Gigachad_Alphamater** (821 users liked this)

Mine's gonna be different from what most people are posting here because my experience has more to do with an actual cryptid than the woods. The woods were involved, but only sort of tangentially. And I can only assume it was a cryptid, fyi.

I think this was around the time a young girl went missing maybe ten years ago, and volunteers were trying to look for her till night-fall came. I was one of those helpers. They warned everyone before sunset that we had to go and we all hightailed it out of the area, but I was an idiot who realized halfway back to my car that I'd lost my keys and I spent an hour after everyone went home desperately trying to look for them. Fortunately, I found them before it got too dark, but I was alone at that point. That's when I realized that everything looked ten times creepier at night. I was convinced that every shadow was some creature lying in wait for me, and so I wasted no time at all racing back to my car.

I got in, had my key in the ignition and was ready to start it up, but something out of the corner of my eye made me pause. That's when I saw them.

I didn't see a lot of details, thankfully—just a figure all in black walking away from the opposite side of the parking lot. Gave me a bad feeling. Anyway, I kinda ducked behind my wheel and pretended the car was empty because I did not want it noticing me. But as I did, I caught a quick glimpse of it, and there was something about the way it inclined its head to the side that reminded me of my brother, Jorge.

Jorge disappeared about fifteen years ago when I was just a kid—one of those juvenile delinquents who didn't like going to school and always wanted to trespass in the woods until the worst finally happened—and he had this habit of cocking his head to one side when he was pondering something, and I could have sworn the shadow did that.

I don't even know what came over me, but I found myself crying quietly. I waited until they disappeared before I mustered the courage to start the engine and get out of there. I'm not someone who cries easily—I barely even cried when Jorge went missing, just felt kind of numb for a while—but that little gesture was enough for me to remember him all of a sudden.

+ **Highestleveldork** (617 users liked this)

I think you refused to let yourself grieve for him until that moment. My condolences all the same, and I'm glad they didn't see you.

+ **CloudmakerSteve** (312 users liked this)

Isn't this like the definition of what a Quiet Brother is?

+ **Highestleveldork** (161 users liked this)

Not sure. I don't think anyone's seen one in a while especially with curfew and the punishment for breaking it. Giga's a real one for telling us.

+ **CloudmakerSteve** (32 users liked this)

Does that mean Gigachad's gonna be punished?

+ **Highestleveldork** (20 users liked this)

I mean, it was an accident? The authorities are strict about a lot of things, but I think he's fine since he was part of a search party and was just trying to be helpful. Plus he did his best not to be seen by the Quiet Brother just like they say in the PSAs.

+ Heavensturn_raiding (1012 users liked this)

Lol at the top entries in this thread being all about the Backward Lady and the woods.

> **+ Venticoffeedumpster** (126 users liked this)
>
> Is anyone surprised? I mean, it's not like we're swimming in murder and crime, disappearing into the woods is about the only unnatural death that's common in Wispy Falls.

+ Seveninabunker (700 users liked this)

Woke up in the middle of the night to find something tall and all in black staring at me from the corner of my bed. I think I was about seven or eight at the time, and I know people are going to dismiss it as some weird figment of my imagination since I was just a kid, but to this day I swear that I can draw that face from memory: stark white and gaunt, with no actual eyes but black holes like it was a cardboard cutout, except the lips were red and stretched wide and it was in no way a mask. Still gives me nightmares every few months or so.

> **+ StaciEx** (551 users liked this)
>
> That's terrifying. Some people say that paralysis demons look different for each person, so maybe that was what it looked like to you?
>
> > **+ Seveninabunker** (685 users liked this)
> >
> > I wasn't paralyzed at all, I could still move and stuff. I remember seeing that and then throwing the blanket over

my head in a panicked hope that maybe it would serve as protection and that thing would go away. Against all odds it worked (I think) because it didn't do anything to attack me, even if I couldn't see it anymore. I stayed that way the whole night till my mom came into my room to wake me up in the morning. Had on a nightlight every day till I was ten after that, but it never came back. I don't think I ever had sleep paralysis that I can remember, just that one incident.

+ **Cozyghosting** (771 users liked this)

Literally opened a can *of worms*. Saw an abandoned RV out in the woods and thought it would be cool to see what was inside. Maggots. Got out as fast as I could.

> + **ReturnoftheFlack** (24 users liked this)
>
> Was it you who found that body in the woods they're talking about in the news now?

> + **[User deleted]**
>
> [This comment has been deleted by the moderator. Reason: Discussing the details of an active missing persons case is not allowed in the forums under Ruling 35.]

>> + **EmmanuelGoAway** (3 users liked this)
>>
>> Don't do this bro, you're gonna get banned.

>> + **EmmanuelGoAway** (0 users liked this)
>>
>> welp

+ **LightParticle121** (-40 users liked this)

TheBackwardsLady is the password. They Just want you to be Afraid of the Woods. They put all the girls there. They Let them go Missing. They Don't Want you going Past the Woods.

> + **SevenHeaventhBeer** (3 users liked this)
>
> Why are you always like this

> > + **LightParticle121** (-23 users liked this)
> >
> > No One wants to know the truth doesn't mean itsnot the truth

Other similar threads in the Sprawl you might like:

discussioncity/

A place to discuss anything and everything about Wispy Falls. Community events, workshops, drill training and more—shout them out here!

> - **Are we really all alone in here?**
>
> **SeventeenAndCounting** (1256 users liked this)
>
> Has anyone ever thought about how weird it is that we are basically in an isolated town and yet for some reason none of us has ever left? You ever wonder what the world outside might be like? Surely there are still some pockets of civilization who'd survived out there, functioning just like we are?

(load 362 comments)

- They're going to lie to us again

Underthebridge (— users liked this)

    They only put that alleged dead body in the woods because they couldn't stop the rumors from spreading and want to take hold of the narrative again. How many times is this going to happen until we all smarten up?? I know this is gonna be deleted and I don't really care anymore people need to keep shouting this from the rooftops

(load 2766 comments)

Two things that I want to point out. The first is that LightParticle121 has some obvious enmity toward the Backward Lady, which I want to delve into in future videos I make, just because of her proximity to the woods, and because she is often the one people blame for the missing people there.

As for me…I don't know who to blame just yet. Only that I want to know more, and I need to know more.

The second is that there are other people beyond LightParticle121 who are convinced that there is some conspiracy afoot. I have reached out to several of them on this forum, including the ones who had posted here and made their criticisms known, but they have yet to answer. So I guess LightParticle121, for now, remains my only and somewhat dubious source.

Oh, and one other thing. I went back in to check the next day. Underthebridge's post was deleted.

VIDEO #3

The Sprawl: Wispy Falls
Message Board

New developments about the body in the woods. I have accumulated all the documentation that I could find about it, because there isn't much on the news discussing this anymore, and it's only been two days, which I find suspicious. As most of the town's communication lies within the Wispy Falls message boards, this is where the bulk of my evidence has been archived, together with the few newspaper sites that reported it. I've also taken the liberty of adding in any private messages I have received from whatever sources.

explainittome/

Out of the loop? Got something you want to ask that everyone already seems to know?? We don't judge here, so come and be enlightened!

Schrodingersbeer asks: So what is the deal with the news about the body in the woods? (serious answers only) (24648 users liked this)

Okay, so I hadn't been paying much attention to the news and whatnot because I've been focusing on my thesis, but I looked up one day and suddenly everyone's talking about this body with like eight hundred conspiracy theories revolving around it. What's the deal? Why do people think this has something to do with the bloodmoon? And someone actually went and looked for the body and now they're missing too? I tried to check the news and even they don't know who the body belongs to, so why are they talking about some guy that got arrested and then went missing or something?

+ **ThisIsNothing** (7039 users liked this)

Here's the video: http://showvideo.wf/385628348

Basically, this was filmed by someone named UsernameGoesBrr. He snuck through the crime scene tape somehow and actually took footage of the body, but no one's heard anything from him since.

As to why the body is important? Here's the kicker: No one who has ever gone missing in the woods ever had their bodies recovered. This is the first of its kind. So of course, everyone is going bonkers trying to speculate if this body was someone who had disappeared, or if this is someone new entirely.

+ **TacoCatFur** (6826 users liked this)

Burying the lede there, kind of. The video recording is from UsernameGoesBrr, and it gets abruptly cut off at the end, which is giving rise to speculation that something's happened to him. And chances are it's pretty bad. This literally might be the only video to exist right now of a close encounter with a cryptid.

+ **BigVanDyke** (3856 users liked this)

Ohhh shit, I just watched it. Rip, I don't think that guy made it.

+ **RailwayDemonSlug** (3472 users liked this)

Bet that he faked it all and is now pretending to be in hiding so he can rack up all the subscribers.

+ **PetLizardMcGee** (824 users liked this)

Sad when this is actually the better outcome.

+ **LightningRodinaBlender** (3245 users liked this)

It got taken down. :(Anyone have another active link, by any chance?

+ **SmellyCat35** (1472 users liked this)

Yeah, I don't think it's working. Pretty sure someone tried to post another link earlier but that got nixed in five minutes.

+ **WheresTheWaffles** (2646 users liked this)

Does a Backward Lady even count as a cryptid? It always felt like she was in some whole new category some-times when I hear people talking about her.

+ **BigBottomsUp** (2246 users liked this)

More like some kind of anomaly, I think, although I have seen people putting her in the same classification, by like three or four scientists that I know. (Source: I work at the university but not in anything that requires me to be smart.)

+ **JellyBeanFish** (846 users liked this)
That's not a body. I watched the video, and it isn't a body.

> + **ChicharonBulaklak** (345 users liked this)
> Can you explain?

> + **HeimlichManure** (836 users liked this)
> Not the person you're responding to, but from the video I saw, it kinda looks like it has three legs. Again, the camera's blurry enough that there could be some confusion, but that's my take on it.

> + **JustHereThirsty** (745 users liked this)
> I mean...it could just be two legs and something else.

> + **Postmeme_God** (254 users liked this)
> Bruh.

(load more comments)

+ **ElvenElvis** (7039 users liked this)
There was a thread early on that got deleted claiming that the body was Adam Morrissey, a criminal who had been arrested for domestic terrorism several years ago and was said to have escaped from the Facility like a year or so ago.

Some people think he managed to escape into the woods and into the outside, but the OP of the thread that got deleted claimed that a lot of the physical features of the dead body closely resembled Morrissey's and then pointed out a scar or a tattoo the dead body had been described as having as similar to what Morrissey was known to have had. That probably wouldn't have gone anywhere if not for the fact that other people also noticed that the only news sites who'd reported on that tattoo abruptly edited it out of their report when they updated the article, so people have started thinking that this is some kind of cover-up.

+ **AllyAllika** (5996 users liked this)

Chiming in to add that there was another user who mentioned having seen the body himself, having gone to the woods to film it for himself. I don't remember his name, but he's some kind of semi-popular streamer whose content is either playing pranks on people or finding some weird places in Wispy Falls and then filming it. Some people who saw the original thread claimed that he'd posted a video of the dead body, except he said it wasn't a dead body—like it was an alien or something. And then five minutes later the whole thread got deleted and the streamer hasn't posted anything since, so a lot of his fans are saying the authorities got to him for knowing too much, and they're hiding him till things go down.

+ **BurgenotSavant** (3016 users liked this)

His username is UsernameGoesBrr, or Brr for short. They've been up in arms over at his subforum here.

+ **FirebrandGodling** (2502 users liked this)

Eh, the Brr sub is very well-known as a hotbed for conspiracy theorists anyway. Just look at the highest rated thread in there. To save you a click, it's Every Pet You Own Has been Implanted with a Neural Device to Monitor your Activities for the Government, and You Owe it to them to Put Them Down.

+ **HavilaDavis** (1282 users liked this)

I'm honestly a little impressed that they spelled most of the words right in that otherwise insane rant. Normally, the IQ level in there barely hits double digits, so you usually just find posts that read more like "Wym globaal warning is rael????" Source: I went on a deep dive in that sub once because someone from there accused me of cursing him with an erectile dysfunction spell just because I told him sunblock actually works. Not even kidding.

(load more comments)

+ **ErwainHeusaff82** (3101 users liked this)

So I'm not really a big fan of all his prank stuff, but Brr does SOME really good content when it comes to those weird places in Wispy Falls that a lot of people don't even know about. I know a lot of other streamers like Wendragon and Culma do that too, but Brr really looks for those hard-to-find (and yes, oftentimes illegal) spots like the supposed ghost circle at Sandleve Park. He's kind of an idiot, but he knows how to grab attention.

+ **MagicalPrincessMargerie** (1477 users liked this)

I mean, even if that streamer dude was kind of an ass, isn't it valid that there's proof that news sites actually changed the details in the story to hide the fact that the dead body might be the Morrissey guy? You can say that his fans are just full of conspiracy theories or whatever, but it doesn't change the fact that they did alter the details. So now I'm wondering why don't they want anyone to know that Morrissey might be dead?? Isn't it good for people to know that he is, since he was a criminal on the run?

+ **allegedlyDellegedly** (2025 users liked this)

No one has any proof that the news sites actually changed their stories, just a lot of claims from people without offering up any proof, much less screenshots. That's the point. People ran website checkers and they didn't find any previous versions of these so-called edits, but people will believe what they want to believe, I guess.

+ **GuerillaintheMists** (2001 users liked this)

But you're wrong! My father's brother's nephew's cousin's former roommate told me so!

+ **HarveyWickman237** (209 users liked this)

Upvote for the Space Attack reference.

+ **GuerillaintheMists** (1467 users liked this)

Just adding to what everyone is already saying, but this makes

42

Brr the 269th person missing in the woods since Wispy Falls was founded. Poor guy, hope they find him soon.

LettermanPriss265 asks: How did we get here if the woods are dangerous? (serious answers only) (74548 users liked this)

So, I'm supposed to write about the history of Wispy Falls, and I decided to write about the Wispy Falls woods. Like I know it's dangerous, but I was wondering, what is it inside the woods that makes them so dangerous? I know there's the Backward Lady and stuff, but then how did the people who founded this town even wind up in the middle of the woods if they were a threat to begin with?

Like there's one book that says that the world outside got overrun by demons or something, so people found monster eggs that can protect us from those, and the woods have some natural barrier that prevents those monsters from breaking in, but at the same time, that makes it harder for us to get out. But then there's this book by Ralph Montegreen saying that's a lie and we're actually in a giant monster egg that's keeping us alive, and in exchange we gotta stay at home during the bloodmoon and stuff, but the world outside is safe and they've been brainwashing us into thinking it's not. What I'm saying is, if we're using these monster eggs anyway, then what's stopping us from using them to get rid of whatever it is that's in the woods?

+ **JarevNikola** (32217 users liked this)

MONSTER EGGS. OP, whatever you do, please do not put that in your paper.

43

+ LettermanPriss265 (21217 users liked this)

I didn't know what else to call them, but from what everyone describes, they sound like they're shaped like eggs.

> **+ Fahrenheit724** (30217 users liked this)
>
> Oh dear.
>
> Abraham Huntington, the founder of Wispy Falls, discovered by accident that there are some special stones and whatnot that repel most of the cryptids outside the forest and keep them at bay (I will point out that even the best scholars in the field admit that "monsters" might be too presumptuous, as no one has ever described what the "creatures" roaming out in the world were, and the founding members had been superstitious enough that they thought talking about them in any capacity might draw them toward the town).

+ LyseAppreciator (26217 users liked this)

Don't even bother. Montegreen's a tinfoil wearer the same as Kleppe, Jordan, and Anderson. They take some of the documented evidence and then fill in the blanks with theories that have absolutely no basis in reality. I don't mind a working hypothesis every now and then, but these people literally pull "facts" out of thin air with no proof other than that they want it to be so.

Source: Actual scholar of cryptozoology and professor at a leading university, but as this is the internet, you're free to take what I say with a grain of salt.

+ **LettermanPriss265** (12217 users liked this)

I didn't actually read the book my uncle read the book, he likes that stuff

> + **ComicBookDonor2** (21206 users liked this)
>
> Very gentle reminder that some of the authors mentioned above have also done things like threaten to bomb busy areas in Wispy Falls, so I don't recommend just going around telling people that family members read their works.
>
> + **LettermanPriss265** (217 users liked this)
>
> Oh yeah yeah thank you my uncle is totally harmless but I see what you mean

+ **BasicallyImHimbo** (26353 users liked this)

Okay, so the way it goes is this:

- monsters attacking the world because of some unseen event that we don't know about anymore because not a lot of records exist

- by a stroke of luck, the people who founded Wispy Falls stumbled upon relics that gave them the ability to protect themselves from the things roaming about, so here we are.

- scientists and historians are slowly piecing together a catalog of cryptids that have existed, and what they do, but since it's hard to research these things, a whole lot of conspiracy theories have started popping up to fill in those gaps. Like they know that doing these bloodmoon rituals helps, but it's not like we're able to do experiments to see what else would work other than what the town founders had stumbled on.

LightParticle121 says: Its all a conspiracy and We Are All in an ExPeriment Now I have PROOF (-134 users liked this)

I finally hacked into the government accounts and saw they are deliberately banning everyone from accessing any IPs outside the city. If there is nothing out there but just monsters, then why would they take the trouble to put any restrictions in place at all? Do it yourself ping 285.46.26.2 that means there are people outside Wispy Falls but they don't want us to know that and that's why everything in the boards is monitored

+ **LeopardSpotsonMyButt** (363 users liked this)

Or maybe this is just basic standard security protocol regardless of whether there are people outside or not.

+ **BirthdayEnvelopesSuck** (235 users liked this)

Why are people even still giving this dude any attention? He's been raving on these boards for years at this point, and yet none of the proof he ever claims he has is actually proof.

An example of all the rational things he's said over the years:

> They are putting things in the water to brainwash us into thinking that the relics are our gods. Penumbra staff puts them in the rivers around us so we can bathe in it and it gets under our skin and into our brains

> Same thing, but with purple pills this time

> There are worms inside the relics they give us that get into our heads while we're sleeping. He has screamed at people daring them to stay up and watch them because they move on

their own and that they watch you when you're not watching them

> The Backward Lady is a plant. She spies on us and tattles to Penumbra and the government when we get too deep inside the forest; you have to not run away.

Here's his most recent one:

> *I have been posting here for Years no one ever listens to me even if I point out the FACTS, I try my best to put out what I know because people deserve to know the truth. Ive said before that Wispy Falls is a Conspiracy and that this is an Xxperiment that the Higher-ups use to Cull the People who don't Believe from the people who are happy to be Fed theyre lyin Shit like that dead Body in the woods. You think Morrissey is a terrorist but he is not hes just another scapegoat that they're using because Morrissey uncovered their secrets and tried to tell people same as me but they caught him and now they're pretending he's a criminal Morrissey has all the Documents Proving that theyre telling the Truth and now the straemer boy found out that the body isnt his body and now they Caught him too.*

+ **Commagraduate** (134 users liked this)

I'm still screaming at "The Backward Lady is a plant"

+ **RetrogradeAmnesiac** (82 users liked this)

Lady really said snitches get stitches.

If you liked this post, you may be interested in:

IsTheGovernment/

Speculating who could be a member of government. All for fun!

> **- This tiny floofy dog?** [image attached]
>
> **Headpats126** (9371 users liked this)
>
> (load 1436 comments)

WISPY FALLS MESSAGE INBOX

From: Storymancer

To: JellyBeanFish

Hey there! I saw your comments on the explainittome/ board and I wanted to ask about your statement where you said that it wasn't a body, because that got me curious. I didn't see the video before it was taken down, but I've been trying to do some investigations into what's been happening with the missing people in the woods, and I wondered if maybe you can give me any information?

From: JellyBeanFish

To: Storymancer

Oh, hey! I recognize your username! You're the streamer who does a lot of videos about exploring places, right? And deconstructing myths? I've watched a few of your videos before!

And yeah, my mom works for Penumbra, and I'm really interested in what she does too. She's one of the scientists there. Want to get into that line of work after I graduate. So I've seen a lot of cryptid cases because of her (I'm working at the Facility for a paid internship rn) and I'm pretty sure the body in that video is a cryptid, not a human body. What do you want to know about it?

From: Storymancer
To: JellyBeanFish

No way, really? Yeah, how were you able to tell? That said, I never saw the video, so I have no idea what anyone saw there, but I do know that none of the bodies of the missing people had ever been found, which is why this seems like a big deal. But didn't the authorities post a description of the dead body? It sounded pretty human to me (Caucasian male, black hair, etc.)

From: JellyBeanFish
To: Storymancer

Do you have a number I can text? I saved the video before it went down. I'll show everything to you there.

VIDEO #4

UsernameGoesBrr's Live Footage

[The film starts with the smiling face of a boy who looks about eighteen or nineteen years old. He has dirty blond hair stuffed under a black cap, and he's wearing dark clothes. He's breathing heavily, and when he speaks, he sounds excited. There is a device around his hat that appears to be some kind of GoPro.]

Brr: I can't believe I'm doing this, but hey! This is UsernameGoesBrr, and I'm about to do something incredibly stupid on this livestream. You know how I enjoy getting tips from my viewers about the places you want me to stake out, right? And that's led me to some of my most favorite videos I've made, ever. Like femra45 giving me the heads-up on that haunted place that they were about to demolish. 3 million views, man! Or hotplatetogo telling me all about that underground sewer right underneath that chapel—there's gonna be a part two for that by the way, because we never really got beyond that door we found inside. And now?

[He pans the camera around behind him to reveal that he is standing near the woods. He is standing on a small trail that had been
cleared for hiking purposes, leading deeper into the cluster of
trees. The light is fading.]

Brr: You know me, always out for new thrills and the best videos for
my viewers. So now I got a tip from a longtime viewer and patron,
simulacrum, and it just so happens to be here in these woods. I mean,
look—

[He fiddles with something, and the point of view now switches
to his own, using the camera on his head.]

Brr: We gotta do what we gotta do for views. Boy's gotta eat. I've been
here lots of times before, and I've never been lost. Made some real fun
videos out of it too. Besides, I'm of the opinion that it isn't right for the
people in charge to not be giving out any information about cold cases
like the ones they got here in the forest. They've already come under fire
for messing up their investigations when it involves missing people. I
mean, seriously—over two hundred cases of people disappearing, and
none of them have ever been found? Dude. That's just being bad at
your job.

So here's what we're gonna do. I'm gonna sneak in, take the shots
we need just to verify that the news is really saying what they're supposed to be saying, and then I'll head out. Victimless crime. Not even a
crime at all, when you think about it. If they wanna arrest me for trespassing or something, then they should have just barricaded the woods
a long time ago. I got sent the coordinates to where I'm gonna go. So the

way I figure it, if I find something, you're gonna see this video up on my page real soon. If not—yeah, win some, lose some.

[Brr starts heading into the trees, confident about where he is going. After ten minutes and seventeen seconds of walking, he looks down at his cell phone to a map listing the coordinates.]

Brr: You think the GPS gets messed up in some parts of the forest? I've never had a problem before. It says that I'm practically standing on top of where I'm supposed to be, but—

[He breaks off abruptly. Somewhere to his left is a faint noise. He does not move, waiting to see if he can pinpoint the location of the sound, but there is no other sound after that.]

Brr: Yeah. Creepy. Don't really know why people even wanna go here, imo.

[He looks back down at his phone.]

Brr: Ah. My bad. Been looking at it wrong. Says I should be turning left right aboooout...

[He starts walking again. Another three minutes and forty-three seconds pass, based on the video's time stamp, before he finally makes a small noise of glee.]

Brr: Ah shit, finally! I see something!

[From a distance, there appears to be a strange heap on the ground. Some discarded clothes are strewn around it, a shirt and one sock visible from where he is standing. He heads toward it eagerly, but his steps falter the nearer he gets.]

Brr: Shit.

[The remains on the ground seem human enough. The camera catches two arms and two legs, and one odd appendage that doesn't seem to fit anywhere else. From Brr's vantage point, it looks like it is connected to a part of its body, but it is not immediately clear where it is attached. The body itself is in the process of decaying. The faint buzz of flies can be heard, and there are white maggots moving across the body.]

Brr: Ohhh shit. Did someone just give me the coordinates to the scene of a crime? Oh shit. Oh shit.

[He does not run away but approaches out of some morbid curiosity instead. He adjusts the camera on his head, trying to see it in clearer detail.]

[Up close, the man is missing half his face. There is no skull, and the remains make it evident that he is lacking a skeleton—his body sags around him like a pile of dirty laundry.]

Brr: Looks like someone just—yanked his spine right off his body. Shit, he looks like some kind of deflated balloon...

[He swings around, startled when a voice seems to call out from somewhere behind him.]

Voice: *Hello? Hello? Is anyone there?*

Brr: Yeah, I'm here! Where are you?

Voice: *I can hear you, but I can't see where you are.*

Brr: Yeah, I'm—I don't know where I am, either, but you sound pretty close. Are you lost?

Voice: *I don't know where I am. Is anyone there?*

Brr: Yeah, I said I'm here! Can you follow my voice or something?

Voice: *Hello? Is anyone there? Who are you?*

Brr: Can you not hear me, man?

[He turns toward what he has decided is the source of the voice and heads for it. He stops and slowly turns around, his camera headset providing a 360-degree view of the area when he does.]

Brr: You hear me now? Where are you?

Voice: *I don't know where I am. Oh my god—*

Brr: [sounding irritated] Oh for fucking—how did you move over there so fast?

[He heads back and pauses. The camera swings down, but the dead man has disappeared.]

Brr: What?

Voice: *I don't know where I am. Is anyone there?*

[Brr doesn't answer this time, but his breathing is faster, more panicked. He looks around desperately, looks down again at the empty spot where the body used to be, and then starts heading back where he came from.]

Voice: *Is anyone there? Who are you?*

[He is almost out of the clearing when he stops short. A silhouette appears right before him, near the trees. It looks oddly blurred, though the trees seem perfectly sharp onscreen. The figure appears to be human-shaped and is wearing some kind of dark clothing. It is staggering like its leg has been injured, its arms swinging across its body like heavy pendulums.]

Brr: Are you okay?

[The figure takes a step toward him, and then another. As it draws closer, you can finally see silk cords that appear to be tied around its wrist and legs. These cords are raised, hanging over the figure as if it were a marionette being pulled and directed on strings, though the strings disappear above the trees several dozens of feet up. Brr takes a step back as it staggers closer.]

Brr: Dude. Dude, what's wrong with you?

[The figure turns its face toward him—an unnatural angle because the head drops down parallel to its shoulder, as if its neck is broken. The voice starts up again, but now it's obvious that it is coming from the marionette-like shadow.]

Figure: *Hello? Is anyone there?*

[And then it lunges toward Brr, who promptly turns around and begins running with a yell. The foliage tilts crazily around him as he trips and hits his hands on the ground before he scrambles up and continues to flee. He turns to take another look behind him—]

[—and sees the creature in its full glory. The human-shaped silhouette staggering along is now out of the shadows, and its resemblance to the deceased person Brr found is clear—the same hair and coloring, the same type of clothes. This figure has a skeleton, but the way it jerks itself forward is still reminiscent of a puppet on strings, an observation reinforced by the thin wires fixed through its shoulders, lifting it at intervals.]

[There is something large, high above the trees. Parts of it are visibly rotting, exposing the ribcage and vertebrae. There is a patchwork of limbs and feet.]

[Brr flees. He runs for his life down the path, branches and sharp thorns scraping his arms as he forces his way through the bushes in a desperate bid to get away. All around him, the voices continue. It sounds like they are coming from all directions.]

Is anyone here?

Who are you?

Oh my god—

[Brr trips again. He tries to get up but falls. He turns to look behind him and sees that a gigantic hand has closed itself over his ankle. He looks up.]

[The puppet is looking right at him. Behind it, the decomposing hulk looms, the jaws agape, eye sockets watching him. The puppet moves its mouth, the skin around it stretching and breaking off, like thick taffy.]

Figure: *Who are you?*

[Brr screams, and the multitude of jaws come crashing down on him.]

[The livestream ends abruptly.]

From: <Storymancer> xxxxxxx@xxxxxxxx.xxx

To: <LightParticle121> xxxxxxxxxx@xxxxxxx.com

Date: 2-4-2243 7:51:13 a.m.

Subject: Re: Re: Re: Re: These Are not Mine AND not Yours

You saw the video that's been circulating, right? About UsernameGoesBrr and that cryptid? Do you know anything about it? I've never seen that kind of cryptid before, if it even is one.

From: <LightParticle121> xxxxxxx@xxxxxxxx.com

To: <Storymancer> xxxxxxx@xxxxxxxx.xxx

Date: 2-4-2243 87:21:0413 a.m.

Subject: Re: Re: Re: Re: These Are not Mine AND not Yours

[Video 1 attached. Click to scan for viruses.]

[Video 2 attached. Click to scan for viruses.]

[Video 1 starts. A logo is visible on the screen of a red moon, followed by a text that reads, "Cryptid Sequence 003: The Father," followed by a voiceover.]

Voiceover: The third cryptid of the rare Oldkeep classification has long been thought to have died out close to thirty years ago, in part because of its size and stature. Of all the cryptids within the Oldkeep family, it is considered the most dangerous, partly because of its ability to camouflage itself, and also because of its ability for mimicry. While its classification name is Cryptid 03-1736, it is more commonly known among researchers as The Puppetmaster.

The cryptid is best described as being divided into two sections: the Bait, also called the Marionette, and the Handler.

[An illustration of the cryptid is shown here. Its base appears to have a human shape, enough to pass for human, and it is referred to as "Bait" on the diagram. Connected to what looks grotesquely like an umbilical cord is a large misshapen shadow drawn to have mouths on its face instead of any other feature. It is easily ten times the size of the "Bait" and is referred to as "Handler" in the drawing. Odd string-like tendrils jut out from the Handler and appear connected to most of the Bait's appendages.]

Voiceover: *Bait* is an apt term for this particular part of the creature. This cryptid feature is able to take on the appearance of a person so that, if seen some distance away, it can be mistaken for an actual human being. It also has the ability to mimic the sound of human voices but is only limited to a few words or phrases that it has a habit of repeating over and over.

The Handler, on the other hand, makes up the core of the cryptid itself. It tends to make its home in dense surroundings such as forests or, in some recorded cases, abandoned sewers and other isolated areas. Such surroundings make it easier for them to hunt.

[A new illustration appears onscreen. The cryptid is shown here as well, with a stick figure representing an average person seemingly conversing with the Bait aspect of the creature. The Handler is hidden behind a cluster of trees.]

Voiceover: Also known as the Father, this puppet master hunts by luring its victim in using its "Bait" and pouncing to consume them once they are within reach.

[The illustration now changes to show an animated version of the Handler leaping forward and consuming the stick figure with its jaws.]

Voiceover: It has long been believed that the Bait is actually the remains of a previously captured victim that the Handler "wears" long enough to entrap another target. As the victim's body decomposes over a period of time, the Puppetmaster is forced to discard it and locate another fresh human to replace it. The difficulty in procuring new victims while making its lair in unpopulated areas has long been thought to have led to the Puppetmaster's extinction.

It has been speculated that the sounds the Bait makes to attract attention are the last words of its previous victim.

[The illustration now changes. The "Bait" is depicted as slowly melting and decomposing until it is nothing but a sludge on the ground, leaving the Handler with no Bait on its end.]

Voiceover: While researchers and scientists have long believed that the last of the Puppetmasters died out decades ago, practical suggestions for potentially encountering Puppetmasters out in the wild shall continue to be part of our daily public service announcements.

If you see a person behaving strangely or moving in a quick, jerky way, distance yourself immediately and alert any nearby authorities. Keep out of its line of sight. Ensure that you are not alone with it.

If you recognize the person behaving strangely, do not approach. It is common for Puppetmasters to target their victims using people they may be familiar with. Leave the area as soon as you can and contact law enforcement.

If the Bait has you in its sights, run away as fast as possible.

If the Handler has you in its sights, lie down on the floor. Close your eyes and pray to any god that you may believe in that it shall be quick.

Thank you for listening to this public service announcement.

[The scene switches after ten seconds into a saved text conversation, subtitles silently documenting what is said at intervals.]

JellyBeanFish has been added to the chat

JellyBeanFish: Hey!

Storymancer: Yo

JellyBeanFish: Thanks for the friend request

JellyBeanFish: This all still feels so weird

Storymancer: Welcome to my life for the past few weeks

Storymancer: Did you get the PSA video I sent you?

JellyBeanFish: I did!!

JellyBeanFish: Where did you even get this?

Storymancer: The crazy dude I told you about from the message boards.

JellyBeanFish: This is amazing

Storymancer: I've never seen this psa before

JellyBeanFish: Me neither

JellyBeanFish: You think he made it all up?

Storymancer: If he did, it only took him like an hour to do

JellyBeanFish: I should probably tell you

JellyBeanFish: My mom works with the Facility too, ok

JellyBeanFish: That's how I was able to pull up the video and send it to you

JellyBeanFish: Apparently that's all they've been talking about in the office and she had it saved in a folder I have access to

Storymancer: What are they saying about it?

JellyBeanFish: My mom doesn't usually talk about the details of what she does at work

JellyBeanFish: I've been inside Penumbra before, though, it's kinda cool

JellyBeanFish: I've been working as a sort of intern there because I wanna follow my mom's career path and be a scientist like her

Storymancer: Ohh congrats!

Storymancer: I'm not smart enough for any of that, that's why I'm just a streamer

JellyBeanFish: Haha!

JellyBeanFish: Even as an intern, they don't really tell us much about what's going on

JellyBeanFish: For the most part, we've been like, cleaning bones

Storymancer: Bones?

JellyBeanFish: Old cryptid bones and stuff

JellyBeanFish: It's pretty cool, but I wish they'd tell us more things

Storymancer: What do they know about the bloodmoon, btw?

JellyBeanFish: That's one of the things they don't usually tell us

JellyBeanFish: But there's a lot of like, moon-related things in here

JellyBeanFish: Personal mugs and desk items and stuff

JellyBeanFish: So I'm assuming they do know something about it

JellyBeanFish: Want me to poke around?

Storymancer: Only if it won't get you into trouble

JellyBeanFish: I'm the daughter of one of their high-ranking scientists. I'm practically a nepo baby.

Storymancer: lol

JellyBeanFish: I'll try. I'll start with one of my mom's coworkers who collects a lot of those red moon decos.

JellyBeanFish: She's the project lead of something they've been doing at one of the labs recently. I don't know much about that either, just that they were hauling in a lot of tanks

Storymancer: Like army tanks?

JellyBeanFish: LOL

JellyBeanFish: No, like aquarium tanks, but they're not exactly aquarium tanks

JellyBeanFish: It's like those big vats where you make mass-produced stuff like syrups and melted chocolate.

JellyBeanFish: But it's not food, it's set up like some kind of weird water terrarium

JellyBeanFish: I'll ask my mom at least

Storymancer: Thanks

Storymancer: I really appreciate all the help

JellyBeanFish: Yeah, I think I'm just as curious about this as you are.

JellyBeanFish: I'll text you again once I learn more, k?

Storymancer: Yeah, I'll let you know if I find out any more things on my end too.

JellyBeanFish: You really think that video is real?

JellyBeanFish: Both of them. That weird PSA you showed me, and the UsernameGoesBrr video

Storymancer: I don't know

Storymancer: I hope not

JellyBeanFish: Yeah

JellyBeanFish: I don't want to think about that thing existing, but it's actually possible

Storymancer: I'll poke around some more and see if I can verify whatever it is

Storymancer: talk to you later

JellyBeanFish: Yeah

[Video 2 starts playing. A silhouette of walking feet then appears on the screen, with a "Cryptid Sequence 002: The Quiet Brother" tagline, which flashes onscreen before the voiceover and accompanying subtitles commence.]

Voiceover: There is something that crawls through the lands every night, and we call it a Quiet Brother.

It is always waiting for the right time to strike. It is attracted to hotter temperatures and fire, and is therefore more prevalent in the city during the winter seasons, as it wishes to enter households to warm itself from the cold.

Its most distinguishing characteristic is the noises it makes as it moves, which resemble the moans and cries of someone in pain, or the cries of a baby, coupled with the sound of something very heavy and large pulling itself across the floor. This is often the only warning that you will hear to indicate that a Quiet Brother is already inside your house.

It is attracted to fire and warmth, as stated earlier. However, it is even more attracted to the average human's body temperature.

[There is a very simple drawing of what appears to be a creature that looks more like an abstract depiction than anything sentient. It looks like a wheel made up of soft tissue, with the edge of each spoke ending in tendrils that resemble fingers.]

Voiceover: Do not be alarmed.

[At its center is something distinctly skull-shaped, with yellow eyes and a long tongue. The creature is hovering over the stick figure of a person lying down in bed. In the next frame it is putting its tongue into the side of the person's head. The next frame shows it slowly forcing itself into the person's body, while the now-awake person is flailing their arms wildly in apparent panic. The creature is persistent and slowly pushes its inhumanly large form into the person, the growing amount of red now covering the bed signaling their progress. The last frame showcases the person now lying still with most of the creature inside of them, the tendrils slowly folding up into the smaller form.]

Voiceover: Welcome it home.

[The next picture shows the blood-drenched human figure now standing up beside the bed, but its neck is broken and hanging off to one side, and there is a prominent yellow eye bulging up from one side of its face. There is a gaping hole on its head.]

Voiceover: Fortunately, these Quiet Brothers are easy to find once they have taken up their nesting spots. Deficiencies in their appearances may vary from abnormal proportions of the eyes, teeth, tongue, and appendages to dragging its legs as if they are broken in several places (though it continues to stand and walk of its own volition). They also aren't quiet, rather ironic given its name. They make unnatural clicking sounds as their mode of communication. Researchers have mentioned the noise being similar to the buzzing of bees. While they are able to mimic human voices and words, they sometimes forget and use these clicking noises when especially agitated.

If you have come into contact with a Quiet Brother, please do not approach. If you knew the former person that the Quiet Brother has taken over, please do not approach. Maintain your distance from the Quiet Brother at all times. Do not listen when it greets you, or when it asks you for help, or when it cries out for its mother. Contact your nearest local authorities.

The incubating time of a Quiet Brother from the moment it enters its human host to freedom is exactly twenty-seven hours, thirty-eight minutes, and seventeen seconds. Every new human that it consumes will accelerate the incubation by two hours and thirty-five minutes. At the end of this period, it will flower.

[The frame returns to the crude drawing of the possessed human. It zooms in closer to its asymmetrical face with its one bulging eye, and the skull slowly begins to break apart, something that may or may not be a flower slowly growing from the split, its petals opening.]

Voiceover: Once flowering has been achieved, we will know peace.

Do not engage with the Quiet Brother. Contact your local authorities as soon as possible, and monitor it from a safe distance.

[The video changes abruptly to a man who has been strapped onto a long table, tied down with ropes and other hospital implements. He is naked from the chest and stomach up. He has no legs below that, and instead has long fat tendrils, about eight or nine, unfurling from a point underneath his waist, not unlike the way an octopus might look. There is no sound in the video, but his head is thrown back like he is screaming. He is pulling frantically at the straps tied to his wrists and forehead. At one point, one of the straps almost comes loose from the force of his tugging, but a few people in hazmat suits hurry forward to keep him fettered, wrestling him back into the cords.]

[His head is grossly misshapen, a large crack running down the center of his forehead, although there is no blood. As the video continues, his face warps as if it is literally coming apart—but the video cuts off before any more can be seen.]

VIDEO #5

Are You Listening?
With Morn Fields

Morn Fields is the closest thing we have to a celebrity who isn't really a celebrity—just basically one of those folks who likes to discuss current events and dissect them for public consumption. He started out as a radio personality, and I know that sounds weird. Like, who even listens to the radio anymore? But he was able to piggyback off his popularity there and branch out into podcasts, streams—he's got a self-deprecating way of talking that makes people comfortable, and from what I've listened to so far, he seems to have a balanced view on most topics that makes him sound honest. He's got strong opinions about some things, but at least he admits his biases about them.

The one thing about him, though, are his horoscopes, which were what started some weird cult following around him. He started reading them out on his show on a lark, but the thing was, a lot of the predictions he made started coming true, and there are a lot of people convinced he can see the future or something. He still reads them because it gives him a lot of engagement, but he started putting up disclaimers with them.

I've even met him before—he stopped by our school once to help out with a fundraising drive or something, I don't even remember what it was anymore. He had a very nice soothing voice to listen to, which was why I was a little surprised to find out that he was a slight man with glasses and somewhat balding hair—nothing at all like I would have imagined him to be. But he was as nice in person as he sounded, and he signed a ton of autographs and took pictures with students even after the principal said he didn't need to. He even gave us a small class in how to break into the business. Nicer than some other celebrities I've met.

Morn Fields is also someone who people trust to explain complicated subjects or the news to them if they were out of the loop for some reason. He's the one I've heard who talked a lot about the bloodmoon and other mysteries surrounding it, so I'm putting some snippets of his shows about them for some background information. This one talks about the most recent news surrounding the body in the woods.

Welcome, viewers, to *Are You Listening?*, Wispy Falls's most popular radio station for your daily news, reasonable opinions, and the best beats. I am Morn Fields, your host for the next two hours while we talk about everything that's been going on with our sleepy little town.

And of course, we can't start without talking about the dead body in the woods, can we?

I know that the township is telling us to ignore it. I know that talking about dead bodies in any shape or form is going to be bad for morale, especially when we've got the bloodmoon coming up in a month, and things are going to be hectic. And I know what you're saying. *Morn, what good would it do to even talk about it? Why are you attracting their ire by bringing it into the spotlight? The town gives us great benefits. They give us a thirty-hour work week and a basic income outside our jobs besides. We have free healthcare, crime is barely existent, and we're living the good life. And all we need to do to keep enjoying these things is stay home during the yearly bloodmoon and never go deep into the woods surrounding Wispy Falls. Why are you trying to get us all into trouble, Morn?*

Well for one thing, I've been talking about the topics the authorities say not to talk about for as long as my show has been on air, and no one's been after me for it. I know that a lot of people on the Scrawl like to complain about how our free-dom for certain speeches has always been restricted, and how it is tyrannical to police what people say and post. I would say that I am the prime shining example of how the government, in fact, is quite lenient when it comes to free speech, considering I have not yet been jailed or murdered and passed off as another missing persons case, which is the usual go-to accusation for those people when they need some fearmongering to make their point.

I like to think that I have gone fairly unacknowledged by most of the town leadership not because I talk about the topics they would rather not be discussed, but because I talk about the topics *responsibly*. Always have and always will. The body, for example. Let me talk about the dead body *responsibly*.

Very little information has been leaked about the incident in general, but here are the facts as they have been reported. The body appears to be a white man in a state of dishevelment, emaciated and very thin, dressed in dirty clothing. Some preliminary autopsy states that he had drugs in his system, and they are likely what led to his demise, which did make me rather suspicious at first. Wispy Falls is not so large a place that people would not have been oblivious to some meth head's den in town, and the closest thing we have nowadays to any psychoactive drugs are those big white mushrooms people like to dig up and eat so they can taste colors for the next three hours.

And if hard drugs are an improbable cause of his death, then we must assume that it is *prescription* drugs that the coroner is referring to, and no one else in town dispenses those medications but Penumbra Corp. I do agree with the many who want to call on any Penumbra representatives to explain how some very carefully controlled drugs from their facilities have found their way into a stranger's bloodstream, and I do hope for their sake they tell their side of the story soon. As much as many in town rely on them for their medical needs, I understand there is a huge shortage of medication currently, and there needs to be an accounting, especially when these drugs are finding their way to miscreants instead of those who actually need them for their quality of life. We've all heard horror stories of those greedy pharmaceutical companies and hospitals of old, back when the world outside still flourished. We were promised honesty above all else, and even though Penumbra has done much to change many of our lives for the better, I would still like to see them upheld to Wispy Fall standards, if only to ensure that no corruption within their corporation is taking place.

Have I been talking responsibly about all this so far? I hope so.

Now, to the infamous video. UsernameGoesBrr was his name, right? Lots of talk about whether or not the video is actually real. There have been amateurs and professionals on both sides of the aisle, with some very well-respected people saying that the video is real on one end, and other just-as-capable people on the other end saying that the video is likely a fake, so no one's sure what to believe at the moment.

The streamer himself had a small following. This UsernameGoesBrr fella. I remember, because I tried to do my research on what he makes content on and discovered that his schtick revolved around exploring abandoned places and pulling pranks on people. The first I can understand and even appreciate, but the second just feels mean, doesn't it? I saw a video where he tried to headbutt random strangers on the street and got clocked. Makes you wonder if they go around asking to be hit because that gives them more views. He's also been accused of faking a lot of the videos he'd posted before. Pretending that there was something chasing him, acting like the Backward Lady had followed him back into the house, things like that. It's a big reason why most people don't believe him. Unfortunately, if you cry wolf a few too many times, no one hears you even when the sheep start disappearing.

He hasn't posted any more content since that video of his got taken down. Because I like to be thorough, I reached out to his family for more information, but they weren't forthcoming about much, so I backed off. As much as I am curious, I'd rather not push when they were so clearly not wanting any more attention on their family, and I'm not gonna be one of those pushy people to keep going at them. If any one of you have any information related to these photos, or if any of you had been brave—or stupid, depending who you ask—enough to actually venture out into those woods and come back with physical proof, then feel free to call us and we'll put you on air!

For his family's sake, I hope he's not shamming, and I hope they find him soon. Me, I'm on the side where I think it might have some grain of truth to it. I know you're thinking *it has to be fake, right*? The town's been pretty good when it comes to the usual PSAs, and I've never heard about this particular cryptid before. I shot the breeze with a few old folks I know who've been here forever, and they've never heard of this…creature puppeteer either.

But Penumbra's been pretty quiet about this as a whole. So have the other leaders, in fact. Only the Police Chief Inspector's put out a statement, and he has to! I think the creature, at the least, might be something the Facility is familiar with. Call it a hunch, but till I get proof otherwise, that's where I'm putting my bet down.

Which brings us to this week's Dear Morn letter, this time from Puzzled Pills over at 281 Kerrich Avenue!

Dearest Morn,

So, I'm sixteen years old, and my mom works as a nurse at the Facility. She hasn't been home for, like, five days now. I know she's pulled some ridiculous over-time before, and I know she's doing a lot of important work assisting the doctors and researchers there to help make the town a better place, blah blah blah. Even if she weren't a nurse there, I've seen enough ads on TV to know that the work they do there is essential. But still, she hasn't texted me anything, and she usually does if she knows she's gonna be clocking in more hours. Five days, though? I'm kinda worried.

And my dad's no help either. He had some surgery earlier this month 'cause he had some kind of tumor or something they needed to get out of him. They said it was just benign and it wasn't cancer. But ever since then, all he does is sleep in front of the television, eat frozen dinners, and then pop some of the painkillers he has. He's not really the type to do a lot of work around the house anyway, you know? But they gave him three months' leave from work and this is all he's been doing. When I ask him to help me with laundry or the dishes or something, he just complains it's too much, and then goes back to watching his shows. He doesn't even seem to care that Mom's been gone for a long time.

The authorities are no help either. I went to them and tried to file a report, but once they heard that my mom works for the Facility, they just sort of laughed and then said that my mom is a hero, but pulling some long hours at work doesn't mean that she's missing, and they hope she's getting paid well for the extra hours. They did agree to call the place and check, and then they came back to me and said she was doing fine. But they didn't even let me on the phone to talk to her directly and ask if she was all right. They just said she was doing something complicated right now, and anything else would be a distraction. I mean…seriously? She couldn't even talk for, like, two minutes?

I don't believe them, and I'm getting kinda desperate here. I know for a fact that they keep a lot of secrets in there, and my mom has mentioned in passing before that if most people knew what she knew, they would freak. So would it be bad of me to, like, just go back to the police and say that she went into the woods and didn't come back or something? Like, yeah, I know I'll be getting into trouble, but at least I'd know she's actually safe! But if not, are there any other options I have to make sure?

Signed, Worried at Home

Well, dear Worried at Home,

You must surely be aware of the pharmaceutical shortage we have at the moment, aren't you? Try as the facility might, they must control the medication count to ensure that everyone who deserves it can have access. Your mother is likely working hard to ensure that healthcare is accessible to all, especially at this critical moment. I would caution against making her life even more challenging than it already is, and that includes potentially filing a false police report that will put her in a very stressful spotlight, even if you did not intend to do that to her. You could well be arrested and imprisoned for a very long time over an impulse decision!

I am sorry that your mother is not home as often as you like. I have received letters from many others over the years who have been in your position: A family member or a loved one works at Penumbra, and they have to sit at home and wait while their loved one toils long hours to make sure that the rest of the town is protected. I know it is difficult, but I suggest waiting it out. And then, once she is safely home, you two should discuss what steps to take in the future if she should be in that position again where she cannot send word back home about how long she will be working at the Facility so that she does not worry you if it happens again.

And in the meantime, it might do the both of you well to force that ne'er-do-well father of yours to help with the chores every now and then!

Need more advice from me? Feel free to write me anytime! Always remember—we take your privacy seriously and will be removing any identifying names from your letter! Remember, you are *never* the problem.

And now here's what everyone's been waiting for—your horoscopes for the day. As always, the show *Are You Listening?*, its host Morn Fields, (that's me!), nor any of the staff can be held liable for anything that we read out to you folks, and any similarities to any people or events are strictly coincidences. And now that we have that out of the way, let's begin.

Today's horoscopes are sponsored by Meats and Things—we have lovely meat and lovely things! More meat for you with twice the quality at half the price, and more things for you, for free!

Aries: Know that Steve is a jerk and you're better off without him. Be especially wary when he stops by tomorrow, because he'll be asking you for a loan to fund one of his money-sinking harebrained ideas again.

Taurus: I don't think there is anything wrong with the carrots. I think your mother-in-law is poisoning you.

Gemini: Look, it's not a figment of your imagination. Someone really is watching you.

Cancer: Lies. The cake is a lie. No matter how mouthwatering it looks, do not eat that cake.

Leo: I know why the chicken crossed the road. Because it knows better than to go into the woods. You should know that too.

Virgo: Doormat. You're a doormat to these people. They are not family. They are enablers who want to take advantage of you for the free labor you provide them. Find a spine and cut them out of your life for good.

Libra: Excel in your work and you will be rewarded soon. Work smarter and not harder, because you know that jackass at the next cubicle is only getting promoted because he's dating the boss's daughter, so maybe get one over on him and date the boss instead.

Scorpio: Liz. The yogurt isn't the issue here. Stop lying or your relationship will never work out.

Sagittarius: Good evening. There will be an accident at the corner of Drought and Miles, and you will be in it. For the rest of these predictions to work, you must be in it. Are you going to let them down? Are you going to destroy so many people's lives simply because you refuse to be where you are supposed to be?

Capricorn: A word of advice: Do not watch that movie. Your ex loves that movie. Will you let her win? Will you allow yourself the mistake of missing her, after everything she's done to you?

Aquarius: Do gather the following: a thimbleful of dirt, five rose petals, three cups of red wine, and a pig's entrails. Bury them in your garden tonight, where the forget-me-nots are. You will receive a pleasant surprise in the morning.

Pisces: On your life, do not look out the window tonight.

Apotropaion: Rest is for the wicked. Wait for a sign in the woods. Tomorrow we open the curiosities.

And that's it for me today at Good Morn! Remember to stay vigilant, stay happy, and stay safe!

[A video begins. It is of a woman tying her hair up into a ponytail, smiling at herself in the mirror.]

The woman: I don't really understand why you're filming me, dear. Is it for another one of those video streams you like to do?

Storymancer's voice, offscreen: I'm just worried about you, Mom. You and Dad.

The woman: Don't be silly. There's nothing to worry about anymore.

[The woman reaches for a pill bottle, popping one into her mouth before setting the medication back down. She turns to smile at the camera.]

The woman: I'll be out tonight with Dad, all right? We're visiting some friends for dinner. Don't wait up for us.

[She laughs and turns to leave. The camera watches as she steps out of the room.]

Storymancer's voice: This was my mom, two weeks after my younger brother, Lee, went missing. Before this, she was barely eating, cried herself to sleep every night, and could barely get herself out of bed, much less think about going out and having fun.

Medication is closely monitored here in Wispy Falls. They don't hand it out this easily, and you need a good reason to take it. Like if you have PTSD from your younger brother's disappearance.

I didn't take any. I felt weird after taking the first one. Like I was floating. Like my mind was numb.

The numbness made me forget about Lee for a bit, so I stopped taking it. Pretended to.

There's something wrong with those pills.

VIDEO #6

The Sprawl: Wispy Falls Message Board

QuestionTheExperts/

Need something explained by someone who studied it? As the forum title states, we'll be featuring experts on a variety of topics both popular and obscure, so you can learn something new!

If you are an expert on a specific topic or niche, feel free to reach out to us!

CuriousCurator says: I'm the new curator at the recently opened Museum of Unnatural Curiosities, now at Seventh and Ninth Street. Ask me your questions! (16293 people liked this)

Hello there! My name is Audrey Withers, and I am currently the curator of the first ever Wispy Falls museum. My primary area of research is the evolution of carnivorous animals, more specifically studying the bones and remains of cryptids we've discovered over the years. I also lead a team working to clean and repair fossil specimens for public display and preserve fossil and subfossil records as well as gather information on previous ecosystems to improve upon modern conservation techniques.

I am here to promote the opening of the museum! Come view our vast collection of varied cryptid specimens starting tomorrow!

I'll be answering questions starting today until tomorrow at 4 p.m.!

+ **IntrepridHungover** (12856 users liked this)

Will the museum have more information concerning the bloodmoon ritual and how that all began? I've always been confused about how that all came around and would appreciate it if someone who has more knowledge than the average resident could help me understand more.

+ **CuriousCurator** (11699 users liked this)

Thank you for asking that! We researchers don't actually know a lot more, since the founding of Wispy Falls has not been well-documented, save for some scraps of journal entries by its founder, Abraham Huntington. What we do know about the bloodmoon ritual relies heavily on his notes which, as every historian will tell you, are subjective. The gist of it is that the world outside had long been overrun by unnamed creatures, the source of which had never been known. Theories have ranged between some kind of virus, a worldwide curse, or changes in the Earth's climate or composition that forced animals to evolve at an alarming and frightening rate, transforming them into vicious predators. We don't have any firsthand documentation offering proof of any of this, as we can't quite venture out of Wispy Falls for the evidence we would require to prove or disprove those theories.

What we do know is that Wispy Falls's founder had accidentally learned how to protect himself while traveling through the dangerous wastelands the world had been transformed into and defend himself against most of the cryptids there. Like him, we often simply refer to his discovery as Stones—*Anaborea excisismus* is our scientific name for them. They emit an odd scent too complex for our sense of smell to detect, but which serves as some kind of horrendous body odor that is off-putting to most cryptids, essentially keeping them away.

Now, here's where the story gets interesting. In his diary, Huntington claimed that he had a dream where he stumbled upon a treasure in the wilds. When he sought out the place using the landmarks he remembered from his dream, he found plant cryptids and some strange stones that seemed to repel them. He learned to breed these plants by harvesting their seeds and finding the ideal environment for them to thrive, as well as preserve and protect the stones. A settlement eventually grew and became Wispy Falls once it was known that the town was nearly impervious to most cryptid attacks. The bloodmoon ritual is a way for us to replenish and reinforce these defenses, and for that we need to ask everyone to remain inside their house in order to not attract any cryptids while we work to further protect you all.

I understand that a lot of people feel like this is not enough information, and I empathize with them. "Why do we have to remain inside our places of residence? If there are monsters about, won't they be able to find us inside our houses just as easily as outside?" I wish I had a better explanation to give, but that has always been the government policy, and it has served us well so far. We do know based on previous data that staying at home does increase your chances of survival. And obviously, being inside the house means you're not in the woods, which means the Backward Lady won't get you.

+ **TentacleTater** (9572 users liked this)

What is the most carefully preserved cryptid you've ever worked on that gave you more information than you thought it would?

+ **CuriousCurator** (9953 users like this)

I suppose it would have to be the Bloat, though admittedly that is one of the rather grosser things anyone would have to study. Bloats are generally more common than other cryptids, and we can learn a lot just from dissecting their remains. Our research tells us that Bloats are capable of surviving harsh environments as long as they remain in their hibernation phase, though they can easily become vulnerable (and pose a danger to other people in the process) once they "mature." In the over twenty-five years I've been studying cryptids, I've only ever been able to bring back one specimen that was still in its hibernation phase, and we needed to go through a lot of clearance to have just that one in our labs! None that we have discovered out in the wild have been in their active phase, though I am glad, given the damage they could cause!

+ **MaxfieldSheffield69420** (6496 users liked this)

How did that go? Did the hibernating one you had accidentally wake up and mutate, and if so, how were you able to contain it?

+ **CuriousCurator** (11699 users liked this)

Fortunately, it did not evolve while we were studying it, though we placed it in a cage with reinforcement to ensure minimal damage if it had. Even that made people antsy, and in the end, we decided to terminate the creature to ensure everyone's safety.

+ **NewFoundGloryman** (5284 users liked this)

You mention cryptid specimens—what has been the most interesting of them to work on, and why?

+ **CuriousCurator** (3759 users liked this)

I actually enjoy working with the carrion pigeon. It's a fairly docile birdlike creature that has the same intelligence as a dog. You can train it to learn tricks and follow simple commands, and they can be quite affectionate if they get used to you feeding them by hand. I have a colleague we jokingly called the "carrion whisperer," since he was in charge of their feeding. It was fun to see them follow him around like ducklings!

+ **NewFoundGloryman** (3645 users liked this)

I do have another question—why are they named carrion pigeons if they don't actually look like pigeons?

+ **CuriousCurator** (2835 users liked this)

When we first began studying them, we realized that their physiology was very similar to the carrier pigeon, despite the differences in size and features, albeit with a very odd twist. A carrion pigeon usually has rotting insides, which makes it harder to study. It's even harder because natural carrier pigeons are extinct. But despite these obstacles, we know that their mating habits and traits are very similar. The pun, then, is calling them a "carrion" pigeon because they mainly feed on corpses.

+ **Magical_Girl_Annie** (11699 users liked this)

Right?? They look more like cassowaries that I've seen in old photos. Those always look like they're challenging you to a boxing match.

+ **BillOfTheFirmament** (10218 users liked this)

What is your opinion about the recent discovery of the body in the woods? Is it an ancient cryptid, or is it that so-called criminal who escaped all those years ago?

+ **CuriousCurator** (10681 users liked this)

As a matter of fact, I do have an opinion on this. The remains wound up being transferred to the Penumbra facility, and I actually got to have a good look at the specimen in particular.

To sum it up—no, it's not the body of Adam Morrissey. What it actually is, is the Bloat. Do you know those dancing balloon figures they sometimes use in car dealerships or to promote the opening of a new store? Well, the Bloat is something like that, except better made, like a life-sized vintage doll but not quite, due to its overblown midsection. It could pass as a human being at first glance, but most people could tell that it is not human with a second look, because the human being in question has been "bloated" up to literally appear round and spheric in shape, even though it retains human features such as eyes, a nose, and a mouth, with two arms.

While that sounds horrifying, Bloats actually take on human appearance as an evolutionary defense. Any other cryptids that choose to attack the Bloat wind up getting poisoned and paralyzed. Then the Bloat drains it of blood, very much like a black widow spider. Fortunately, Bloats are also stationary, growing where they stand and unable to move. This makes it less likely humans will be harmed. Bloats also generally have a lifespan of only about a month—once it consumes another cryptid's blood, it generates a new seed to sprout as it dies off.

It's easy enough to mistake a dead Bloat for a human. I know there's a video going around, but the lack of skeletal structure on the remains proves that it's a Bloat.

> + **LightParticle121** (-1831 users liked this)
>
> Not a Bloat. They know how to Control Them. they Control Them ToReplace you at Home So they can. Monitoor you. The people They want Train to lead the Next generation, they Will replace your Family first soThey can Control you. They can make Headless from their Labs And

Quiet Brothers and Eggs and Weepers You Arre One of Them

+ Jess_Jones1983 (2645 users liked this)

Have you ever seen a Weeper? Seeing what little they leave of their victims is nightmare fuel enough.

+ Milktea_StrawberryMatcha (1385 users liked this)

Seconding that. One time I heard someone crying when I was walking home, and my first thought was that there was a lost child nearby. And then I realized it was the middle of the night, most people were asleep, and the chances of a child wandering around at that time were very small. I ran all the way home, locked the doors and covered the windows, and just lay underneath my blankets till morning. Once or twice, I could have sworn I heard a couple taps at my window, but morning came without incident. I still think I had a close encounter with one of those.

+ Jess_Jones1983 (406 users liked this)

Yeah, glad you made it out of there safely. My parents have always told me to keep running and never stop till you get home if you hear a child crying. Maybe there really is a kid out there, but better be safe than sorry, right?

+ OmniscientGarlic (5638 users liked this)

If I were to find some cool fossil or bone or anything like that, where would be a good place to let you or your team know?

+ **CuriousCurator** (4246 users liked this)

Send me an email with the photo of whatever it is that you've found. My team and I usually get something once every two or three weeks from people who just wanted to show us something cool that they've seen when they're out on walks. We don't disparage anyone from doing so because it's such a great opportunity to learn if there are any new areas we've never even thought about looking at otherwise!

+**HeavenlyEgg** (3245 users like this)

Do you consider the Backward Lady a cryptid? Have you ever tried to find her as part of your research?

+ **CuriousCurator** (2724 users liked this)

The Backward Lady is a bit unusual in that she doesn't quite fit our typical prerequisites for determining a cryptid. The others we study fall under a category of creatures, but the Backward Lady is unique in that there is no other like her, and she is probably the only one of her kind, which means all our customary research collecting evolutionary patterns doesn't matter. That said, I have more than a few colleagues who are very interested in studying her, though from all the evidence people have gathered about her, it would seem to be useless to put her in any restraints or holding cell, due mainly to her incorporeality.

+ [Comment has been deleted by the moderator for violating the forum rules.]

+ **AmoebaAmorsis** (257 users liked this)

> Lol.
>
> Someone's jealous.

> + [Comment has been deleted by the moderator for violating the forum rules.]

> + **SpongeBoss_SquareRants** (145 users liked this)
>
> > Go home, girl. You drunk.

+ **Yolelehihoo** (136 users liked this)

> Why do these weirdos keep popping up every time there's a science AMA?

> + **IHavethePower** (23 users liked this)
>
> > Do you really have to ask or was that a rhetorical question?

WISPY FALLS MESSAGE INBOX

From: Storymancer

To: Yolehehihoo

Hi there! I saw your comment on the Sprawl where you were in a thread about the museum AMA. You were responding to someone whose replies have been deleted by the moderators, and I was wondering if you remember what was being mentioned in that specific post?

From: Yolelehihoo

To: Storymancer

Hey, I know you! You're that streamer who does a ton of those haunted places videos, right? Awesome!

And yeah, I did talk to the person, and as a matter of fact, I took a screenshot of it at the time because I wanted to show a coworker of mine who loves conspiracy theories what a kook that user was. I'll attach it here.

[Screenshot of a Wispy Falls comment thread is attached.]

+ **HederaRose16** (-27 users liked this)

Please do not give this woman and her museum any more attention than they already have! I am the scientist who used to work on this project and this is nothing but a front! It's a distraction from the Morrissey incident and made to have you believe that it was cryptid bones they found in the woods and not his body! They want you to think that everything is okay! Screenshot this reply asap, because you know they'll take this down as soon as they see this, but to anyone who actually wants to know the truth, I swear I can give you all the information you need if you can prove to me that you are not one of their spies.

> + **AmoebaAmorsis** (257 users liked this)
>
> Lol.
>
> Someone's jealous.

+HederaRose16 (-12 users liked this)

I resigned my position voluntarily. This woman and the people behind her are actively trying to use all of you as fodder for an even worse cryptid that none of you even know!

+ SpongeBoss_SquareRants (145 users liked this)

Go home, girl. You drunk.

+ Yolelehihoo (136 users liked this)

Why do these weirdos keep popping up every time there's a science AMA?

+ IHavethePower (23 users liked this)

Do you really have to ask or was that a rhetorical question?

VIDEO #7

Storymancer's Video Blog Entry: An Analysis

At first glance, yes, the moderator had every right to delete the user's comments for being rude and for not posing any actual questions. But to be banned from the forum entirely? I've seen worse users who've all but bullied and stalked other people on the boards and still continue to keep their accounts. And while some can argue that all those other problematic accounts simply slipped through the cracks, it was the speed with which they banned user HederaRose16 that did attract my attention.

So, I decided to go down that rabbit hole and see what I could find.

To start, the username itself. A quick online search did not come up with any promising leads, but I wasn't deterred. The username was pretty unique, not something they would have come up with at random—my guess is that there's something in their name that can give me a clue as to who they are, even though that was a long shot.

So, back to my snooping. They mentioned that they once worked with the museum curator, Audrey Withers, albeit in a much higher position. The Facility has a list of their current and previous employees, but a look at their website turned up nothing. None of the listed names there seem to have any correlation with the username below. Since they were so quick to delete their account, I assume they're aware of who did it and scrubbed their page just as quickly.

No problem, though. Just set the search engine to look for previous iterations of the page, and voilà! It tells me that the page was updated only two days ago—which is roughly the same time the AMA happened and HederaRose16 posted. So, all I need to do is find out what the difference between that page and the current one is and—aha! Here we go—one name had been taken off, Ivy Delgado, and that's my answer. Ivy, a plant that is also commonly known as a hedera. Not a coincidence!

So now we have a name. Searching the name *Ivy Delgado* doesn't turn up much—just names of other people who don't seem to have anything to do with the Facility. But going back and checking out previous pages comes up with an Ivy Delgado who graduated from Wispy Falls University, has a doctorate in cryptic physiology, and had previously worked at the Facility for the last twenty-eight years. Much more promising!

All her social media, however, appears to have been scrubbed, and likely not by choice. Obviously, her email linked to the Facility no longer works, and now I'm frustrated. We have a name and yet I'm coming up with nothing!

And then I had a burst of inspiration. Her username was HederaRose16. Surely the rest of her username isn't random either. And I was right.

It took long enough, but I think I have my answer. I pored over quite a few links and paid for website crawls and investigative sites to get the name I needed but, yeah. According to the site, there are three Ivy Delgados in Wispy Falls. One is eighty-six years old and in a nursing home, the other is nineteen years old. Which leaves Ivy Delgado, forty-five years old, whose last known address is at the Rose Apartelle, Apartment 16.

Guess where I'm going next??

But first, a quick conversation with someone who was slowly becoming an ally of mine in the search for the truth. I make a point to showcase this conversation with JellyBeanFish simply because she has an in with the Facility through her mother, and also because she's much more familiar with cryptozoology than I am. She reached out to me shortly after that Question the Experts post went public.

JellyBeanFish: She's lying.

Storymancer: Who?

JellyBeanFish: My mom. CuriousCurator.

JellyBeanFish: That's not what a Bloat is.

JellyBeanFish: Bloats hate sunlight. They also move, but very slowly, the same way vines or a tree's roots would. The place where Brr found those remains was right in a clearing where the sun was shining down on it without any cover. Bloats would rather choose to hibernate and slowly move deep beneath the ground until they find a dark place where they could grow and wait for other cryptids to hunt. She should have known that, but she was lying.

Storymancer: How sure are you about this?

JellyBeanFish: Very sure. I think you're right. I think there's something they're trying to cover up.

JellyBeanFish: That's why I'm starting to think there might be something about that other source of yours. That LightParticle121 guy. Maybe he didn't fake that video. Maybe it really is that alleged criminal who went missing. Do you

know anything about this Morrissey guy??

Storymancer: I found several newspaper articles about him.

Hold on, let me grab one for you.

[A link to a website article is attached.]

EXTREMELY DANGEROUS

Convicted murderer and terrorist escapes
from restraining facility: Police Chief

A man convicted of murdering three people who was serving
three life sentences has escaped from the Wispy Falls restraining facility, authorities said.

There is currently a manhunt underway for Adam
Morrissey, forty-five, who escaped from the Lighthands
Restraining Facility at approximately 9:45 p.m. local time
Monday, officials said.

He was last seen at the Springtime gasoline station around
1:25 p.m. Thursday, according to the Chief of Police's office,
who warn that Morrissey should be considered "armed and
extremely dangerous."

"He is a depraved individual and an utterly vile waste of
space fit only for the gallows. He is a sick man and he must
be stopped at all costs, for he has nothing to lose and only his
freedom to gain," Police Chief Apartow told reporters at a press
briefing on Thursday.

Morrissey was convicted of three first-degree murders for

fatally stabbing his wife and two children last November, officials said. He was also charged with one count of arson and multiple counts of attempted murder for planning to blow up the Penumbra facility shortly after, though charges were dropped after his conviction for murder.

He had no chance of parole.

JellyBeanFish: So he was never caught?

Storymancer: Nope. This was the last time that the news ever mentioned him. He escaped four months ago, nothing since then.

Storymancer: The odd thing is that I've never heard of the guy. We don't have a lot of murders in town, and if there were any, everyone would be talking about it.

Storymancer: I had to go through a lot of older news articles to find anything about this dude, and the only thing I found was a really short article that mentioned he'd been in prison for almost twenty years. I can understand why no one remembers him now.

JellyBeanFish: So what it also means is there's a chance that Morrissey is the body they found, and they're passing it off as a Bloat.

Storymancer: Why would they hide it, though? Wouldn't it be good to announce that he's finally been found, and that he is dead?

Storymancer: Are you saying that your mom's in on this too?

JellyBeanFish: I don't really know you beyond our texts here, but I'm going to be up-front with you, okay?

Storymancer: Sure.

JellyBeanFish: My mom's been acting strange for the last few months. She's always been busy with work at Penumbra, but before she always found time to get home early enough to have dinner with me. But in the last few weeks, I've barely seen her. Most of the time I'm asleep when she comes home, and there have been days when she's even spent the night at the Facility. She started working weekends. I've seen her maybe twice in the last two weeks. When I ask her what's wrong or why she's been working so hard, she just sighs and tells me she's doing her best, and that it'll be done soon and we can spend more time together. But I doubt it's going to get better, especially since she's now in charge of this museum I hadn't even heard of until I saw that forum post. She never told me she was going to be placed in charge of the museum, ever. She would have told me.

JellyBeanFish: I don't even see her when I'm interning there anymore. I send her a text when I'm ready to leave, and she always tells me to go on ahead and that she'll be home soon. But she's never home soon anymore.

Storymancer: I'm sorry.

JellyBeanFish: Hah, yeah.

JellyBeanFish: I don't know anymore.

JellyBeanFish: She doesn't even pick up her phone when I call. She always apologizes, but...

JellyBeanFish: This isn't like her at all.

Storymancer: What are you going to do?

JellyBeanFish: I want to confront her later, but I don't even know if she's coming home.

JellyBeanFish: I'm going to go to the Facility after school for the internship. I think I'm going to find someone there and insist they bring me to her.

Storymancer: I hope her workload gets better.

JellyBeanFish: Yeah, me too.

JellyBeanFish: You got any new information to tell?

Storymancer: Ivy Delgado. Tell me everything you know about her.

JellyBeanFish: I've met her a couple of times before. She's nice. She was my mom's boss, but I think she resigned like a few weeks ago.

Storymancer: No scandal or anything like that?

JellyBeanFish: No. But she just didn't turn up one day, and then one of the higher-ups announced that she was leaving and they had a going away celebration for her. I wasn't invited of course, but I don't think Mom was either. She never said anything about it, at least.

Storymancer: I think something might have happened to her.

JellyBeanFish: Why?

Storymancer: A hunch.

JellyBeanFish: You're really focused on investigating this, aren't you?

Storymancer: No offense to you or your mom, but I think they've got something going on at the Facility that they're covering up.

JellyBeanFish: You're not one of those people who thinks it's all a big government conspiracy where they're putting poison in the water to make us obedient, right?

Storymancer: Still too early in the investigation to say.

JellyBeanFish: Uhh

Storymancer: I'm kidding.

Storymancer: Partly

Storymancer: What, you never suspected they could be doing things just for profit instead of being the good Samaritans their ads keep saying they are?

JellyBeanFish: Of course I did, they're a conglomerate, pretty much

JellyBeanFish: But every company is out to make a profit, they're not the only ones

JellyBeanFish: But I do want to help you. Why else would I be sending you videos even though I know you're trying to find stuff to take them down with?

Storymancer: You're an intern with Penumbra, and your mom works there. Why are you even helping me?

JellyBeanFish: I have friends who've lost family to the woods too. I didn't like how they handled their investigations. And that video...

Storymancer: Brr's video?

JellyBeanFish: Even if that video is fake, it still feels like it was made by someone who knows cryptids well. More than any other average person would be able to know. They must have at least worked at the Penumbra facility in the past to get some advanced knowledge of similar physiologies, right?? And I don't know any other place in town where he could have learned all that.

Storymancer: I've got a plan.

JellyBeanFish: Do I get to hear it?

Storymancer: Not yet. I'm gonna see if it pays off first, and then I'll share what I've found with you after.

JellyBeanFish: Good luck. Let me know if you've found anything there.

[A home video plays of two boys laughing as they cling to monkey bars, trying to goad each other into letting go first. They appear to be in a playground, though they are the only two people seen on camera. The older boy is wearing a plain blue shirt and khaki pants, and the younger wears a red shirt and ripped jeans. After several seconds, the boy in the red shirt loses his grip and falls to the ground. Seeing this, the boy in the blue shirt promptly lets go as well, landing on the ground and bouncing back up before the other boy could. He picks up the boy in the red shirt and half-carries him, shouting, "I'll protect you! I'll protect you!" while the younger kid squeals in glee.]

Storymancer: Sometimes I look through these old videos and watch Lee the way I remember him. We were each other's best friends. Some days it's still hard not to let go.

[The boy in the blue shirt finally sets the boy in red down, and then tugs insistently at his arm, gesturing toward the nearby slide.]

I don't want to take the medicine. I've seen my parents take it and zone out, even though they seem to go to work and function well enough. When I took it that first time, it was almost like I'd forgotten about Lee. Like I was the only kid my folks ever had or something. It was a weird feeling. And then it wore off and I remembered him, and I felt so guilty. I always wondered why Mom and Dad didn't feel guilty and just kept taking it anyway...

[The boy in blue helps his younger brother up the slide before climbing after him, laughing as they both skid down.]

I really miss you, Lee. I'm doing this for you.

VIDEO #8

Storymancer's Video Stream:
An Abandoned Building

[It is nighttime. A video camera slowly pans over a building. There does not seem to be any kind of activity within. A voice, clearly the person holding the camera, speaks.]

Storymancer: Well, this is the apartment building I think Ivy Delgado is currently living in. I have no way of actually contacting her since all her social media accounts appear to be wiped, and she gave me no clues as to what her email is, if she even has one. So, I decided to take the plunge and visit her myself, just to see if she really does know something about the Morrissey incident and whether or not the so-called body in the woods is an escaped criminal like she and some conspiracy theorists are claiming, or if they really are just cryptid bones.

[The camera approaches the front door. The person hesitates.]

Storymancer: Well, that's weird. I don't think there's any light inside. Is it even—oh!

[He gives the door a tentative push, and it opens easily but reveals a yawning darkness within, with no light in sight.]

Storymancer: What the hell?

[There are some fumbling noises before he produces a flashlight, which he switches on, carefully splaying it into the room within. There does not seem to be anyone inside.]

Storymancer: Yeah, this is creepy. I kinda wanna back out now, but since I'm already here... Hello? Anyone home?

[No one responds.]

Storymancer: Oh, make myself at home? Don't mind if I do. Just don't be a demon or anything, all right?

[He steps through and shines the flashlight across the walls, finding a small switch nearby. He flicks it on, and the room is immediately flooded with light.]

Storymancer: Oh, shi—haha, I wasn't expecting that. Good. Good. Hello?

[There is no answer. The camera shifts again as the person ventures farther in. There are several more rooms inside; he enters one, which is revealed to be a small lounge area. There is no one here.]

Storymancer: Kinda weird that the whole building would be sitting in darkness like this if there are still people living here. Are there? Maybe I made a mistake...

[He moves toward a small area where the elevators appear to be located. Hesitantly, he presses the button and gives a slight start when it blinks green, and the elevator slides open without warning.]

Storymancer: Ah, shit. That scared me...

[He steps inside, and the doors close behind him. The camera pans over to the buttons on the right, showing numbers ranging from 1 to 12. He presses 4 and there is a soft whirring sound as the elevator begins moving up. He says nothing until it finally stops and the doors slide open once more, revealing even more darkness along the corridor before him. The flashlight moves slowly across the hallway, flicking from door to door. There are no other sounds beyond the faint noise of his feet across the wooden floor and the sound of his breathing.]

Storymancer: Man, I should've asked someone to come with me...

[The flashlight rests on each apartment room number. It moves to number 11, and then number 12, moving farther along until it reaches number 16. But just as he steps in front of the door, an odd shuffling noise from somewhere behind him makes him turn around.]

Storymancer: Who's there?

[There is no one there. He waits a few more seconds, and then turns back toward the door. He knocks tentatively, and then reaches a hand out to open the door, and the knob turns easily in his palm. The door swings inward.]

Storymancer: Oh my god...

[The room is in complete disarray. Tables have been overturned, and chairs have been broken in half. The flashlight beam moves over the walls, revealing that parts of the wallpaper on one side of the room appear to have been ripped out. None of the furnishings remain standing, and broken pieces of what is likely plates, jars, and other glassware are scattered on the floor. It looks like someone had torn the place apart, ensuring that nothing was left to salvage.]

[The camera trembles slightly as the person steps in and closes the door behind him. He moves carefully over the carpeted floor. There are some faint crunching sounds as his boots step on some of the small bits of crockery. He pauses over some scattered pieces of paper, which have been torn out of a notebook. He crouches down and shines his light over them, before picking one up and reading the words written there.]

Storymancer: "If you find this, then know that I am likely lost and there is little hope for me. I have tried to outrun and outwit them at all turns, but I know it is only a matter of time before they find me anyway. They control everything in Wispy Falls, and the only options I have are to sit here and wait for them to arrive, or take my chances beyond the forest and into the unknown outside. Knowing what awaits me once the Facility arrives, I would rather risk the latter.

"But if you are someone who is suspicious of the Facility as well, about how their intentions seem too earnest to be true, then please know that your suspicions are not unfounded. Be as the ethical divinity, who demands moderation from his followers and self-knowledge, so that they can observe moderation, and so alongside the aesthetic necessity of beauty run the demands 'know thyself' and 'nothing in excess.' Be not like the man who, through his knowledge, pushes nature into the destructive abyss, to experience in himself the disintegration of nature.

If you find me here, I beg you—say a little prayer over my body and hope that I am in a far better place now. We are—"

[The note ends here. After a pause, the paper disappears from view. Rustling sounds indicate that the cameraman may have placed it inside one of his pockets.]

Storymancer: Well, that didn't make much sense at all. Not signed, but it had to be Ivy Delgado's notes, right? But what did she even mean...?

[He picks up the other scattered pieces of paper, obviously intending to take them back with him. He turns another piece of paper over and sees it is a photo of a middle-aged woman with curly black hair, brown skin, and dark eyes.]

Storymancer: I guess this is her. Ivy Delgado. But the rest of these papers look like they were torn out of textbooks. Nothing out of the ordinary. Suppose I should bring them back and read them through, just to be sure. These the clues she left behind, or did someone ransack this room and take away all the evidence she'd been planning to give?

[The flashlight moves across the rest of the room but, short of the notes, does not find anything else of interest. He moves across the room, toward the wall where the wallpaper had been destroyed. The camera pans briefly to the left, and then to the right, finding that the wallpaper on either side remains intact. He places his hand on the wall, trying to follow the ragged tear of the wallpaper, and then stops abruptly when his fingers come into contact with a series of jagged-looking scratches scored deeply into the surface. They look like they could have been made by some large animal similar to a bear or lion, though much bigger. The marks begin at the upper wall close to the ceiling and end more than halfway down.]

Storymancer: Holy shit.

[He moves across the wall and finds what looks like a small Renaissance painting of several cherubs flying amongst the clouds. He carefully brings it closer to the flashlight to reveal that most of the cherubs' eyes have been cut out from the cloth, leaving holes in their wake.]

Storymancer: Fucking creepy.

[There are more paintings leaning against the wall instead of hung, and he looks through them quickly. All remain undamaged and consist of Renaissance-like paintings depicting satyrs, gods and goddesses, and Greek festivals. He murmurs the titles of the paintings aloud as he goes through each one, the flashlight shining on a small piece of paper taped to the side of each frame.]

Storymancer: Dance of the Satyrs. The Maenads. Dionysus and Apollo. Ethical Divinities. Wait...

[He fishes out the piece of paper again and quietly reads through part of it.]

Storymancer: "Be as the ethical divinity, who demands moderation from his followers and self-knowledge, so that they can observe moderation, and so alongside the aesthetic necessity of beauty run the demands 'know thyself' and 'nothing in excess.'" Is that a clue?

[He sets down the flashlight so it faces the painting in question, while he pulls out a pen knife. He turns the painting toward the back, trying to feel along the canvas for any bumps. He makes a startled sound when he sees that the back of the canvas has already been ripped out.]

Storymancer: Someone got here first, huh?

[Just to be sure, he peels the canvas back, but there is nothing hidden there. He checks the frames, searching for any hollows, but does not find anything.]

Storymancer: Shit. Whatever Dr. Delgado was trying to hide, they must have gotten it...

[He looks down at the piece of paper he has again.]

Storymancer: You know what. Let me copy and paste this whole thing.

[The video stops briefly. When it resumes again, he sounds smug.]

Storymancer: That whole ethical divinity thing. Know thyself and nothing in excess. It's a Friedrich Nietzsche philosophy. I don't have enough brain cells to understand this, but his whole thing is that you need disorder and a heck of a lot of emotion in your life in order to improve and appreciate the importance of logic and harmony as concepts. Or something like that. But get this—the harmony thing is represented by a god called Apollo, and the disorder thing is represented by a god called Dionysus. Apollo and Dionysus!

[Eagerly, he takes out the Apollo and Dionysus painting and begins to cut open the canvas. He makes a satisfied sound before reaching into it and drawing out a USB drive.]

Storymancer: Ha! To that one commenter who said I was a moron—fuck you too!

[He pockets the USB, and then stands to approach the bathroom next. As he draws closer, he makes an audible, horrified sound. The camera moves toward the mirror, where a dark red smear takes up half the surface, obscuring his own reflection. It looks dry.]

Storymancer: Shit. Is that blood?

[He turns the flashlight toward the shower stall, and then hesitates when the camera focuses on something that appears to be huddled on the ground. Cautiously, he moves closer. It seems to be a sack of some sort, but nothing about it indicates what could possibly be inside. He steps into the stall and, with shaking fingers, starts to open it.]

Storymancer: Please no please no please no please no—

[The sack's contents turn out to be an assortment of empty shampoo bottles and other toiletries. The cameraman exhales.]

Storymancer: Haha. R-really fooled me there—

[A sudden thump against the door leading into the apartment makes him jump. The flashlight and camera both spin toward the door. A series of heavy, hard blows resound against the frame, far too loud and far too strong for a normal human. With a quiet gasp, he scrambles out of the bathroom, instead finding a small closet in the corner, opening it, and then hurriedly closing the door behind him. He turns off the flashlight and waits in the darkness, the camera picking up nothing.]

[The blows continue, growing louder. And then, with one final hit, there is the sound of the door splintering. Storymancer lets out a pained gasp.]

[Something heavy treads across the room. There is nothing on the camera to indicate what it is, or even if Storymancer is able to see it from his hiding spot.]

[The heavy footsteps continue. There is a pause, as if the creature has stayed still and is listening intently for noises from elsewhere. The cameraman stifles his quiet whimpers. Whatever it is moves again, and the footsteps sound closer, seemingly stopping before the closet. There is dead silence from Storymancer.]

[The heavy treads start up again, but this time it sounds like it is moving farther away. Storymancer says and does nothing until the last of the footsteps recede into the distance. Even then, three more minutes pass before he slowly inches open the closet door a crack, just to check if the thing that had been in the room with him had left.]

Storymancer: Fuck. Fuck. Gotta get out!

[He flicks the flashlight back on and slips out of the closet noise-lessly, moving very slowly. He plays the light around the room once more and lets out a quiet sigh of relief. He pauses when the flashlight takes in what remains of the door. It looks like it has been blown off its hinges.]

Storymancer: Fuck.

[He steps out of the apartment, moving the flashlight from left to right, but there is nothing else in the hallway with him. He starts moving, quicker now, back where he came from, toward the elevators. He hits the button and watches it glow green before turning around nervously to check behind him, though both the flashlight and camera reveal nothing else out of the ordinary. He is breathing heavier now.]

[Finally, the elevator doors slide open. He slips inside as fast as he can, pressing the ground floor button and hitting the one to close the elevator doors, though it takes a few seconds before they actually do. They slide shut—]

[And then—just before they close completely, *something* lumbers from around the corner and hurtles toward him, and Storymancer screams. The flashlight is still aimed at the elevator doors, and the camera only has a moment or two to register what it is—a thick shadow of a creature roughly ten feet tall, with burning bright lidless eyes, a maw that stretches obscenely over its features, so wide that it seems like it spans the length of two eagle's wings, jutting away from its body. Its spindly fingers are thin and long as the rest of it is stocky and squat, and it begins to slide across the narrowing opening between the elevator doors, ready to throw them wide open—]

[Only for them to close anyway. The elevator begins its gradual descent back to the ground floor, but there is a small thump as Storymancer slides down to the floor in fright, trembling so hard the camera shakes along with him, the flashlight's beam bobbing up and down. There is a small ding, and the elevator opens once more, this time to reveal the lobby.]

[He wastes no time scrambling to his feet. He hurls out of the elevator and across the room, pushing the main doors open without bothering to look around any further, and sprints out into the night, not stopping until he is several blocks away, the camera focused on his running feet and the ground below.]

Storymancer: Fuck, fuck, fuck. What was that, what was that, what was that—

[The video ends there.]

VIDEO #9

Are You Listening?
With Morn Fields

Welcome, viewers, to *Are You Listening?*, Wispy Falls's most popular radio station for your daily news, reasonable opinions, and the best beats. I am Morn Fields, your host for the next two hours while we talk about everything that's been going on with our sleepy little town.

I feel like I have an apology to make. The last time I spoke to all of you about this issue, I was quite gung ho about the remains they found being our runaway criminal, and I am sorry for misleading my viewers. I took the information that was available on hand, but unfortunately, I did very little to cross-check those claims. In my defense, both the initial assumption the remains were human, and the administration's later clarification that the remains were actually of a previously unknown cryptid, are, in fact, both technically accurate.

Even so, that was my bad. Goes to show that even if you try to get as much information as you can, it still pays to cross-check. I'll do much better next time, and I will at least be accountable for what I said!

Is everyone excited about the new museum opening up? The one with the so-called cryptids that no one's ever seen before? Good thing there's nothing left but the bones, or else we'd be in trouble, eh? I've heard horror stories about some of these beasts reanimating as long as they still got a heart or some of their organs intact, and I'd rather not see anything like that set loose on the town if I've got something to say about it.

And yes, I know what a lot of people are saying. The Facility has received its share of criticism over the years, and some of it is even valid. But this current mess regarding what I'm going to now call the Flesh in the Woods seems nothing more than a miscommunication error. Some citizen sees remains, gets excited, and thinks it's human, and then the news spreads and embellishes with every retelling before any official announcements have been made. What's that old saying? That lies spread around the world three times before truth has a chance to put its hat on? I might be butchering that, but I'm sure you get the drift.

And like I've said so many times before, I talk candidly about things on my show, even when people don't want to hear it, even when there are some hard truths that need talking about. They talk a lot of smack about the authorities attempting to censor some social media, but so far they haven't found the time to censor me, although I am sure they know it would cause a hubbub if they did try to cancel my show. That said, I have not been harassed or threatened by anyone in authority, and nor have they done anything to take my show off the air, so I would hope that despite having some differences in opinion, Wispy Falls's administration would be welcoming to opposing views.

Which is why I am asking every one of you to please visit the goddamn museum first to view "the body" before anything else!

I have. It opened earlier today, and I was among the curious who'd gone over to visit and find out what the fuss is all about. The flesh they found in the woods was on display and, folks. Folks! If that exhibit doesn't blow your mind, then I don't know what will. I can see now why they call it a Bloat. Imagine a human being expanded to grotesque proportions simply because there are no bones or muscle mass to prevent one from doing so. The worst part is that it somehow still looked human. The descriptions are similar to what the news had been reporting—black hair, brown eyes, etc. No tattoos that Adam Morrissey supposedly has, but I do not think tattoos could survive the way that skin expanded…

And that's not even the most interesting monster they have for display in there! I implore you folks.

Which again brings us to this week's Dear Morn letter, this time from over at 281 Kerrich Avenue!

Dearest Morn,

My girlfriend and I live in an apartment building with seven other people (with shared walls and a communal garden at the center), and our landlord is refusing to do anything about an infestation in our walls. It started around three months ago, when we would wake up to hear something crying late at night. For the first couple of weeks, I thought it was one of my neighbors, because I know one of them just had a baby. But a chance encounter with the family in question made me realize it wasn't their baby and that they, too, were hearing the noises coming from somewhere inside the walls, which they had also assumed was coming from another tenant.

We decided to meet with the other neighbors and they have also been hearing this same cry around the same time we had. When we talked to our landlord about this, he insisted that no one was crying and it must be either the sound of the wind or from some other house. Given the way the rest of the other houses have been structured in the neighborhood, we all found that unlikely. To the landlord's credit, he insisted on spending the night in the only empty apartment there, and we didn't hear any crying that night.

But I would say about five days out of the week we hear the crying, and it seems to grow louder and louder every day, and it's no longer just at night. We tried to ignore it at first by wearing headphones and earplugs, but it came to a point where not even that helped anymore. Shortly after that, one of my neighbors claimed that he could see black mold growing out of his ceiling—another guy and I took a look, but we couldn't find the mold, though he was insistent that he always saw it near midnight forming out of the corner of his wall. It wasn't long before another neighbor started saying the same thing.

We were worried that perhaps there might be some carbon monoxide leak somewhere and it would affect the apartment, so we sat down for a meeting with the landlord again. Unfortunately, he was very belligerent and refused to listen to any of our complaints, instead threatening to sue us for slandering him and telling lies about the place he owned. This came as a surprise to us, especially because our landlord was this really easygoing, laid-back person who was willing to come and do repairs when something broke, and he was now acting a complete 180 from what he used to be. We have considered calling someone to report the health code violations, but someone suggested that we ask for your opinion first since you've talked about how to deal with bad landlords in the past. Do we try and talk some sense into our landlord again, or bypass him and call the authorities?

Signed, Infested Tenant

Dear Infested Tenant,

My producers have, in fact, already called the authorities on your behalf once they received your message, simply to confirm that everything is as you say it is, and then also to alert law enforcement as soon as possible.

This is not a slow carbon monoxide poisoning.

There is either a Quiet Brother or a Weeper in your house, and your landlord is already a lost cause either way. If you were worried about his abrupt change in personality, then look no further as to why.

I am sure that most of you are already aware of what a Quiet Brother is, but for the sake of those listening who have been living under a rock this whole time, I will make a brief summary. Do not look at a Quiet Brother. If you believe there is a Quiet Brother in your house, run and keep running until you have reached the nearest station and alerted the people in charge. If you hear a baby in a house where no baby cries, then leave immediately and contact the authorities. A Quiet Brother cannot talk, but its ululation is like an infant's wails. Do not investigate.

I am frankly a little disappointed. Everything you've described is a textbook description of what a Quiet Brother is, and yet none of your neighbors even thought to make a report? Was the abrupt change in the personality of your landlord not enough confirmation? Why didn't the cries throughout the night make any of you realize what it is? And one of your neighbors is a family with a newborn, even! How irresponsible have all of you been?

Unfortunately, it is now out of your hands. Some of my listeners right now may have seen the news report earlier today of a neighborhood block in lock-down, and that very little information about it has been forthcoming. While I suppose I should not confirm nor deny if that incident has anything to do with the letter I am reading today, I will instead use this as a cautionary warning for the rest of you. Please. Better to be safe than sorry. If you hear something crying and cannot pinpoint its source, there is an available hotline—let me say it now, for the rest of you to take note: The emergency number is 111—that allows you to call in quickly and have a team of experts sent to your location within the next five minutes. Do *not* let the situation worsen to the point where black mold now protrudes from your domicile and everything now needs to be liquidated and the area fumigated. That poor child.

While it may likely be too late for the people involved, I believe that the area has been successfully closed off and the target annihilated, which means it is now safe to stay. I believe there ought to be a report coming in the next few hours talking about that. Still, let this be a warning to everyone! Please be more mindful about your neighbors and the people who live around you. Remember that we're all in this together, and everyone's safety means your safety!

Need more advice from me? Feel free to write me anytime! Always remember—we take your privacy seriously and will be removing any identifying names from your letter! Remember, you are *never* the problem.

And now what everyone's been waiting for—your horoscopes for the day. As always, the show *Are You Listening?*, its host Morn Fields (that's me!), nor any of the staff can be held liable for anything we read out to you folks, and any similarities to any people or events are strictly coincidences. And now that we have that out of the way, let's begin.

Today's horoscopes are sponsored by Everything At Tony's! We have it all—spices, chewing gum, musical instruments, produce, bottled water, rations, guns, hair products, makeup, couches, beds, snacks, gasoline prices, pets, swimwear, books, lamps, and more! If you want everything, then why aren't you at Tony's?

Aries: Tell me, is it Steve again? I warned you countless times about him, but it always seems to go in one ear and out the other. How many times are you going to let him walk all over you until you finally muster up the spine to say no to him? We're done after this. I'm tired of trying to save you when you don't want to be saved.

Taurus: Ah, but I told you so.

Gemini: Keep watch. A secret admirer will be leaving roses and lilies at your doorstep tomorrow. Deliver them to your nearest law enforcement agency so they can look into it.

Cancer: Even though you feel healthy, it might be time for you to see your family physician. There is something growing inside of you that you may not like.

Leo: Choose not to answer your phone today. Do not

answer it tomorrow. Do not answer it until next week, when you may accept any call between 1:00 and 3:00 p.m. on a Tuesday.

Virgo: A PSA: Someone is about to rob you at the corner of Tenth and Seventh. Be smart and rob them first.

Libra: rweu2746395hhhdytsfr.

Scorpio: Ever always, there is Ogtha. No other love can compare to that which is Ogtha.

Sagittarius: Oh, but your cat *is* judging you. Ensure that you give him food at the proper time, and change his litter whenever possible. You would not like to know what he is planning.

Capricorn: Forgo the bath and take a shower instead. Do not look into any bodies of water for the rest of the week.

Aquarius: So have care; there is something in the forest. There is always something in the forest.

Pisces: Might not be wise to bring a gun to a knife fight. You will be arrested. You will all be arrested.

Apotropaion: Why not visit the new and marvelous Museum of Natural Curiosities today? There are over 300 exhibits for you to peruse, including ancient cryptids of the seas and skies dating back over a hundred years! Our experienced guides will give you a walking tour through three floors of wondrous curiosities, with over two hours' worth of discoveries at your fingertips! Come and enjoy our Cryptid Cafe, where you can have burgers, fries, and our famous Bloodmoon Coffee at affordable prices! Get a little slice of history today at the Museum of Natural Curiosities!

And that's it for me today at Good Morn! Remember to stay vigilant, stay happy, and stay safe!

VIDEO #10

Public Service Announcements

JellyBeanFish: Holy crap

JellyBeanFish: Are you okay?

Storymancer: I feel a bit shaken still but yeah, I'm good

Storymancer: I think I have a rash, though. I put some cream
on it and it looks all right now. I guess I'm allergic to cryptids.

JellyBeanFish: There's a cryptid right here in our town? And of
that size?

Storymancer: Do you know what it is?

JellyBeanFish: I think so, but it's been a while since anyone's
had it.

Storymancer: What do you mean?

JellyBeanFish: A long time ago, there was one kind of cryptid
you could actually keep as a pet

Storymancer: As a what now

JellyBeanFish: I know it sounds ridiculous, but it was mostly
harmless.

Storymancer: It's a cryptid, none of those are mostly harmless

JellyBeanFish: Yeah well, this one got approved for some reason.

JellyBeanFish: That one's called a Regret.

Storymancer: Wait, no it isn't. Aren't they supposed to be small?

JellyBeanFish: They're small unless you don't take very good care of them. And then they grow to be the size of a building and will try to eat everyone they can find.

JellyBeanFish: You actually went to her apartment? They evacuated everyone there. Said there was a bug infestation they couldn't get rid of, so they paid for everyone else to stay at some hotel while they looked for another place. That was before she went missing.

Storymancer: And then they just released that Regret in there?? It almost ate me!

JellyBeanFish: They're immortal. They don't eat because they need to, they eat because they want to.

Storymancer: Well, shit.

JellyBeanFish: You really sure you wanna push through with this?

Storymancer: I've come this far and I'm not stopping now.

Storymancer: I've been going through everything I could find in Ivy Delgado's USB

Storymancer: It's been wild

Storymancer: Let me upload them so you can see

JellyBeanFish: That's a lot

Storymancer: Yeah, I think I'm beginning to understand why the Facility is after her.

JellyBeanFish: You're sure about that?

Storymancer: Yeah, go and have a look.

JellyBeanFish: You should take a break.

Storymancer: I'm fine

JellyBeanFish: No you're not. If I'd seen that thing with my own eyes, I would have freaked

JellyBeanFish: I'm not telling you to stop investigating, I'm telling you to de-stress for awhile

Storymancer: Yeah, maybe I will

Storymancer: I don't want to go back there, but someone needs to know about that

JellyBeanFish: I'll talk to my mom. I won't tell her anything about you or that it was you who found it

JellyBeanFish: I know they can send someone there to get rid of it

Storymancer: Okay

JellyBeanFish: I'll look through the documents, and then we can talk once I'm done, k?

JellyBeanFish: Go have some ice cream and watch some silly videos or something

Storymancer: Yes, Mom

JellyBeanFish: Pfft

JellyBeanFish: Are you back?

JellyBeanFish: Here's something! I was looking through the rest of the videos that your friend, LightParticle, sent you before

Storymancer: 100% not my friend

JellyBeanFish: And here's a PSA about Gentle Regrets!

[The video begins with a "Cryptid Sequence 001: The Gentle Regret" title that flashes onscreen, with an oddly accurately detached eye like one might see in medical textbooks. It is animated, and it beats frantically.]

[This one also has a narrator's voice, and it sounds pleasantly cheerful and upbeat with its subtitles.]

Voice: Welcome once again to our ongoing series of Know Your Cryptids, one of the ways Wispy Falls is committed to keeping you educated about the world we live in. Don't worry; you'll be safe here.

For today, we will be discussing the very reclusive *and* very elusive Gentle Regret. Now, what is it, exactly?

[A much more detailed artist's sketch is shown onscreen, depicting the cryptid. It looks similar to a big mouse, except it has large, bulbous eyes, curved ears on top of its head, and a long tail, scaled like a lizard's, though the rest of it seem to be composed mainly of fur.]

Voice: Cute little things, are they? Well, the Gentle Regret in many ways does live up to its name. It is a friendly creature that likes to be cared for and enjoys being fed food and water just like your average cats and dogs. It is very playful by nature and highly intelligent. You can even teach it tricks!

[A short scene, clearly a family's home video, is shown. The camera owner is not seen onscreen. His hand is holding a small ball, and he tosses it toward a wall. Immediately a small rodent-like thing scampers toward it, grabs it with its two hands, and carries it triumphantly back over its head, chittering happily. The owner takes the ball and scratches affectionately at its head, and the happy noises increase. He tosses the ball again, and the cryptid heads off to retrieve it again.]

Voice: You're probably wondering why this creature might be dangerous. It doesn't look like a cryptid at all! It doesn't look dead, it seems friendly enough to humans, and most importantly, it doesn't look like it's going to kill you. So why the classification?

[The video returns to the detailed image of the Gentle Regret, along with a much more comprehensive anatomical chart. It depicts the inside of the cryptid, where it is shown that the inside of the Gentle Regret is composed of one giant eyeball, apparently leaving no trace of a digestive or nervous system, enclosed within a small skeletal frame where bones are only prominent in its tail, small arms, and feet.]

Voice: Truly a nature's wonder, though one may even argue it actually goes against it. There is nothing about its physiology that makes sense. Based on what we know about science and basic anatomy, this little creature isn't supposed to exist. It cannot possibly exist. And yet here it is.

You might be curious as to where to get your hands on such a charming creature. That is simple enough! The Gentle Regret has no natural habitat. It does not procreate the way most mammals do—there is still some debate among scientists as to whether it could procreate at all, given that none have ever been found in the wild for study, and that it does not have genitals or a reproductive system. There have since been tests and experiments on Gentle Regrets, but none have ever been observed multiplying, whether through normal breeding or by mitosis.

Some people might call it an abomination. But in many ways, it is far more docile and eager to please its owners than even your friendliest pet. That said, there are, of course, proper ways to care for the Gentle Regret just as there is a proper way to care for any animal.

[Another short video appears of it happily consuming the remains of a watermelon.]

Voice: First, DO feed it fruits and vegetables. These are its favorite foods and, based on previous studies, are very nutritious for them. While it is still debatable where exactly these nutrients go, given its abnormal physiology, it is believed that the eye within its form absorbs not just these for sustenance, but also what an average body would normally consider waste. Gentle Regrets do not produce natural waste products such as urine or feces, which makes them a popular household pet to take care of!

That said, DO NOT feed them any of the following items: dirt, meat, corn, chocolates, ice cream, carbonated drinks, paper, household electronics, ceramics, glass, other pets, dishwashing liquid, and bricks. Unfortunately, these curious little critters have a habit of nibbling things they should not be nibbling, and then wind up getting sick for anywhere between a few hours and a few days, though they are often able to recover soon after that. Allowing them to eat too much of these items may even result in an addiction, allowing them to consume up to over fifty times their body weight, and they will grow in size accordingly. You don't want to be homeless, do you?

[A video shows a simple illustration of a Gentle Regret and a house, with the latter slowly disappearing in small chunks as the former feasts on it, the creature's size growing larger as the house shrinks, until it is many times its former size.]

Voice: Second, Gentle Regrets like to take on the habits of their owners. An active owner who enjoys hikes and walks will find their pet will be more than happy to accompany them outside and keep pace until their owners grow tired. In contrast, a lazy owner who sits on the couch the whole day will also result in a Gentle Regret who will refuse to move for days on end, instead staring at its master at all hours of the day, from morning until midnight, watching them slumber. Gentle Regrets have no ability to sleep themselves, so they will continue watching, and watching, and watching, and watching, until their owner finally rises.

[There is a short video with yet another simple illustration of a Gentle Regret staring at its stick figure owner in a bed while the sun rises and sets rapidly through a window, night taking its place before it transforms back into day again. All this time the creature does not move and continues to stare at its sleeping owner.]

Voice: A Gentle Regret is more than likely to take on their owners' demeanors as well. A happy owner will result in a happy Regret, a sad one will result in a melancholy pet, whereas an owner who has too many emotions bottled up inside of them—those with so much anger that it is threatening to burst out from their bodies and overwhelm them in sudden fits of rage...

[The animation does not change. The Gentle Regret continues to watch its owner as they lie sleeping. The background begins to carry a faint tinge of red before the animation disappears altogether.]

Voice: Do regulate your emotions better and reach out to a therapist or a counselor before you take on a Gentle Regret as a pet. An unhappy pet will choose to eat many things they are not allowed to eat, with unfortunate results.

Third, and last—you may NOT have two Gentle Regrets under the same roof!

[The video flickers abruptly to the silhouettes of two of the cryptids facing each other, with a banned sign over them both. The normally jovial tones of the narrator changes and now sounds unexpectedly hysterical, and he is all but shouting while some kind of microphone feedback is heard screeching in the background.]

Voice: Do not allow them to be in the same room together! Do not allow them to eat each other! There will be death! There is death! Death! They will find your remains, and smile!

[The animation disappears without warning as well, and the

narrator's unhinged screaming switches to its usual friendly and gentle cadence, as if nothing out of the ordinary has happened.]

Voice: Remember these three things, and it is guaranteed that you will have a wonderful time with Gentle Regrets as pets. These creatures are known to live for close to one hundred years, which means there will be no need to mourn your pet. They will take very good care of your body once you have shuffled off your mortal coil. Be responsible pet owners.

[There is a final video of a real-life Gentle Regret staring straight at the camera without moving for five minutes before the tape ends.]

JellyBeanFish: omg

JellyBeanFish: What was all that

Storymancer: Ikr

JellyBeanFish: Why do they have so many PSAs

JellyBeanFish: I've never seen any of these before

Storymancer: You know more about these than I do.

JellyBeanFish: Not these PSAs

JellyBeanFish: I know what these cryptids are, but I've never been shown any PSAs about them before

JellyBeanFish: I mean, it's probably because these look pretty old. The animation seems dated.

JellyBeanFish: This is the cryptid that I was telling you about. The one that people could keep as a pet.

Storymancer: The one in Ivy Delgado's apartment

JellyBeanFish: I think so. The Gentle Regrets.

JellyBeanFish: Except someone screwed up and fed it the wrong stuff like the PSA says not to do

JellyBeanFish: But again, I've seen a lot of the old videos the Facility made years ago, but I've never seen these

JellyBeanFish: The quality and the way this video was made reminds me of the one that your conspiracy theorist friend sent.

Storymancer: The same kind of production values, you mean?

JellyBeanFish: Yeah

Storymancer: Why was Ivy Delgado's life in danger because of these, though?

JellyBeanFish: Did you see the last video? This one?

[The new video shows the same darkness that had been shown in the earlier video, but this time more movement can be clearly seen, and it is coming from whoever owns the camera. They appear to be struggling, as if wanting to get out, and the darkness seems to ripple around them, ebbing and flowing so that a few faint sources of light occasionally peek out from that darkness. The video then suddenly halts on its own, and the footage warps and stays like that before ending.]

Storymancer: Yeah, that one confused me. You know what this looks like to me? It looks like someone's trapped inside a really heavy-duty blanket or cocoon and is trying to fight their way out. But why is this on the same drive as those other videos? Was it a mistake? Was it maybe someone taking a video on their phone by accident who forgot to delete it afterward? Or is there some hidden meaning to this?

JellyBeanFish: It had to be something if Ivy Delgado was risking her life for these.

JellyBeanFish: I can say though that the video about the pet cryptid is accurate, and it would have been something that would have been recommended for people to follow.

JellyBeanFish: I'm not sure about the other videos, though

Storymancer: You talked about the production quality being similar to the one LightParticle121 sent. Like they were made by the same people, or the same company?

JellyBeanFish: Yeah, it gives a vibe like that first video you showed me was part of a series like this one.

Storymancer: I've been trying to contact him the last couple of days or so, but he hasn't responded. He hasn't posted anything on the message boards either.

Storymancer: But my hypothesis is that he'd worked at the Facility before, and either had a falling out with them or went on the run for some reason. I tried looking him up based on the information I got about him, and no luck.

Storymancer: You're of the same mind as me that Brr's video is real, right?

JellyBeanFish: I think so.

Storymancer: What do you think?

JellyBeanFish: I can make a guess that these were PSAs that were made some years ago

Storymancer: If you say the PSA about your pet cryptid has all the right info, then I'm guessing that the rest of these PSAs are the same. Except they were never released to the public, that much I know

JellyBeanFish: Yeah?

Storymancer: So why would they choose not to?

JellyBeanFish: I've seen PSAs they did release, but they weren't as informative as these ones.

JellyBeanFish: The ones I've seen shared on social media sites only give general overviews. "Avoid at all costs," etc. Nothing about going into details with a cryptid's anatomy.

JellyBeanFish: I looked through the PSA videos in the stored hard drive. These provide a lot more detail.

Storymancer: What I'm thinking is that they don't want people knowing too much about these cryptids.

JellyBeanFish: I think the same thing.

Storymancer: I think that Ivy Delgado planned to have people find these videos. Maybe she was thinking to upload them. What are the chances that there's some kind of cryptid army coming, and she wants us all to be prepared?

JellyBeanFish: If there was a cryptid army coming, then why keep everyone in the dark? Wouldn't it be easier to train people?

Storymancer: What if they don't want to train people? What if they want to put people in danger without being accused of it?

JellyBeanFish: What do you mean?

Storymancer: It's not a coincidence that LightParticle121 has been claiming that people are being used as fodder. That he is calling out the authorities for exposing certain people to cryptids to keep the rest safe? Rebels and people who disagree with the government and stuff like that?

JellyBeanFish: You mean the one where he says we're all an experiment? And that the government is responsible for having people disappear to feed them because they're vocal against them?

Storymancer: Yeah

JellyBeanFish: The brother you lost was only seven years old, right?

Storymancer: Yeah, but he was sick. Maybe they want to give up the people with a ton of liabilities first. Pretty much every family or loved one who lost someone they care about to the forest has had some kind of illnesses.

JellyBeanFish: Oh.

JellyBeanFish: You're right. I have a friend who lost a mother to the woods, and he said that she has some form of cerebral palsy.

Storymancer: Until I find proof otherwise, I want to run with this theory, because it makes sense. Why would they choose not to release any of those PSAs if they didn't want people in danger?

JellyBeanFish: Or why even make them in the first place? But I think I know why.

Storymancer: What do you mean?

JellyBeanFish: We were taught something about the Penumbra and its founder. Abraham Huntington. Here, let me pull up an entry about him.

[Link to an article about Abraham Huntington is attached.]

Abraham Huntington (pictured, on right), the founder of Wispy Falls, has long been considered the father of modern cryptozoology and was responsible for the classification of cryptids.

BACKGROUND

Not much is known about Huntington before the calamities that forced him to take up traveling, but what is known is his interest in cryptid evolutionary traits and habits. Huntington traveled during the peak of the calamity, believing that their combined knowledge would be more than enough to keep him alive.

FOUNDING OF WISPY FALLS

Huntington was fond of keeping a diary, and the few pages that have been found and preserved list several hardships he withstood during his journey, including numerous cryptid attacks. He would also document his first encounter with a Quiet Brother.

"Picked up one of the many unusual-looking rocks that abound in this place. Most of the others are as large as I am, with streaks of some red running through them. Soon enough however, a thing tried to stalk me when I tried to make dinner. It called out and pretended it was my friend, but it appeared to be repulsed by these odd stones. Ever the scientist, coupled with possibly a dash of foolishness, I set to work pushing most of these stones outward, and it seemed to succeed in making whatever it was retreat."

The site soon began attracting more travelers seeking sanctuary, and the encampment eventually grew into a small-sized town. Huntington began keeping the stones around their territory, and then planted trees to further camouflage their town, which they eventually named Wispy Falls because, according to Huntington, "There was a nice waterfall around here back when things were still green and normal, and it was one of the prettiest places I remember."

DISAGREEMENT

It was rumored that Huntington had a falling-out with some of his deputies over how they wanted to run Wispy Falls. Huntington was keen on being proactive, training people to fight cryptids, while many preferred a more defensive approach, instead choosing to avoid coming into contact with the creatures as much as possible and relying on the defenses.

Huntington eventually set up a hospital/research institute that dedicated itself to studying cryptids as well as the protective stones. The place became known as the Penumbra, though over the years it has been referred to as simply the Facility. The bloodmoon practice came about as a result of these studies, with everyone in town advised to remain inside their homes for three days and three nights. Very little has been stated as to why leaving their residences is prohibited, but a good majority of missing persons cases in Wispy Falls begin during the bloodmoon, when people who flout the restrictions mysteriously disappear.

Huntington died ten years after the founding of Wispy Falls, aged forty-seven years old, of a stroke.

Storymancer: Yeah, I'm sorta familiar with this. That's what they teach us in school, more or less.

JellyBeanFish: They disagreed about how to run Wispy Falls, right? And those videos looked really old. Like pulled from some old video recording advice that hasn't existed for decades. Maybe—I'm guessing it would be Huntington— wanted to teach the public about how to fight against the cryptids, but some of his people disagreed, thinking that it would only make people panic.

Storymancer: That would track, I guess. But what's so important about them now that Ivy Delgado would be keeping them in a USB?

JellyBeanFish: Maybe there's some hidden clue in them?

Storymancer: Wouldn't it have been better if she'd just written it out for us in that same USB drive?

JellyBeanFish: Not if she thinks that people are after her, maybe? I don't know.

Storymancer: They would have just gotten rid of the USB, or destroyed it. But the fact that I found it means that maybe they weren't even aware of it when they were chasing her. Maybe their goal was just to get rid of her and not even bother to look through her stuff. Or they were swayed by the decoy Delgado put in, drawing attention to one of the other paintings instead of the right one. I mean, if I could find it, then they should have with all the hi-tech stuff they got, right?

JellyBeanFish: Maybe they were in a hurry. Just because they're scientists doesn't mean they know anything about philosophers, so maybe they made a mistake there. Maybe they couldn't control the cryptid they set loose there, which is why they closed that whole building.

Storymancer: Hey.

Storymancer: HEY.

JellyBeanFish: ???

Storymancer: That Morn show

Storymancer: Didn't he read that one letter

Storymancer: Where there was, like

Storymancer: Someone who had a Quiet Brother inside their apartment building who killed and replaced their landlord

Storymancer: And they needed everyone evacuated or something

JellyBeanFish: Oh, yeah!

JellyBeanFish: You think that was Dr. Delgado's building?

Storymancer: They sounded hush-hush about it. It would explain why it's not even in the news.

JellyBeanFish: You could be right.

Storymancer: I think I am

[Attached: a video of the closeup shot of the Gentle Regret, zoomed in on its tiny claws. It then switches to footage Storymancer had taken of his time investigating Doctor Ivy Delgado's apartment— specifically, the one scene where his camera jerks up only to see a massive claw attempt to pry the elevator doors back open, a claw much larger than an average person's head, but curled in the same way as the Gentle Regret's are.]

Storymancer: The PSA said that this Gentle Regret, if not cared for properly, can grow many times its size

JellyBeanFish: You're not doing anything stupid again like going back there.

JellyBeanFish: Let me talk to my mom, or find someone at work

Storymancer: All right.

JellyBeanFish: Don't do anything!!

Storymancer: Nice to know you care :)

JellyBeanFish: shut up

JellyBeanFish: I'm going to watch the last video

JellyBeanFish: There must be some clue in there we're overlooking

JellyBeanFish: I'll find it

Storymancer: Hey

Storymancer: Thanks

JellyBeanFish: Haha

JellyBeanFish: We're in this together now, right?

[A video plays. It features a living room with comfortable-looking furnishings, complete with a large sofa, a long table, and a small mantelpiece. A woman's voice is talking as the camera approaches the sofa, where two young children are fast asleep.]

Woman's voice, offscreen: Oh. Oh, Marty, come here. Look at this.

[The camera focuses on the two sleeping boys. They have their arms around each other while they sleep, a thick blanket over their legs.]

Man's voice, offscreen: Well, if that isn't precious.

Woman's voice: I'm taking a video. They're so sweet every time they're like this.

Storymancer's voice: Lee usually went to my room when he had a bad nightmare. He always felt better when he shared the bed with me, and I'd keep the both of us awake, making up stories to entertain him for most of the night. And then, because obviously we would both be tired because we hadn't gotten much sleep, we'd wind up falling asleep the following afternoon just like this.

Woman's voice: I wish they'd never grow up. That they could just be our two perfect boys like this.

Storymancer: No shit, Mom. That came true for at least one of us.

[The younger boy yawns and snuggles deeper under the blankets without waking his brother up.]

Storymancer: I need to know where you are now, Lee. I won't stop till I know where you are.

VIDEO #11

Ivy Delgado

[The video starts with an image of a frightened-looking woman staring into what appears to be the camera of a handheld phone, given the way it trembles on occasion as she grips it in her hand. She has dark skin and black hair and wears glasses. She is wearing something that could have been a lab coat, though it is smeared in what appears to be dried blood. The left side of her face is also smeared in the same red. She is speaking rapidly and occasionally glances over her shoulder as if to see if anyone is behind her. She appears to be in a long white hallway of some kind, similar to perhaps a hospital or a laboratory.]

Woman: My name is Ivy Delgado, and I want this on record. I have suspected for a long time that the Facility is not what it seems. While they have always claimed to be at the forefront of revolutionary medicine and research to improve the longevity and health of the people here in Wispy Falls, I have every reason to believe that their objective is something far more vile. And while I understand that all this may already sound incredible, I now have proof.

[She looks nervously behind her again before stopping beside one small door. She takes out an ID and holds it up against a device on the wall beside it, and it makes a quick humming sound. The door slides open.]

Ivy: Four hours ago, the Facility was compromised.

[She steps into a small room that looks sterile and neat. There are bookshelves filled with thick volumes on one side of the wall, but the rest of the space appears to be occupied by long tables with several test tubes and beakers of assorted sizes. Most of them are filled with liquid of varying hues and colors. Ivy ignores all of these and instead moves toward a wall devoid of any furniture. She presses at some invisible latch there, and part of the wall slides open.]

Ivy: They brought in a new cryptid specimen today, one I've never seen before, never even knew existed. I told them it was a mistake to bring it inside the Facility, and I don't care how many walls there are between us and the creature, it was too dangerous. But they refused to listen. The Director refused to listen. Said that they, in fact, had encountered one other like it in the past, and that it was too valuable to be contained anywhere else. And now—

[The room she steps into is filled with surveillance equipment, including one wall that was full of active security cameras and a complicated-looking control panel before it.]

Ivy: I don't care about my job anymore. I need to show people what they actually do here.

[The phone camera is set down to one side of the control panel and shows her typing something rapidly on a console there. She nods to herself, and then picks up the phone again, her face once more taking up the screen.]

Ivy: This is footage of what had happened five days ago. I'm calling up the video.

[The phone camera moves now to focus close-up on one of the monitors. On the screen, Ivy's figure is recognizable. Standing beside her is a man in a lab coat with glasses. He has brown hair and a pinched face. But the screen is centered on a very large metal table surrounded by other men and women in the same white coats, likely scientists or doctors.]

[There is something strange on the table. The monitor is oddly blurred even when it is focused on the thing there, so anyone watching is unable to clearly see it for what it is. What is apparent is only that the thing is massive and shaped like an ovoid, with thick veins running along its sides. It seems to shift and ebb as if it is breathing.]

Ivy on the screen: I cannot help but stress the danger that you are putting us all in, sir! I'm not talking about the staff here, I'm talking about everyone else in the city! We have no idea what this creature might do! We don't even know if our protective gear will be enough to—

[The man she is arguing with raises a hand to silence her.]

Man: As much as I respect your knowledge, Dr. Delgado, I assure you there is no danger to the city nor to its citizens.

Ivy: How can you say that with any confidence? We know nothing about this! What if it's worse than a Quiet Brother? What if—

Man: *You* know nothing of this particular creature. But we do.

Ivy: What?

Man: We have encountered one other like this in the past. There is no need to worry yourself over this, Dr. Delgado. We have everything here under control.

[One of the people in a hazmat suit near the large ovoid makes a sudden gesture with his hands, catching the man's attention.]

Man: Ah. If you would please step away from the operating table, Dr. Delgado, and join me instead behind the observation deck.

[The man takes Dr. Delgado by the elbow and begins to steer her firmly toward another smaller room on the left with a thick glass partition. The others in hazmat suits follow, and the last one closes a heavy steel door behind him, sealing them off from the rest of the area where the ovoid is.]

Man: Are we finished running the tests?

[One of the hazmat suits speak up.]

Hazmat: Yes, sir. All diagnostics confirmed. Everything is as it should be.

Man: Good. We shall require a—

[A warning sound blares unexpectedly through the room, coupled with red flashing lights. Dr. Delgado visibly starts, but the man with her appears calm.]

Dr. Delgado: What's going on?

Man: At ease, Doctor. All is as it should be.

[A door on the opposite end of the room slides open, and a man runs inside. He is dressed in a loose white shirt and pants, but the rest of him looks a mess. He is carrying an ax in his hands.]

Man: [speaking an unfamiliar word, softly] Hellenos.

[The newcomer doesn't stop. He makes immediately for the ovoid as if that had been his target all along, the ax raised over his head. He begins swinging the ax wildly, bringing it down on the ovoid. The sound is not apparent over the screen, but it looks like the ovoid is made of a softer substance than it looks. The ax sinks down into it as if the latter were made of flesh instead of the hard shell it resembles.]

Dr. Delgado: What is he doing? Mr. Threnody, we need to get him away from there as soon as—

Man: It is too late.

[The assailant does not seem to care that he's attacking a cryptid. His rage is focused on the thing before him, though his attacks seem to have no effect. He raises his ax again—]

[The ovoid's shell cracks—or rather, folds into itself. Something from inside of the ovoid then moves. The monitor blurs when it refocuses on the creature, it and the man becoming distorted onscreen. It is difficult to make out what is happening, only that something from within the creature has reached out toward its attacker and has caught him. There is a heavy thunk as the ax falls from the man's hand.]

[The man is screaming, but the words are inaudible. It is hard to make out what the ovoid is doing to the man, but the shape of the latter appears to fold in on itself, much like the creature had when it had first emerged, but in ways a person was not meant to fold. There is a gurgling noise coming from the man, followed by a sound like a dishcloth being wrung out and then, inevitably, a splattering sound. Spatters of blood hit the security camera looking on, half of it stained red. The man's blurred figure onscreen no longer resembles what a human being ought to look like, his limbs twisted in absurd positions, body contorted like a ball. He is no longer moving, nor does he make a sound.]

[There is a slithering noise as the ovoid retreats back into itself, its blurred shape sliding back in and dragging the man's remains after it before the shell closes up around them both.]

[The reinforced glass of the observation room has also been splashed a bright red, the liquid dripping down. Dr. Delgado backs away until she is braced against the wall behind her like her legs could no longer hold her up. She is trembling uncontrollably. The man beside her continues to watch the scene before him with little surprise.]

Dr. Delgado: Oh my god... Mr. Threnody, what do we—

Man: Tell the others to wait five minutes, and then enact protocol 346 as a containment measure. Clean up what you can of the body, but you are not to touch the cryptid. Monitor it for any other signs of movement. If any are detected, you are all to evacuate the immediate area. It should have retreated back into its hibernation now that it has been fed, but it may not have been enough, so we shall err on the side of caution. Once the cleanup is done, you are to burn everything in the crematorium—all your masks, equipment, gloves, everything that was used to clean up the mess. Do you all understand?

[A murmur of voices assenting from among the crowd of hazmat suits. The door slides open and they trickle back out into the area and soon get to work with minimal fuss.]

Dr. Delgado: Now that it has been fed? Now that it has been fed?! Do you mean that you planned this all along?

Man: Of course not. I have no idea why that madman was wandering about unattended. I am putting out a Facility-wide alert to identify the remains and—

Dr. Delgado: No. You knew who he was.

Man: My dear doctor—

Dr. Delgado: You really want me to think that anyone could just burst in here with nothing but an ax and not be stopped and arrested long before he reached this room? I know those hallways, and I know how many security access codes you need just to get halfway across! That was Morrissey, wasn't it? You were holding him somewhere in the building. You let him escape for this. Why did you let him die? That was—that was brutal. It doesn't matter if he was insane, he didn't deserve to be butchered like—

Man: Thank you for your time, Dr. Delgado. It must have been a long day for you, and I am thankful for your insight on the pair of cryptids you had successfully dissected for us earlier. Now I believe it is time for me to leave for another meeting, and I advise you to retire for the day.

Dr. Delgado: Mr. Threnody, what is that thing?

Man: You are dismissed.

[The security camera freezes. The phone camera now returns to Ivy Delgado's terrified face.]

Ivy Delgado: I know what it is now. I accessed everything I could while I still had the clearance, because I knew for a fact they would come after me sooner or later. But I don't care. I know what it is. And now everyone has to know too, for their safety. And here is what happened literally an hour ago.

[She accesses the control panel again. After a moment, the security cameras flicker out, only to be replaced by different scenes, each more horrific than the other.]

[Camera one shows several bloodied bodies lying motionlessly on the floor.]

[Camera two shows half of the face of a clearly-dead woman, her eye staring blankly at the monitor above her. The other half of her face is ruined beyond recognition, more blood vessels and tissue than any skin that exists.]

[Camera three shows half a body facing away and sitting on a pool of its own blood.]

[Camera four shows a person frantically backing away from a door behind him before hiding inside one of the lockers in the room, barely fitting inside but finally able to after some struggle, and the phone camera Dr. Delgado is using slowly veers to focus on the door. There is no sound, but you can see the door the man had just locked bending at intervals, as if to indicate that something massive is throwing its weight against the frame or is pounding at it with such force it will break down soon. There is no movement from inside the locker, and no outward sign the man is making any sound that might attract his unseen stalker. After a few minutes, the door stops bending, but several more minutes pass before the locker door slowly inches open. The man climbs out and looks around fearfully, and then cautiously approaches the door. He presses an ear against it, his whole body relaxing when it is apparent he hears nothing. He takes a deep breath and then slowly taps at a numerical keypad on the side of the wall, allowing the door to slide open noiselessly. He takes a step outside.]

[And immediately something long and dark lunges at him from outside the room, slamming the poor man's body onto the floor. It is a shadowed being with no features, save for something that should be a mouth on what should be its face, stretching to reveal

156

red gum-like crevices. It is three times the length of its victim. The man tries to fight back, but it is of no use. It is clear he is screaming, though the security camera does not pick up any sound. The shadow flings its arm out, and something bloody is tossed across the room. It does it again, and again, and again, ripping something out of the man with every gesture.]

Dr. Delgado's voice: Oh my god...

[The man is no longer moving. The shadow hunches over his broken form, the maw on its face moving rapidly. Dr. Delgado makes a whimpering sound.]

[The shadow pauses. Slowly, it turns to face the camera. It does not appear to have eyes, but it is staring into the monitor and at Dr. Delgado. There is movement as Dr. Delgado begins to back away from the screen, breathing rapidly. The shadow does not move at first. It only continues to watch her.]

[And then in less than a second, it twists its body completely so that it is facing the camera and it lunges at her. Its thin fingers pass through the screen, as does part of its face, the maw emerging through the monitor to snap at her.]

[Dr. Delgado does not wait. She immediately turns and begins running for her life, pushing a button on one of the walls as she runs, and turning around long enough to see that the shadow is completely out of the monitor but not fast enough to stop the door from sliding shut on its face. Dr. Delgado pauses, still recording the now-closed door, which begins to bend and fold in the same way as it did in the room with the security camera. Dr. Delgado immediately turns and starts running again, showing a blur of feet and the floor of the hallway as her breathing grows harsher. She strives to keep her voice low, but her clear panic is making her tone rise several octaves higher despite her efforts.]

Dr. Delgado: That thing is what killed most of the personnel inside the Facility. They've ordered a lockdown, but all that did is trap us in here with it! Any calls to the higher-ups are being ignored, and we have no way to contact the rest of the outside world! It's like they're planning to entomb us with these creatures—I don't even know how many have been kept in here all this time! There's a way out, I know where it is. I just had to get that footage recorded first, because I know no one's going to believe me and they're going to pretend nothing ever happened—

[She pauses as she reaches an intersection. She looks around fearfully, the camera swinging around to reveal nothing but darkness, with only emergency lights above to provide an additional light source beyond her camera. Finding no one else, she turns left and begins to walk rapidly down the corridor, her breathing rapid.]

[She pauses at an intersection to take stock of where she is, the camera swinging back and forth from one darkened hallway to another similarly darkened hallway, as if she is trying to remember where to go. Having made a decision, she turns left and travels through a few more series of corridors before winding up in front of an unmarked door. This time, it requires a keycode and a retina scan before she can open it, and the room beyond it is no longer a sterile-looking laboratory area but instead something more akin to a storage space with a series of steps leading underground.]

Dr. Delgado: I have to leave them behind. They might already be dead. There's nothing I can do for them now... There's nothing I can do...

[She heads down the stairs. The phone camera trembles as she turns on a flashlight before starting to move through a series of unmarked tunnels. Though artificially hollowed, very little has been done to develop the area further.]

Dr. Delgado: This is an escape route they showed us before. It's what most of the personnel in the Facility are taught to use in cases of an emergency, but I'm not entirely sure if anyone else has been able to escape through these tunnels. I—

[She breaks off abruptly when an odd clattering sound echoes from behind her, somewhere up the stairs. She grows quiet immediately, and then begins to silently but purposefully move deeper into the tunnels. There is no other light source available save for her flashlight, and her breathing seems loud as she steps cautiously through. The walls of the tunnel are made of some kind of steel that, while sturdy enough, bears traces of rust. The ground is a faint red color paved well enough for the surface to be artificial rather than made from natural means.]

[For the next several minutes she does not utter a word. There is nothing else other than the darkness looming before the scientist as she continues to walk, and it is dark enough that one cannot see beyond a few feet in front of them, with only the play of the flashlight against the walls occasionally breaching the gloom. But the doctor continues, choosing diverging pathways without pause, as if to indicate that she is familiar enough with the area to know her way.]

[All too abruptly, there is another faint clatter of noise from somewhere behind her. She immediately turns away from the path she was taking and instead turns right onto a smaller path. There is a small crevice on the wall large enough to fit an average person, and the camera shudders as she begins to squeeze herself into that space. The cranny is deeper than it looks, and she manages to get several inches away from the opening by the time she stops moving and switches off her flashlight. She waits.]

[For the longest time, there is no other sound, but Dr. Delgado makes no attempt to leave her hiding spot. Her breathing is slow and steady, but she does not move a muscle, and the camera is trained on the opening before her.]

[There is an odd slithering noise, one faint enough that the sound would not have been caught on camera had it not been so quiet. And then there is a heavy thudding sound, rhythmic and constant. Something large and heavy is moving closer, with one foot carefully placed on top of the other, followed by an odd dragging noise.]

Voice: It is all right now, Ivy. We managed to contain the incident. Foolish of us to lose control over it, when there was a chance we could have lost the moon. There is nothing to fear anymore. The inhibitors went down and it caused the other creatures to panic, trying to get away from its scent. We have rounded up all the cryptids, and they are safe in their respective chambers. It is safe. You are safe.

[Something moves slowly past the crevice where the doctor lies hidden, accompanied by a heavy shuffling sound. It appears to be a man in a lab coat, and he looks exactly like the man who had been in the previous video, talking to Dr. Delgado and in charge of the staff wearing the hazmat suits. He is still wearing his lab coat, oddly pristine, but something appears to be attached to the back of it resembling a rope or a thick vine. He looks around, his expression worried.]

Man: Dr. Delgado? Are you here? We managed to clear out as many of the staff as we could—the ones we've been able to find, at least, but one of the security cameras caught you leaving here as well. Are you all right? We had to fall back, but we're waiting at Exit 305. We have a team of enforcers already there, and some medics for those who've been injured. Are you okay? We have no footage of you leaving, so we thought to make sure you weren't lost in here, or hurt.

[Dr. Delgado says nothing. The man looks around and shakes his head.]

Man: If you can hear me, then please head out to Exit 305. Please be all right, Ivy. We'll be waiting for you.

[The man then does a curious thing. Instead of turning around and walking back the way he came from, he instead takes a step backward, and then another step, continuing like this until he is out of the camera's perspective, the shuffling sound returning. Still the doctor doesn't move and waits until the slow tread fades away, and even then she continues to wait for another half hour despite nothing happening.]

[Finally, she emerges. She shines her flashlight in the direction the man walked off to, but there is no one else in sight. She turns back toward the original direction she intended and began walking faster than before.]

[Nothing else happens as she traverses the tunnels, until she comes upon a metal door with a handle and a keypad on the wall. She inputs a series of codes and then finally lets out a gasp of relief as the door swings open. She steps forward—]

[A hand lands on her shoulder and spins her around. The phone camera reveals the man staring back at her, human in every way save for the eyes, which have no eyelids.]

Man: Where are you going, Ivy? Where are you going, Ivy? Where are you going, Ivy?

[With a scream, she shoves hard at him, and surprisingly he stumbles back. She spins back around to race outside and yank the door shut behind her before the man can follow. She stands still for a moment, trembling at her near escape.]

[From beyond the door, the man speaks up again.]

The man's voice: Where are you going, Ivy? Where are you going, Ivy? Where are yougoing, Ivy? Whereare yougoingIvy? Where areyougoing where areyougoing whereareyougoing—

[The camera whirls around as Dr. Delgado begins to run again, and here the video ends.]

VIDEO #12

Advertisements

Storymancer: How did you find it?

JellyBeanFish: How did I find it???

JellyBeanFish: The guy who got fed to that weird egg was Morrissey, wasn't it?

JellyBeanFish: It looked like him based on his mugshot.

Storymancer: I think so too.

Storymancer: The events line up. The date stamp in this video says this happened three weeks ago, and the body showed up less than a week after that. And then Ivy Delgado posts something on the message boards as a cry for help, and then she winds up missing. Of course, they do their best to cover it up so no one else knows there was even an incident at Penumbra. But now we're on the case.

Storymancer: I don't think it was an accident that he escaped. The way the staff acts, and from how that manager dude reacted in Ivy Delgado's video, it's almost like they set some of those patients loose deliberately.

JellyBeanFish: I thought that too.

JellyBeanFish: I've never seen this before. But about three weeks ago, like you said, there was a lockdown within the Facility itself. It never made the news, but there were some cryptids being studied that got loose, and they killed some people in there. I only know this because I was accompanying my mom at the time when the siren started going off, but we were near enough to the entrance still that we were able to get out. It didn't look like anything was going on inside when you were standing outside. You can't hear the warning alarms, there's no one running out screaming. But I knew something bad had happened because mom didn't go in to work for three days. She told me not to mention it to anyone because it was classified, and I didn't think much of it. That must be the incident in Ivy Delgado's video.

JellyBeanFish: That man who died, though. He said something like "Hellenos." What is that?

Storymancer: I tried to look it up.

Storymancer: The closest word to it I've found was from the name Helen, who was some mythological half-goddess who was born from an egg and had men fighting over her enough to start a world war with.

JellyBeanFish: Born from an egg...

Storymancer: You think Morrissey worked there before too?

Storymancer: Any information about his work history has been scrubbed.

Storymancer: The same thing that happened with Ivy Delgado. They scrubbed hers too.

Storymancer: And what was that thing looking for the doctor?

Storymancer: That wasn't her supervisor. Mr. Threnody, she said? He had bugged out eyes

JellyBeanFish: A cryptid. I don't know what cryptid he turned into, but I'd bet money on it.

Storymancer: And you think they're the ones who got to her?

JellyBeanFish: If the Facility was responsible for killing her, then I think we might be in trouble.

Storymancer: It's not too late for you, you know.

JellyBeanFish: What?

Storymancer: You can get out of this. No one knows you've been helping me, but I've spoken so many times that they know about me.

JellyBeanFish: I'm not going anywhere.

JellyBeanFish: We're in this together and that's how it's going to be.

JellyBeanFish: If they're raising cryptids in there, then the public's gotta know.

JellyBeanFish: Besides, you're cool

Storymancer: hehe, thanks

JellyBeanFish: Seal of approval from me. The last thing I'm gonna do is leave now that it feels like we're getting close.

Storymancer: I'm gonna watch through some of these again and see if there's anything I missed. And maybe take some cough medicine.

JellyBeanFish: You got a cough?

Storymancer: Just a small one. When I get stressed, I get sicker easily.

JellyBeanFish: My mom's probably not gonna be home

    tonight either. I'm gonna try and grill some of her coworkers

    tomorrow and see what I can find.

Storymancer: Thanks. Stay safe.

JellyBeanFish: :)

JellyBeanFish: I found some things too.

Storymancer: Good morning to you too

JellyBeanFish: Good morning

JellyBeanFish: I found some things.

Storymancer: I see that.

JellyBeanFish: I have gotten my hands on the most bonkers of

    yoga studio ads

Storymancer: What do yoga studios have to do with anything

JellyBeanFish: Apparently a lot

JellyBeanFish: Look, let me show you.

[The video begins with a bright blue sky over a green meadow. A babbling brook is situated just in front of the camera, the soft, serene sounds of flowing water pleasant to hear.]

Good morning, and welcome to Inner Peace Yoga, from Skyflow Studios, the largest and most popular yoga studio in the world. Today, we are here to practice some calming yoga techniques before you turn in at night, to more effectively regulate your sleeping habits and your circadian rhythms. I am Ingris Everwater, and I shall be your teacher for today. Let us begin.

    To start, spread your knees as wide as possible, and then walk your fingers forward to extend both your arms in front of you. Rest your forehead against the mat, close your eyes, and imagine yourself floating into the ether, weightless and free. You are one with everything around you. You are a finely honed instrument and yet also as light as a feather. Now, inhale and exhale, keeping your breathing light, and observe your body. Look into your mind. You are safe here. There is nothing that can harm you or take you away. You are as a baby in your mother's womb, where everything flows back to you and sustains you. Imagine that this is your universe, and that this is how it must be.

While there may be no one who is out to get you, everyone will dearly miss you should you ever be gone.

[The scenery changes. The waters take on a reddish hue. The sky darkens and the ground takes on a sickly, tar-like appearance. The sound of running water does not cease.]

Imagine a flowing red river that travels endlessly and relentlessly through the galaxy. Imagine that everything within it has all the sustenance and joy you will ever receive. All the happiness you might experience, all the experiences of luxury you have ever hoped to have, all the desires you keep secret even from those who love you the most—all of it is made possible by this flowing red river. Now imagine all of it pouring into you. You are the most beautiful being in the universe. You are the driving force of the world and the center of everything. You are worshiped, you are protected, you are nurtured. This is how we save you. This is how we love you.

[The video goes black. In the darkness, there is movement. It looks like something is struggling underneath a thick cloth that envelops it. The noises from the babbling brook are gone. Instead, there is a steady rhythmic sound, much like a heartbeat.]

And now, imagine yourself giving even just a tenth of everything you have experienced back into the world, giving back even a small percentage of what you have just received. Channel that energy back into the universe, because if karma is real and if there is some god out there who loves us to such an extent, then it is only fair that we love him back in turn. We are loved and we are cherished.

[The movements within the darkness visibly increase, panicked, frantic.]

We are made possible because of the red river. Continue to channel that newfound energy and let it fuse first into our very beings, and then push it back out so that it may dissipate in the air and be returned to the cycle of the lifestream. We are and we are and we are.

[The screen goes fully dark. Slowly, the sound of the stream returns. The blue sky reappears, as does the meadow.]

Now, open your eyes. Do you not feel refreshed? Do you not feel as if the red river flows inside of you, giving you the boost you need to go to bed relaxed and at ease, so you can wake up tomorrow morning full of spirit and zeal? I know I have. Thank you for joining me, and check with us again tomorrow when we'll show you techniques for dealing with exhaustion and stress from your daily lives. Until then, may you find your inner peace.

Storymancer: Okay. First of all, what the fuck

Storymancer: Second of all, you're right. That's an absolutely bonkers yoga ad

Storymancer: Where did you even get this

JellyBeanFish: You're not gonna believe it

JellyBeanFish: The Facility made it

Storymancer: What? They make advertisements for yoga studios now?

JellyBeanFish: They don't just make the ads, they own the studio

Storymancer: What? They own Skyfall Studios? My mom goes there!!

JellyBeanFish: They don't let people know they own it. This is just one of the videos they show during their yoga sessions.

Storymancer: And no one finds it weird?

JellyBeanFish: You can ask your mom about it.

JellyBeanFish: One of my mom's coworkers goes to that studio too. She says she doesn't really remember much of the video, because by then she's in this weird meditative stage. She just remembers the sky and the stream.

Storymancer: Yeahhh, that's weird.

JellyBeanFish: You notice anything else about it?

Storymancer: You mean the part where everything starts bleeding?

JellyBeanFish: I mean, that's creepy. But the one after it.

Storymancer: Like there's something struggling in a sack?

JellyBeanFish: Yes!

Storymancer: Wait

Storymancer: WAIT

Storymancer: That was familiar

Storymancer: It was one of the videos on Ivy Delgado's USB drive

JellyBeanFish: YES

JellyBeanFish: It's the exact same one

Storymancer: You're a genius

Storymancer: How did you even know how to find that?

JellyBeanFish: I was trying to find out what else Penumbra has
investments in

JellyBeanFish: My mom's coworkers got real excited because
she thought that meant I wanted to join her in yoga

JellyBeanFish: She gave me a list of other companies that
Penumbra owns too

JellyBeanFish: I've been looking through them for the last
couple of days

JellyBeanFish: This is the next weird one I found.

[Attached video plays.]

Tired of getting constantly bitten by wasps? Exasperated at the thought
of going into your garden and seeing them wreck the plants you've been
caring for for weeks and even months? Would you do anything just to
make sure you never find a wasps' nest in any corner of your house?
Then look no further!

Our Wasp-aways blasters are guaranteed to ensure that none of
those terrifying buggers dare go near your house again! All you need to
do is take a spatula and slather it up, and then throw it at the irritating
wasp and voilà!

[Onscreen, a man smiles at the camera and hefts up something that looks like a rifle but is not quite one. He points toward something behind him that appears to be a person standing quietly. The latter's head is bent down so you do not see his face, which seems intent on staring at the floor. His skin is an odd shade of gray. Without hesitation, the man lifts his rifle and carefully aims it at the gray-skinned man and pulls the trigger.]

[There is a loud bang. The man twitches backward, and for a moment a bit of his features can be seen—only one giant eye. And then he topples over onto the ground.]

The wasp will mutate into a tiny quietus, which as we all know is mainly harmless and will do far less damage to you or your garden than a normal wasp ever could. From there it is simply a question of taking the nearest knife or ax you can find and chopping it down so they will simply disappear back to wherever it is that they come from! Easy enough!

[The man calmly takes an ax and turns to the body, still offscreen. He lifts the handle and slowly and methodically starts to chop away at the unseen corpse. The screen shifts after five seconds.]

But don't take our word for it!

[A woman with a very large hat hiding half her face comes onto the screen. She is dark-haired and smiling broadly.]

Woman: I couldn't believe it until I tried it myself. I'm not very good at shooting things, but the gun itself seems to have had a mind of its own. It was so easy to use, and I shot down every annoying wasp to ever come near my prize roses!

[Another scene shows a happy-looking man with dark skin and a bald head.]

Man: Came at a fair price and with so many bullets I haven't run out so far! Good thing that none of the wasps came back after a few days of using it, and I am going to recommend this product to every friend of mine who has the same wasp infestations that I do!

[Yet another scene shows another older woman with gray hair and glasses.]

Older woman: Thank you so much, Wasp-away! Exactly as they promised! And now I've just won first place for my petunias because I didn't have to worry about the pests!

And that's not all! For a limited time only, you, too, can take advantage of our ongoing sale! For only $29.99, you get three of our Wasp-aways for the price of one, and a supply of bullets for one year! This is the first and only time we'll be offering this special deal, so what are you waiting for? Get one now and protect your home and garden!

Storymancer: The hell

JellyBeanFish: Haha

Storymancer: Yeah, I definitely would have remembered this one

Storymancer: What weirdo in upper management even approved this

JellyBeanFish: I dunno, it probably would have worked with old folks

JellyBeanFish: I know a bunch who are just waiting for the chance to legally shoot something

JellyBeanFish: I mean, I understand. I have a gun. My mom taught me how to shoot. She said in her line of work, she's learned to make sure to have every chance you get to defend yourself.

Storymancer: That's kinda badass. She took you out to shooting galleries and stuff instead of your dad?

JellyBeanFish: I don't know who my dad is.

JellyBeanFish: She said it didn't matter that I didn't have a dad, I had her. I figured it was a bad breakup or something

JellyBeanFish: But the thing is, I checked and this commercial *did* air. Like, thirty years ago.

Storymancer: REALLY.

JellyBeanFish: Wasp-away was a bestseller even for people who didn't have wasps.

JellyBeanFish: As it turned out, it was just a front. The ad was supposed to be for wasps, but what people actually did was buy it as protection against cryptids that had gotten inside Wispy Falls then or something

JellyBeanFish: I tried looking it up online, but I couldn't find anything.

JellyBeanFish: I did talk to a few people who are old enough to remember then and who still work at Penumbra, and they confirmed that it was just a way for people to arm up because there was a huge cryptid scare back then.

Storymancer: Which cryptid was it?

JellyBeanFish: They never really knew.

JellyBeanFish: But there was an incident where one whole family went missing in their own house

JellyBeanFish: Their mom was the only survivor. She'd slept through the whole thing and had no idea what happened

JellyBeanFish: I think there were security cameras too, but they never showed them publicly. But rumors were it was bad.

Storymancer: So, I'm guessing they did find the cryptids that did it?

JellyBeanFish: Everyone I talked to wasn't sure. It was the only reported incident. There weren't any other attacks after that

JellyBeanFish: And then a few weeks later someone accidentally shot someone else, thinking they were a cryptid, so the ads were pulled

Storymancer: Yeah, I kinda figured that was gonna happen even before you told me

Storymancer: What's the connection, though?

JellyBeanFish: There is no such thing as a quietus wasp. That's not a cryptid that exists.

Storymancer: Oh

JellyBeanFish: Most people assume there are new species of cryptids that they don't know about, and then they just take people's word for it if they sound like they know what they're talking about

Storymancer: Like me

JellyBeanFish: Hah

JellyBeanFish: That cryptid was real, though. The gray-skinned one

Storymancer: Wait, they filmed an actual cryptid??

JellyBeanFish: I think so

JellyBeanFish: Most people don't want to play a cryptid in movies, much less commercials

JellyBeanFish: It's why they're usually like, CGI and stuff, instead of them showing a real actor's face

JellyBeanFish: No one wants to be mistaken for a cryptid. A lot of people aren't the sharpest, and there were incidents a long time ago where someone got killed because people saw them in a show and thought they were really the cryptids they played

Storymancer: Yeah, makes sense

JellyBeanFish: No one's gonna risk that for a commercial that turned out to be real popular too

JellyBeanFish: That was the Quiet Brother. In the last stage before it's at its most dangerous.

Storymancer: They held a cryptid captive just to make that commercial?

JellyBeanFish: Wait. Hang on.

JellyBeanFish: Okay, back.

JellyBeanFish: I enlarged his face and tried to make it look clearer.

[A screenshot of the Quiet Brother is posted, magnified enough times so that its face fills the screen.]

Storymancer: Ew, but okay.

JellyBeanFish: He looks familiar...

Storymancer: I'm looking, and I'm not liking it.

JellyBeanFish: I KNOW I've seen him before.

JellyBeanFish: I just don't remember where!

Storymancer: Facility. Maybe?

JellyBeanFish: I'm not sure yet. Maybe.

JellyBeanFish: They executed a real Quiet Brother on a
freaking ad, though????

JellyBeanFish: You get into contact with your friend again?
The conspiracy theorist dude?

Storymancer: He's my source, and definitely not my friend.

Storymancer: Sometimes he's a fountain of information, sometimes
he disappears for days and weeks on end, who knows

Storymancer: I think he knows what's going on, but trying to
get answers out of him is like pulling teeth.

JellyBeanFish: We need to know who he is.

Storymancer: I'm working on it

Storymancer: You found anything else?

JellyBeanFish: Yeah, this one's the most disturbing one to me
imho

*[The third video posted to the chat is obviously an infomercial for
a certain prescription medicine.]*

Always tired? Feeling adrift in a world you feel you do not belong in? Do
you think that none of your friends and family ever seem to understand
you? Then let us help.

Everyone knows what it feels like to be sad. To be miserable. To feel like you're not doing as well as you should.

Somnium helps you find more meaning in your life and gives yourself the boost you need to live your life to the fullest. Somnium is a natural booster that will help you fight all the bad thoughts in your head and suppress the worst parts you hate about yourself. Let yourself be washed away by nothing but good feelings. You never have to worry about anything in your life ever again. Remember, here at the Facility, we care.

Side effects may include: gentle thoughts, vivid daydreams, general feelings of satisfaction and completion, a happier disposition, death.

Storymancer: In their defense, all prescription med ads are supposed to be vaguely threatening.

Storymancer: I guess Penumbra makes this too, but it's more of a given since they're pharma, right?

JellyBeanFish: Do your parents take them?

Storymancer: Yeah, I've seen the pills in their bathroom.

Storymancer: They've been taking them since Lee passed away. My mom was constantly sleeping before, and it helped turn her into a semi-normal person.

JellyBeanFish: I'm sorry.

JellyBeanFish: My mom takes it as a kind of energy boost. I was kinda suspicious about their claims that there are no major side effects, but I haven't actually seen any negative issues with my mom about it.

Storymancer: It does say death is a side effect.

JellyBeanFish: I asked about that. Mom said some marketing executive was probably being cheeky when they made the ad since it's so vague.

JellyBeanFish: But here's the part that makes me suspicious

JellyBeanFish: They've prescribed it to every family who's had a member turn up missing in the woods

Storymancer: What?

Storymancer: I mean, they did give us a prescription for free, but—

JellyBeanFish: Have you ever taken it?

Storymancer: Yes, but I didn't like it so I sort of stopped. It got my mom up and moving about, but she and dad have been kinda weird since. I didn't want to take it and be the same way. I did once and didn't like how it felt.

JellyBeanFish: What do you mean by weird?

Storymancer: It's like they've forgotten all about Lee. They're back to how they were before Lee died, but it's like they don't even acknowledge him anymore. My folks even took some of his stuff and put it down in the basement. Dad needed an office, so they turned his room into one.

Storymancer: I didn't take that well.

Storymancer: It was like they didn't care anymore.

JellyBeanFish: Oh

Storymancer: I mean, yeah. That's what the meds are supposed to do, right? They're supposed to make you normal. Like the way you were. But I don't want to be the way I was, because being the way I was means I don't care that my brother is gone.

JellyBeanFish: I think that was a deliberate choice.

JellyBeanFish: They don't want people complaining about how nothing's been investigated. If the families of those who went missing don't care, then they have even more reason not to do anything.

Storymancer: I think you're right

Storymancer: Shit

Storymancer: I need to think this is over

JellyBeanFish: Take all the time you need

JellyBeanFish: I'm sorry

Storymancer: Not your fault

Storymancer: I just...shit

Storymancer: I'll talk to you later.

Storymancer: I found some new stuff

Storymancer: LightParticle121's still giving me random crap

Storymancer: But he gave me several more videos.

[The video attached is a PSA.]

We interrupt this program to deliver to you your friendly neighborhood public service announcement by the hour on the hour until further notice.

As always, we are reporting on sightings of Quiet Brothers that may have infiltrated our barriers and found their way into our community. Please do not be alarmed, and remain calm at all times. The chances you actually encounter one are slim.

It is important to remain at home from 6:00 in the evening until 4:00 in the morning, and this shall be a mandatory curfew for all until further notice, excepting those who have been granted special privileges to work past those hours.

If you see a person exhibiting strange behaviors, including but not limited to shuffling their feet slowly, walking backward, or having trouble enunciating themselves clearly due to an enlarged tongue, do not engage. Instead, put as much distance as you can between yourself and it until you are safely back home. Do not open your doors to anyone you do not know, or to anyone you do know who is nonetheless exhibiting similar characteristics.

If you see that this person has successfully infiltrated your house, do not panic. Alert law enforcement when you can and keep a phone constantly with you for this express purpose. Until they arrive, hide in any small, enclosed space available to you, even after you believe it has gone away.

If you recognize this person who continues to behave strangely, please do not approach. This is not the friend or family member you know, may they rest in peace. If they have assumed their features, then it is too late for them, but not too late for you.

Do not listen to it when it attempts to speak. The voice that comes from its mouth is not your loved one. Everything that leaves its mouth is a lie. Do not listen to it for your own safety. Do not seek to communicate with it in any way, no matter what threats it makes or promises it offers.

If you are backed into a corner and have no choice but to defend yourself, the easiest form of execution would be to use a gun and aim directly into its mouth. You will know you are safe once it is done twitching on the floor, but until then, remain ever vigilant until it no longer moves. Even then, you must keep an eye on the creature, because in some cases they may just pretend to be dead.

Most importantly, do not look at what lies behind them. If you see what it is, then you are already lost. Please note that there will soon be law enforcement at your house to question you about the creature while they open an investigation. Every encounter must be reported to the authorities, or you will be arrested for withholding vital information contributing to the safety of our community.

This has been an important public safety announcement. We now return to our regular programming.

> **JellyBeanFish:** I remember this. That was a PSA that frequently played during the news segments, right?
>
> **Storymancer:** How about this one, then?

[Another PSA video plays.]

We interrupt this program to deliver to you your friendly neighborhood public service announcement by the hour on the hour until further notice.

As always, we are reporting on sightings of Quiet Brothers that may have infiltrated our barriers and found their way into our community. Please do not be alarmed, and remain calm at all times. The chances you actually encounter one are slim.

It is important to remember that these Quiet Brothers are mostly harmless. If you do not engage with them, they are not likely to engage with you. Simply look away when you see one in the vicinity and continue to do so until you have arrived in the safety of your home.

These Quiet Brothers will appear very much like an average person, with an innate ability to transform into the features of people they have already preyed upon. While they are excellent mimics, they are not able to completely replicate certain human features. Their tongues remain elongated as in their natural form, which means they have a much more difficult time keeping them hidden in their human mouths. They also have a habit of shuffling backward instead of turning around and walking when opting to move to an opposite direction.

They are fond of warm temperatures and will often choose to enter a home for this purpose, especially if it is raining or cold outside. Ignore them. More often than not they will nestle themselves in one corner and sleep for roughly six to seven hours, after which they tend to leave in the early hours of the morning. It is believed they have evolved their ability to mimic the human body to appear pleasing or safe for the express purpose of finding temporary sanctuary in one's household by taking one's thought patterns, selecting a familiar face within one's mind, and recreating their faces as a means to persuade humans to allow them to stay.

The quietus will attempt to speak on occasion. Do not engage with it, but simply nod as if the garbled conversation they are trying to start makes sense. Do not make any sudden movements toward it or raise your voice and use loud noises. Do not use any form of violence against them. While they themselves are not homicidal, they startle easily and will break down walls in their bid to get away from you, and may cause unnecessary property damage in the process.

More importantly, do not look behind them.

This has been an important public safety announcement. We now return to our regular programming.

JellyBeanFish: That's not right.

JellyBeanFish: That's the exact opposite of what you're
supposed to do.

Storymancer: But it looks like it was made by the same
production company.

JellyBeanFish: Yeah, it does.

Storymancer: Why would they make two completely opposing ads?

JellyBeanFish: Remember Huntington? Some people didn't like how he handled the town dealing with the cryptids, right?

JellyBeanFish: What if they were trying to put out inaccurate information about the cryptids so it would affect Huntington's reputation? He was in charge, so the blame would have fallen on him.

Storymancer: All we know about him we learned from these sites, but do you ever think he might be some kind of manufactured hero? Even in what little they give about him, it's said he never liked public appearances, and except for the diary—which could be a fake, who knows—a lot of the information about him is from secondhand sources. It's no secret that Penumbra is pretty much the government here, but even then they don't really put out any information. Have any of the older folk there ever met him? Has your mom?

JellyBeanFish: Nope. The dude Ivy Delgado was talking with in her videos, the Threnody guy? He's the person I know in charge and has some position in government, but I don't know anyone else. But they treat him like a hospital director, not the person in charge of the whole town.

Storymancer: Yeah, bet. We need to know more about Huntington.

JellyBeanFish: Good luck. The Facility is likely the one place

that would know all there is about him, but like you said—
they focus more on the cryptids than on the town's founder.
I don't think I've even seen a plaque or a wall or anything
dedicated to him.

Storymancer: I'm hoping our current investigation will lead to
more eventually. I'm more focused right now on the missing
people in the woods, and what's happened to Dr. Delgado.

Storymancer: Wait though, I got one more thing to show you
that LightParticle sent.

[The final video is what appears to be a children's program called
Mr. Happy. An introduction begins to play with upbeat music
before a smiling man appears onscreen, waving merrily to viewers offscreen to their applause. He is enthusiastically upbeat and
cheerful for a man in a spider costume with a small cut-out in
the cloth for his face. His additional four legs dangle uselessly on
either side of him.]

Mr. Happy: Hello again, kids! My name is Mr. Happy, and welcome to
the happiest place in town! You know what they say—when Mr. Happy
is around—

[The camera pans to the children seated in the audience, cheering
as they sing out.]

Audience: —He'll turn your frown upside down!

Mr. Happy: You know you know you know I will, hahaha! But now kids,

I want to talk to you all about a very serious thing every one of you ought to know. Do you know what this is?

[He steps back, and magically enough, a small whiteboard drops down from the ceiling via chains fused to its upper corners, with the word "BURROWER" written in large block letters across its surface.]

Audience: Burrower!

Mr. Happy: That's right! It's a cryptid called a Burrower! Now, since everyone in Wispy Falls have been doing such a wonderful job of protecting our town, Burrowers have not been seen around these parts for nearly ten years! That's a very, very long time! Why, I must have been the same age as most of you when that happened, and I remember it very clearly!

[The whiteboard gets pulled up again, and this time a small stage is dropped down with several finger puppets popping up from behind the curtain. One of them has the semblance of a small child, while the other is like a smaller version of Mr. Happy.]

Mr. Happy: When I was very young, there was a Burrower that ran amuck in the city for a day or two. Do you know that Burrowers are very bad cryptids? There are some good cryptids that will leave you alone, but then there are also some who are not very nice. It's like how there are good people but also bad people sometimes! So when I was just a very small Mr. Happy, I was hiding in my bedroom like the government was telling us to. My mom and dad weren't in the house at that time because the announcement came when they were at work and I had just gotten home from school. But I was a very good child and knew when to obey the people in charge. So I went and hid under my bed, of course!

[The puppet-Mr. Happy shuffles toward a bed prop, and then burrows himself underneath, though his face is still sticking out.]

Mr. Happy: Well, small Mr. Happy was really unlucky that day, because at that time the Burrower decided to pay my house a visit!

[The spider crawls as menacingly as a spider puppet can, pausing to look around the "bedroom" as if looking for someone. The puppet-Mr. Happy is trembling.]

Mr. Happy: I was very, very afraid that would be the end for me, but I didn't make a sound. Not one bit! I curled myself into a ball and then waited for the Burrower to go away, because that's what they said I should be doing!

[The puppet-spider behind him pauses and then turns toward the bed. Immediately its long arms jut out and grab the puppet-Mr. Happy, dragging him out of the bed even as the boy is struggling frantically.]

Mr. Happy: The authorities were also very, very good at what they do. In almost no time at all, they were able to track down where the Burrower was and realized it was inside my house! Before the Burrower could find me, they were already banging at the door. The Burrower moved away from the bedroom because it was attracted to all the noise being made downstairs, and it was then that they finally captured it! Zapped it quite well, even!

[The puppet-Mr. Happy behind him continues to be dragged away from the bedroom by the spider puppet, not stopping until they have disappeared behind the curtain again. The small setting is lifted upward, disappearing above Mr. Happy.]

Mr. Happy: Later on, the authorities told me what a brave boy I was! And so did my mom and dad when they were finally able to return home, and they hugged and kissed me a million times! That was how Mr. Happy knew this was a bad Burrower, and that all of us should do our best to hide when most of the other cryptids are around, right?

[A different set of music plays, though still upbeat.]

Mr. Happy: All right, kids! It's that time again where we go through the list of do's and don'ts when it comes to finding a cryptid of your own! Do you want to sing along with me as we learn together?

Audience: Yeahhh!

Mr. Happy: And here we go!

[Mr. Happy starts to sing as he dances around the podium he is standing on. He is not a very good dancer, and his moves look more like an awkward marionette being jerked around on strings as he wobbles around.]

Mr. Happy:

When there's a giant eye just sitting
*   there and staring back at you*
And you're all by yourself at home
*   with no one else around,*
Do you leave the house and scream
*   and run into the night,*
Or are you a brave boy or girl to stand your ground?

Audience: Stand your ground!

Mr. Happy: You're absolutely correct!

When there are shadows on the wall and
*   they're far too long and thin,*
Your parents aren't home but your
*   mom is calling you inside,*
Do you tell them to clean up 'cause you
*   don't know where they've been,*
Or do you find a closet or any other small place to hide?

Audience: Hide!

Mr. Happy: Excellent! Now here we go!

Something odd is going on because you're seeing you,

They're standing across from you

   and you don't have a twin,

Do you call the authorities, they know what to do,

Or do you kill yourself instead so you

   know that they won't win?

Audience: Kill yourself!

Mr. Happy: Correct once again!

[The song ends and Mr. Happy stops dancing. He bows low to his audience.]

Mr. Happy: I'm afraid that's all the time we have left for today, my lovely little things! Until then, remember me, Mr. Happy! Because when I'm around—

Audience: My frown turns upside down!

[The audience cheers. Mr. Happy turns to beam at the camera, but for a few quick moments, his mouth blurs downward unnaturally before it lifts back up again. The video ends here.]

JellyBeanFish: That is the most disturbing thing I've ever watched

Storymancer: ikr

JellyBeanFish: It looks like a really old kid's show. Like from twenty years ago.

Storymancer: Thirty-five years ago, according to Mr. LightParticle.

JellyBeanFish: And technically, his instructions are right.

JellyBeanFish: The PSA is accurate. Burrowers are more cautious if you stand your ground, and you earn yourself more time for authorities to arrive if you called them. If you run, its instinct is to immediately chase you.

JellyBeanFish: But if it doesn't see you, it's better to hide

JellyBeanFish: And if it's progressed to the point where it's stalked you long enough to adopt your features, then it's too late to do anything. You'd be dead before any enforcement arrives.

Storymancer: I don't know why LightParticle would send me this.

JellyBeanFish: Because he's a weirdo?

Storymancer: A weirdo who knows a lot more than what he lets on

Storymancer: I'm going to post this on the message board.

JellyBeanFish: They might ban you for it

Storymancer: If there's a chance someone out there might know and reach out, I'll take it

Storymancer: I'm creating a second email just for that, so it won't get back to me. Hopefully.

JellyBeanFish: I hope you know what you're doing

Storymancer: It's just a message board, and I'm a nobody. I don't think they're even gonna ban me for it

VIDEO #13

Colde Trial

Storymancer: Hahahhahaah they banned me!!

JellyBeanFish: I TOLD YOU

Storymancer: Worth it, someone reached out to me

Storymancer: I'll copy and paste it here.

WISPY FALLS MESSAGE INBOX

From: ThrowAway2745

To: MrHappyFan

I Believe that you reached out to me before about the Body In The Woods, but I never responded. I thought at first that you were like the REST OF THEM, and that you only wanted the attention but did Not want to look further beyond what they show you with your eyes. But now that you have seen Mr. Happy, I realize that you are serious like me when it comes to finding out the Truth.

I was once a part of the Facility myself, just like your Ivy Delgado. I was one of the few who were lucky enough to GET OUT before they put their hooks into me. It was a long, long time ago, and maybe they think I am too old to do anything against them, hahaha. But I remember Mr. Happy. The Facility also created Mr. Happy, just like they have created every TV program for the past fifty years. But Mr. Happy was one of their pet projects, because unlike their other shows that cater to brainwashing the adults, they intended to use the program to brainwash the children.

The Facility approved it at first. They thought they could get away with explaining some dark realities in a fun way. But that's where they underestimated both Mr. Happy and their audience. Children will be children, and children will always be asking questions. There were other episodes that they tried to destroy beyond the one you showed. Episodes where children in the audience began speaking up and asking Mr. Happy why the authorities say they should remain still and not move when Mr. Happy told them that a Quiet Brother would find them faster that way. Or asking why they were supposed to say hi to the Backward Lady when they know that everyone who saw her always turned up missing. Mr. Happy was giving the children conflicting information with what he says in contrast to what the people in charge wanted him to say. And yes, it was deliberate.

The man who voiced and played Mr. Happy did not like the directions he was given, you see. The Facility wanted him to lie. To make the creatures a little more palatable, so they did not need to feel too afraid. But he wanted the children to know the truth of how to fight these creatures, even if it meant they would have to kill themselves, for example. The parents didn't like that.

So in the end, they decided to put an end to Mr. Happy and his show and then tried erasing all of it from existence.

But then there are the renegades. There are always the renegades. The ones who keep questioning and questioning, even after they become adults. The Body in the Woods was one of them. Your Ivy Delgado was another. But sometimes the renegades who are questioning things are still children. Still not good to demonize, even after Mr. Happy was done. So instead, they will do one of two things. They will either find a way to make sure the renegade child no longer exists to question their beliefs, or they will extend an olive branch to them if the child is a particularly intelligent one, and they will offer them a place in their Facility. An invitation to be one of them and share in the power. You would be surprised to learn how many choose that path.

I hope this is enough to Clear Up Matters when it comes to Mr. Happy. And no—not even I knew what ever happened to the man who played him. But it is not hard to think that his fate is the same as many others who opposed Penumbra...

But I need more Proof from you that you are not one of them, and that you are not a Spy sent to find out Who I Am. As Proof that I am Who I Am, I will send you this video I think will Convince You that I once worked at the Facility.

194

JellyBeanFish: I am not sure how, because he's a bit more coherent...

JellyBeanFish: But he sounds even more unhinged than your LightParticle friend

Storymancer: Yeah, but we finally have some information. It sounds like he knows what he's talking about, and he verified some things. He makes some sense

JellyBeanFish: For someone who's trying to avoid the Facility though, he's not really staying under the radar, is he

Storymancer: Maybe he wants to risk it to warn us

JellyBeanFish: Maybe he's a plant and they want to find out about us the same way they trapped Dr. Delgado.

Storymancer: Well, Dr. Delgado obviously wanted to stay under the radar too, but she risked it to post on that message board.

Storymancer: That's why I need to find her

Storymancer: As long as we can corroborate what they're saying, I'll give them the benefit of the doubt. In any case, he does confirm the point that the town is just Penumbra's test subjects, and it's the same thing LightParticle's been claiming

Storymancer: Plus, he also sent me something

Storymancer: It's wild, watch it

[Video begins with a title: Colde Trial. It fades to reveal three simultaneous video feeds showing side by side on one monitor. The first video is the largest, taking up half the monitor, and it seems to be security camera footage of one house. The second video takes up half of the remaining space and features a series of logs that seem to be describing the activities and events going on in the first screen. The third video is a black screen that says LIVING ROOM.]

[The first screen shows what seems to be a family inside their house. There is a father and a mother, and a son and a daughter approximately seven and ten years old. There is a large dalmatian stretched out on a rug before the television, dozing off. The son is nestled against the dog's side, while the daughter is lying down on one of the two couches in the living room watching the show, which appears to be Mr. Happy. The two adults take up the remaining couch. The mother is also watching the show, though she looks bored. The father is scrolling through something on his phone. The room appears to be a well-used and comfortable one. There are family pictures lining the walls and a mirror over a small side table. Tastefully decorated vases and paintings indicate that the owners of the home are well-off.]

[The second screen reads: Subjects 1, 2, 3, 4, 5, and 6 are watching television.]

[The first screen switches to a bedroom. The third screen now reads MASTER BEDROOM. The second screen reads NO ACTIVITY. The first screen then switches to another bedroom, one that is messier and has toys strewn around. The third screen reads BEDROOM 1. The first screen moves again to yet another bedroom, this time neater and full of stuffed dolls. The third screen says BEDROOM 2. The second screen reads NO ACTIVITY for both cases. The first screen moves back to the living room, and the second and third screens resume their previous descriptions of Subjects 1, 2, 3, 4, 5, and 6 who are watching television and LIVING ROOM respectively.]

[On the first screen, the mother is now massaging her forehead.] "I have a headache," she says and sighs.

[The father does not even look up from his phone. "Why don't you go upstairs and lie down for a bit, honey," he says. "You've had a long day."]

["I suppose," the mother says, and glances down at her son. "I think that's enough Mr. Happy for you for one day, Jason."]

[The son looks up at her and whines. "Mom, can't I watch just one more?"]

["You've watched six today," the mother says firmly. "It's about time you go and rest your eyes. You and Squirrel can go take a nap for about an hour or so."]

[Jason grumbles but stands up obediently. The dog gets to its feet when the son does and wags its tail.]

["See?" the mother points out, getting up herself. "Squirrel wants to rest too. Go on, now. The sooner you nap, the sooner you can wake up."]

[Jason trots to the right of the screen, the dog following. After a moment, the mother follows.]

[The second screen now reads: Subject 2 heading upstairs to master bedroom. Subjects 4 and 5 heading upstairs to child's bedroom.]

[The first screen moves again, this time to a bathroom. There is a tub on one side of the room, with curtains half-drawn across the area for privacy. There is a toilet bowl and a sink with a mirrored medicine cupboard above the latter. The second screen reads NO ACTIVITY and the third screen says BATHROOM. The mother enters with a long sigh, rubbing tiredly at her eyes. She moves toward the mirror cupboard and opens it. She takes a medicine bottle out and pours purple-colored pills into her hand, which she downs quickly. She leans her hands on the sink and watches her reflection for a few moments, and then sighs again before turning to leave.]

[The second screen now reads: Subject 2 2762626262. The third screen reads: Subject 2 leaves.]

[The first screen then moves to the mother entering the master bedroom, the third screen title again changing to reflect that. She sighs and crawls into bed without bothering to take off her shirt or her shoes, instead lying on top of the covers on her stomach and her face down. She stops moving.]

[The third screen reads MASTER BEDROOM. The second screen reads: Subject 2 taking a nap.]

[The first screen now shifts to the son and the dog entering the former's bedroom. The son pets the dog and then kicks off his slippers, burrowing underneath the covers so only part of his head can be seen. The dog leaps onto the bed on top of the covers and settles itself down, resting its head on the bedsheets.]

[The third screen reads: BEDROOM 1. The second screen says Subjects 4 and 5 taking a nap.]

[The first camera then pans back to the living room. The father is still scrolling through his phone, and the young daughter is still watching.]

["Dad," the daughter says. "Our teacher says that we should be covering up our windows and mirrors because there are monsters in the area. Why do we have to?"]

["Are you sure that's what he said, honey?" the father asks, apparently only half-listening.]

["Yeah! He says that the cryptids can get in through the mirrors and your reflection, so you have to make sure that you throw blankets or something over them so that they can't get in that way."]

["I don't think that's right, sweetie. I'm pretty sure all the broadcasts are saying the opposite of that."]

[The daughter frowns at her father, and then shrugs and turns back to the television.]

[The first screen abruptly switches to what looks like a large storage space. The rest of the room is filled with cardboard boxes of different shapes and sizes placed haphazardly on the floor, leaving little room for one to move across with ease. There is a cleared area near a set of stairs leading up the farthest wall by a washing machine. The second and third screens say NO ACTIVITY and BASEMENT, respectively.]

[The screen switches again, this time to another storage space. There are even more boxes here despite the smaller area, and the ceiling slopes down with a tiny window at one end. The second and third screens now say NO ACTIVITY and ATTIC.]

[The screen moves briefly to the master bedroom, where the mother has not moved, and then to Bedroom 1, where the son is turning a little under his sheets, clearly unable to sleep. The dog has lifted its head and is motionless, staring at something offscreen.]

[The screen returns to the living room. The phone in the father's hand suddenly begins to ring. He looks down at it, annoyed, and answers the call.]

["Yeah Maddox, it's Dave," he says. "Didn't we already discuss this? I know there's not much you can do right now since the neighborhood quarantine hasn't been lifted yet, but I was hoping you could pull some strings and—" He trails off and then frowns harder.]

[The man's voice is still being recorded, though the screen switches to Bedroom 2. Nothing appears to be present there, but the second screen now reads: Subject 6 has entered the room. The screen switches back to the living room, where the father continues to speak into his phone.]

["That wasn't part of our deal. I'm a valued member of the board, and not just some schmuck you can boss around whenever you feel like it. I spearheaded the Maple Protocol. It's my show, and I don't intend to leave it to someone else just because I can't get out of the house for the next few days—"]

[The father breaks off to stare at something in the mirror. He speaks into the phone again. "Hey, Maddox—I think I should call you later. What? Well sure, I can stay on the line, but I think it would be better if I could—"]

[He pauses again and rises to his feet, striding toward the mirror. He stares hard at it for a few seconds, and then shakes his head and turns away. The reflection in the mirror takes another second or two before it does the same. "Yeah, it was nothing. Look, I gave you all the information I had with the promise that I was going to keep leading this project. I've been working hard on this for the last three years, and we're getting close. At least give me the chance to see it through myself. I'm not going to sit by and let someone like you take the credit, Threnody, all right? This is my hard work, not yours."]

[He hesitates a third time. "As far as I can tell, yeah. We've been successful so far with all the tests. People can imprint on it in the same way ducklings do to their mother, except it's like a reverse hatching—or to make a better comparison in this case, people can imprint on it if we act quickly. Seven or eight years tends to be the sweet spot, but any older than that and they'll still be questioning things. Out of two hundred families to date, eighty-five percent react favorably to what we want. I know you're impatient, but at least let me up the number to ninety so I can give you a more accurate—"]

[He breaks off abruptly, stares right into the security camera, directly at the first screen, and doesn't say anything for a long time.]

["You didn't," he finally says. "You broke into our security cameras. You would—"]

[Someone screams, and the father whips his head back toward the stairs just as the daughter looks up in alarm.]

[At the same time, the first screen switches to Bedroom 1, where

the boy is rolling around in his bed and screaming in terror. The
dog is on all fours, haunches raised and teeth bared at something
in the room, barking loudly. It tries to leap from the covers, but
it crashes into something invisible mid-air and falls to the floor,
whimpering loudly. The boy scrambles toward the dog, trying to
grab it and pull it back up to the bed, but finds himself sliding
backward across the sheets as something invisible drags him
toward the closet beside his bed, doors slamming shut once he's
inside.]

[The screen switches to the master bedroom, where the mother
does not move from her prone position despite the noise going
on. The second screen reads: NO ACTIVITY.]

[The screen switches again to the attic. The second screen reads:
UNUSUAL ACTIVITY.]

[There is nothing trying to get in through the window.]

[The father dashes into Bedroom 1 with the daughter close behind
him. The dog is already at the closet, pawing and whining at the
door.]

["Oh my god, Ethan? Are you there? Oh, shit—" The father pulls
uselessly at the closet door's handle, but it refuses to budge. He
starts slamming his shoulder into it with all his might, while the
daughter looks on, horrified. The son's screams are evident over
the rest of the noise and show no signs of stopping.]

[The first screen switches abruptly to the basement. Though nothing appears to be moving, the second screen reads: ACTIVITY DETECTED. UNKNOWN SUBJECT.]

[The screen switches back to Bedroom 1. The father has finally succeeded in breaking down the closet door and pulling the terrified boy within into his arms, hugging him tightly. He is still gripping his cell phone tightly in one hand, and he lifts it up to his ear now and begins to yell.]

["What the hell are you doing, Maddox? This is my family! How dare you bring them into this just because I—"]

[Something reaches from inside the closet, wraps its arms around the father, and drags him. All he can do is toss his son onto the bed before the closet door slams shut. Now it is the son's and daughter's turn to scream, pounding futilely at the closet door. The dog is no longer barking. It has turned its head and is instead watching the security camera in the bedroom, staring directly at the screen.]

[The first screen unexpectedly flickers in and out, and then shifts abruptly from morning, where all of the action took place, to nighttime. The rest of the house is silent. The first screen moves from living room to Bedroom 1 to Bathroom to Bedroom 2, but there are no signs of anyone else in the house. The second screen reads: NO ACTIVITY in every room. The camera moves to the master bedroom, where the mother is still lying on the bed, not having moved from her position at all.]

[The camera stays with her for several minutes until she finally stirs and then sits up to stretch, humming contentedly. She leaves the bed and shuffles off toward the bathroom. She looks refreshed. She looks younger for some reason. She examines herself in the mirror and smiles at her reflection. The camera follows her through the rooms, down the stairs, and finally at the living room where she exits the house.]

[The basement and the attic are still, but the second screen now reads: EXTREME ACTIVITY in both areas, though nothing moves.]

JellyBeanFish: omg

Storymancer: Yeah

JellyBeanFish: That's a Burrower!

JellyBeanFish: I've never seen footage of them before...

JellyBeanFish: That poor family

JellyBeanFish: And I know him.

Storymancer: The father?

JellyBeanFish: His name is Simon Colde.

JellyBeanFish: He was the Director of Human Resources at the Penumbra until like five years ago.

JellyBeanFish: I met him during one of those bring-your-kids-to-work-days when I was seven. He was really happy I was so interested in cryptozoology and told me he was looking forward to working with me at Penumbra in the future.

JellyBeanFish: They told me he'd retired...

Storymancer: Yeah, right. Sounds like another cover-up.

Storymancer: I tried tracking down the person who sent me that video, but he'd deleted his account. No information I can grab from it, nothing I can find in any web caches that could give me an idea of who he is.

Storymancer: Him having that Colde video just means that he's legit. But I don't have any other way to contact him for anything else.

JellyBeanFish: I can at least verify that's Simon Colde.

JellyBeanFish: He must have done something to make the higher-ups mad...

JellyBeanFish: At the very least, he knew something.

JellyBeanFish: He must have. That other person he was talking on the phone with—he called him Maddox. Maddox Threnody. The director. The one who was talking to Ivy Delgado in that other video.

Storymancer: Oh.

JellyBeanFish: I feel awful.

Storymancer: More likely he was fine with keeping everything a secret, same with the rest of them, till he was in the line of fire. Don't feel bad about him just yet till we know more.

Storymancer: Did you see those pills the mother took before she napped?

[Photo attachment: a zoomed, slightly blurry, closeup shot of the purple pills in the mother's hand, followed by the medicine bottle it was taken from inside the bathroom cabinet.]

Storymancer: Don't you think that looks familiar?

JellyBeanFish: The drug. Somnium.

Storymancer: Yep.

Storymancer: She was the only one taking it, and she's the only one who seemed to have survived

Storymancer: That's gotta be something

JellyBeanFish: Are you saying that maybe the pill prevents cryptids from attacking them?

Storymancer: I'm about to make a really far-fetched guess here.

Storymancer: The stones in the woods keep cryptids away, right? Did they ever tell you at the Facility why?

JellyBeanFish: Oh, that's easy enough to answer.

JellyBeanFish: It's all about the pheromones inside of them. Scientists still do not quite know what they are made of, but they do act as a deterrent to monsters.

JellyBeanFish: If you've been to the museum, they explain more.

JellyBeanFish: The best guess that it could have some similarities to large trees that used to exist, and the most widely accepted theory is that the stones are some kind of shed-off scales from a creature we don't even know of yet.

JellyBeanFish: The main theory as well is that these "stone" cryptids died out just because there weren't enough nutrients for them due to their size, so essentially they wound up starving themselves.

JellyBeanFish: And the main evidence we have is in the pheromones. The stones are still exuding some kind of scent that lets lesser cryptids know there's a predator in the area, and they flee. Obviously, we can't detect it, but they can.

Storymancer: What kind of predator is that, then? Announcing your presence to your food doesn't sound like a good evolutionary trait.

JellyBeanFish: There's a debate going on right now that maybe this cryptid only releases that scent after they're dead, to prevent prey from eating their remains. Someone even suggested that prey who consume them might turn into these kinds of stone cryptids themselves, and it was their way to prevent competition since they had a hard time finding food already.

Storymancer: What if there were other uses for these stones?

Storymancer: Like say, grinding some of them up and using them as food supplements?

JellyBeanFish: You seriously don't mean

Storymancer: I got my folks' pill bottle and I'm reading the ingredients

Storymancer: They take Somnium too.

Storymancer: It lists all the usual vitamins, but who the hell would even investigate and file anything against Penumbra if they added anything else and not put it on the label? Their pharma director could also be the person in charge of the town for all we know.

JellyBeanFish: It makes sense when you put it like that...

JellyBeanFish: But my mom's been taking it too!! They prescribed it to her because she'd been feeling stressed about her job lately. Is that why she seems so withdrawn from me?

Storymancer: Somnium is the prescription that the Facility gives all the people who lost family to the woods. After my parents started taking it regularly, they started acting like that mother in this Colde trial. It felt like they didn't really care about my brother anymore. That's why I stopped taking it after that one time.

Storymancer: She acted that way too. My mom. She smiled at herself in the mirror nearly the same way. That's what caught my attention. Before she'd started taking Somnium, she'd been crying nearly nonstop. To see her so relaxed and happy so soon after...

Storymancer: There's something else

[Attached: a short screencap of the trial video. The image is the basement, with the second screen on one side still reading EXTREME ACTIVITY. It is zoomed in on one corner of the basement. There is a distinct shape hiding behind one of the stacks of boxes there, though it is difficult to see more clearly, save that it has bright yellow eyes and very long arms that at first glance had blended with the shadows of the basement. Those arms are shown extending upward along the walls, reaching the ceiling above it.]

Storymancer: What are the chances that part of the basement also happens to be underneath Bedroom 1 on the second floor? I'm willing to bet a lot of money it is.

JellyBeanFish: It is. That's a Burrower who took Simon Colde...

JellyBeanFish: Let me show you one of those PSA videos you found that talks about the Burrower.

[The first video begins. A silhouette of hands cupped together appears onscreen, with "Instructional Video: Burrowers" super-imposed over it, along with a smaller "brought to you by Mainville Productions" tagline. A series of texts begin to fill the screen.]

Do you know where your children are? Have you searched for them under the floorboards? Have they been found inside your closets? We have been receiving numerous reports of unidentified dangerous organisms, and we encourage everyone to be on the alert. They have been termed Burrowers, and they are coming for your kids.

These creatures are fond of burrowing into the ground right underneath your houses and tend to thrive in dark places such as basements. The Oldkeep classification system called them "Sisters" in keeping with the rest of the cryptids in that species, but Burrowers have become the more popular term for them in recent times, given the horror movie of that same name that was made nearly ten years ago and is long considered a cult classic.

[A rough caricature of an extremely thin, shadow-like figure with bulging eyes is now seen lying down under a drawing of a typical house.]

It is unknown if they are composed of muscles, tissue, skin, or other organs, save that they closely resemble shadows and often camouflage as such. A closer inspection, however, reveals that they have bulging eyes and, when threatened, rows of rotting teeth, which seems to indicate they may at least have a limited bone structure.

The Burrowers, however, do not approach their victims directly.

Instead, their arms are able to extend and slip through cracks in the floors and walls, with nerves in their bodies that allow them to seek out hidden places in the rooms of the house. Often they prefer closets and other small places to lie in wait. While they favor smaller targets like toddlers and children, they have also been known to take adults when confronted by the element of surprise.

It is not known quite what happens to their victims once they have been captured, but there have been no known cases of anyone surviving these encounters once they're taken, and any remains from the attack have yet to be discovered. Dissecting the remains of Burrowers that have been retrieved by our special forces, however, has yielded traces of DNA of known victims, though the manner in which they had been consumed is still yet to be determined.

[The video now flashes a Know What To Do segment before more text begins to scroll.]

If you suspect there is a Burrower in your basement, leave the premises immediately and contact the nearest local authorities.

If there is something inside your closet or your pantry, keep your distance and vacate your house as soon as possible.

If you wake up and see eyes staring down at you, it is already too late.

Sacrifice other people in the room if you wish to distract it long enough to get away. It has a natural preference for small children and pets. Sometimes it is necessary. Do what is necessary.

[The video ends.]

Storymancer: You think that's the thing that got them?

JellyBeanFish: At least one of them, yeah

Storymancer: The video is titled *Colde Trial*. What was the trial? How a family would respond when there's a Burrower in their house—or is it to test to see if the pill works? Do you know when Somnium was first sold?

JellyBeanFish: Let me check

JellyBeanFish: Eight years ago

JellyBeanFish: I met him ten years ago

Storymancer: The meta on this video says it was taken ten years ago too. Somnium wouldn't have been public yet then. So if that video happened shortly before his "retirement," then it sounds like they were one of the last families to have been tested for that.

Storymancer: brb, just gonna grab some medicine

Storymancer: Here's what I think.

[Attached: a short clip of the attic in the video, where the second screen reads: EXTREME ACTIVITY.]

Storymancer: I have gone through this part of the footage over and over for hours now. I can see nothing out of the ordinary in the attic, but the Extreme Activity warning tells me otherwise. What could possibly be hiding in here...?

Storymancer: Do you see anything?

JellyBeanFish: No...

Storymancer: A riddle for another day.

Storymancer: Gonna pore though the footage again. You better get some rest.

JellyBeanFish: You should too

JellyBeanFish: I appreciate everything you're doing

JellyBeanFish: I'm worried what this might mean for my mom too

Storymancer: Don't worry about anything till we get more proof there, kay?

JellyBeanFish: yeah

JellyBeanFish: But don't push yourself either

JellyBeanFish: You still feeling sick?

Storymancer: Just a bit.

JellyBeanFish: HYDRATE.

Storymancer: Yeah yeah yeah

JellyBeanFish: I'm serious, go get some rest

Storymancer: Haha

Storymancer: I'll rest when I'm dead

Storymancer: But fine, I will

VIDEO #14

Wispy Falls Message Board

Cryptozoology/

Your one-stop source of information for anything monsters!

InnovativeObscurity says: Opinions of the Cryptid Museum from the Point of View of a Professor of Cryptid Sciences (3291 users liked this)

For starters, I teach cryptid biology at Archaeon University, and I thought it would be a good thing to stage a trip with some of my students to take a tour of the museum. Very few of them have actually seen any of the specimens up close, given the rarity of any being found, much less shown to the public. I decided to use the opportunity to help educate them further about the marvels of cryptids' unusual physiology so they can finally see for themselves what they look like beyond just the pictures in their textbooks or in released government files about the creatures.

And while I cannot deny that the museum provided a delightful experience for my students, I cannot help but see glaring oddities in some of the displays and exhibits there. For instance, the remains recently found in the woods appear to be missing the main torso and half of the arms, based on the muscular tissues I could see, but the display's description claims it is fully-formed and intact. The bloating might make it more difficult to determine, but I do not think scientists of Penumbra's caliber would make that mistake, much less put that mistake on display.

I think my main point of contention, however, was the covered statues that had been left in the exhibit for the bloodmoon. Everything in that room is wrapped in sheets—why would you open this to the public when it was made obvious none of these displays were ready for public viewing yet? I found it unreasonably odd that they were already stationed around the room, yet we were prevented from approaching any of them, much less seeing what is underneath the covers. Can you give us an explanation? The museum guide said they would be ready soon, but it's been nearly four days since our visit, and from what I have been told, nothing has changed.

Quite frankly, I was a little disappointed. We still know very little about the bloodmoon. I had been hoping the exhibit meant some of the researchers at the Facility had finally made a breakthrough, so it was crushing to see that we have been deprived of any new knowledge on that score. Why would they be covered? If there had been anything wrong with the specimens themselves, would they not have been kept away from the public instead of positioned there like they are about to be revealed? What are they? If they are to help us understand more of the bloodmoon origins, then why are we being denied the opportunity? Why tease us with covered statues when we are prevented from ever looking under them?

+ TurtleSoupChowder (1226 users liked this)

I do admit I also find it odd that they would choose to place statues and other artifacts on display but then choose to cover them up. Why even exhibit them in the first place if so?

> **+ InnovativeObscurity** (3291 users liked this)
>
> Exactly my point! I had been excited to learn there would be a room devoted to the bloodmoon, and so I was more than a little disheartened to see that we ended up having even more questions than answers upon leaving the museum than entering it.

+ LettuceIntotheDeep (899 users liked this)

That's weird. Maybe there were some problems with some of the displays, so they're not able to announce any set schedule for viewing them yet? I've worked in a few places where it's important for a collection to be seen in its entirety rather than in small portions. Otherwise, you lose the whole context of what the collection is.

> **+ InnovativeObscurity** (717 users liked this)
>
> Even so, why put them out on display if it wasn't ready to begin with? I admit that it's more the disappointment that's spurring me to make this post in the first place. But even so, they gave us no real timeframe as to when we can expect that particular collection to open.

+ LittleBeats36 (584 users liked this)

Considering it's a new museum and also the first one dealing with cryptids, I'd give them the benefit of the doubt. It's hard enough to put together a collection of something so rare, much less have enough for a whole museum. There are probably some things going on behind the scenes we don't know about that they might be having some problems with, so I'd say in a few months' time they'll have solved them and we'll finally have an exhibit celebrating the bloodmoon.

+ **ChemicalImbalance** (344 users liked this)

I'd be frustrated, too, if they put up all the signs saying the exhibit was open, only to find out that the exhibit wasn't even ready.

+ **BeefcakeMilkshake** (200 users liked this)

Hopefully in the coming days they will put something up to clarify what's happened. I've visited myself, but I actually stayed clear of the bloodmoon exhibit. I thought it was still under construction because of all those covered statues, lol. But I did like the skull collection on the second floor, and I do like how they give you unlimited free drinks at the cafe and a little keychain if it's your first visit.

+ **JellyBeanFish** (21 users liked this)

That's because my mom is the head curator of the museum and she's being stonewalled by the higher-ups into doing things that she doesn't really want to do! They wanted to put up news of the exhibition even though it isn't ready yet because they want more people coming so they can boast that it's a success! That's why they said the bloodmoon exhibit is ready when it's not, because they can at least count on more people coming in to see! They're utter crap for forcing my mom to take the heat for all of this and I don't think it's fair!

+ **ChemicalImbalancezone** (91 users liked this)

    Are you really her daughter or just a troll?

+ **ElvenHootie** (51 users liked this)

    I am not sure you should be badmouthing your mom's place
of work so publicly.

+ **CafeBooyah** (36 users liked this)

    lol

Storymancer: I saw your post, you okay?

JellyBeanFish: Yeah

JellyBeanFish: Maybe

JellyBeanFish: I had a fight with my mom

JellyBeanFish: She admitted that people went over her and
made that exhibit without her permission

JellyBeanFish: And she's letting them

JellyBeanFish: That guy who made that post is a well-known
professor

JellyBeanFish: He might sound polite, but this is actually the
academic equivalent of dunking on her.

JellyBeanFish: And she's just letting him!!

JellyBeanFish: They're whispering at work today

JellyBeanFish: Saying that she's a pushover

JellyBeanFish: It's not her fault!

JellyBeanFish: I don't understand why she's just taking it,
normally she'd push back

Storymancer: Heyyy deep breaths

JellyBeanFish: I don't like the idea that my mom is a part of this. They picked her because she's an up-and-coming professor and she's willing to do anything it takes to make her name in the field, and I don't like it.

JellyBeanFish: Yeah, I'm biased.

JellyBeanFish: She rarely comes home anymore and sleeps in the Facility most nights. And then they disrespect her like this even though she didn't give the order

JellyBeanFish: It feels like I lost my mom because of this.

JellyBeanFish: But thanks to you I do know there's something fishy going on in there, and I don't care what they say.

JellyBeanFish: The whole vibe in there is weird nowadays. Like people are constantly chirping about how great it is to work there, and it starting to feel like a cult, you know?

Storymancer: Like maybe they're taking Somnium?

JellyBeanFish: Heh

JellyBeanFish: And don't worry about me getting in trouble, lol.

Storymancer: That just makes me even more worried

JellyBeanFish: They didn't even ban me from the forums

JellyBeanFish: But I got something

JellyBeanFish: Somebody sent it to me after I posted, but he deleted his account after I downloaded it

Storymancer: What is it?

[Attached: The video that follows is of darkness. There is nothing that can be seen or heard, save for some heavy breathing noises that appear to belong to whoever it is holding the camera. After a while, those noises are replaced by some faint whimpering before, finally, a male voice begins to whisper.]

Male voice: It's coming. It's coming. It's coming. I can feel it inside of me, aching to get out. The moon is coming. Something breaks. Soon the eggshells of our memories will be cracked open, and we will see the child. We are mothers. We are all mothers. God help us. God help us. God is dead, and we are trapped in here with His killers.

Storymancer: What the hell is that

JellyBeanFish: I have no idea

Storymancer: The moon is coming? The eggshells of our memories? He sure is cracked, yeah.

JellyBeanFish: I tried to look at this video frame by frame, tried to see why it was so dark, nothing. It's a far too grainy video, so for the moment I can't do much but leave it like this.

JellyBeanFish: I tried to send out another email to the guy asking what it was and why he'd sent it to me, but he hasn't emailed back yet. I'm not sure if he will.

Storymancer: You know his username?

JellyBeanFish: QuietInCandlelight

JellyBeanFish: I don't think you'll get much out of it.

JellyBeanFish: It's a new account made within the last 24 hours. No information listed, no profile pictures or anything

Storymancer: A lot of people want to tell us things but don't wanna have anything traced back to them, huh

Storymancer: How sure are you that this isn't just some dingbat who wants to mess with your head

JellyBeanFish: There's more stuff he sent that makes me
believe him

Storymancer: What

JellyBeanFish: Let me post them

[Attached: a picture of a pristine-looking laboratory.]

JellyBeanFish: Look familiar to you?

Storymancer: Hey yeah! It's the same lab from Ivy Delgado's
video, down to the mug on the counter there!

JellyBeanFish: You remember that much detail?

Storymancer: I've been staring at it and other photos for hours
every day. At this point it kinda sears into your brain

[Attached: a photo of a mug in the background of Dr. Delgado's
footage that clearly says "World's Greatest Phrenologist" with a
human anatomical skull drawn behind it.]

Storymancer: Look at that chip on one edge of the rim. It's the
same chip in both, which means it has to be the same mug.
This is just telling me that your source is the real MVP, and
the evidence they're giving you is in the same laboratory
Dr. Delgado was at—which means it's the same laboratory
within the Facility.

Storymancer: I changed my mind. I don't think this person is
sending you stuff just to screw with us.

JellyBeanFish: I'll upload the rest of the photos he sent.

JellyBeanFish: Maybe you'll see more here than I have yet

JellyBeanFish: Word of warning though

JellyBeanFish: Some of these pictures are...awful. Like, NSFW kind of awful

Storymancer: If you're sending nude pics, I wanna let you know that's illegal since we're minors—

JellyBeanFish: Ha ha ha. I mean gory stuff.

Storymancer: Nah, I can handle it. You think I can't handle it?

JellyBeanFish: Just giving you a heads-up

JellyBeanFish: Here

JellyBeanFish: There's gonna be seven photos in total I'll be sharing today, and three of them taken in the same area. I'll save the most horrifying ones for last, just so you can adjust to some of these photos because...

Storymancer: That bad?

[Attached: Photo shown is what appears to be a seafood hatchery of some sort. It is a room with a large number of tanks filled with murky water. There are several pumps located in one area with heavy pipes connecting them to most of the tanks.]

Storymancer: That's in the Facility?

JellyBeanFish: It's somewhere I don't have access to, maybe

Storymancer: What are those tanks?

JellyBeanFish: I've seen some old photos in textbooks

JellyBeanFish: It looks similar to these except it's for something called fishing

JellyBeanFish: Except fish don't exist

Storymancer: How sure are you that this is really the Facility?

JellyBeanFish: Look at the layout. Then look at this.

[Attached: a screenshot of the security camera footage from Dr. Delgado's previous video—that of the large tissue-like egg surrounded by people in hazmat suits. The small room where Dr. Delgado and Dr. Threnody was waiting in is slowly superimposed on top of the hatchery photo, showing their dimensions and appearance are exactly the same.]

Storymancer: You're right. It's the same layout.

JellyBeanFish: Maybe the Facility should be a bit more creative when it comes to their typical room layouts, huh? Not gonna lie, I still don't know what these tanks are for.

JellyBeanFish: But I did some research about what hatcheries are, and what kinds of equipment they're supposed to have, and this looks very similar to them. The same kinds of tanks used for broodstock

Storymancer: What's that?

JellyBeanFish: Kinda like a process which encourages a better development of a fish's, uh, gonads. So they can make better breeds of fish, or something like that.

Storymancer: Hahaha, I'll bet

JellyBeanFish: I doubt very much that these tanks have any kind of fish inside

[Attached: Photo now shows a closer look at one of the tanks, and it is obviously not a fish. Instead, a rock large enough to fill up most of the tank's parameters is sitting at the bottom.]

Storymancer: What, they're breeding rocks?

JellyBeanFish: I have no idea what those are.

Storymancer: Are they rocks, or are they like, eggs?

Storymancer: Is this a freaking nursery of baby cryptids?

JellyBeanFish: We don't know where cryptids come from!

JellyBeanFish: Given their constitution though, that's not likely!

JellyBeanFish: Cryptids don't reproduce!

Storymancer: Well, I don't know what else those could be!

JellyBeanFish: Maybe some new kind of specimen they found and are incubating?

Storymancer: WHY THOUGH

Storymancer: Why would they make more cryptids

JellyBeanFish: These are guesses, calm down

JellyBeanFish: There's a chance these are doctored photos. Maybe they're real, maybe they're not. But we just need to be open to all possibilities

Storymancer: Including baby cryptids

JellyBeanFish: Look

[Attached: photo of a rock lying on a metal slab with what appears to be a heating lamp directly over it. The rock, however, is not a rock—it has been sliced open to reveal something very soft and rubbery within the craggy surface, not unlike a pink jackfruit. The insides also have a hollowed-out area, like something had been scooped out of it with a similar shape to that a very large avocado seed might leave behind.]

Storymancer: Ew

Storymancer: I don't want no living and breathing alien fruit

Storymancer: Please don't tell me they mix that in our food without our knowledge.

Storymancer: Blegh. And you're saying the last three are worse?

JellyBeanFish: See for yourself.

[Attached: three photos side by side of what could only be described as lumps of flesh. Some facial features can be seen, but it is an otherwise soupy caricature of what a human is without bones. It is similar to the early pictures of the body in the woods, but higher-quality images. Some people in hazmat suits are in the act of loading one of the lumps into a steel barrel.]

Storymancer: This was a bad day to have eyes

Storymancer: The heck were they used for.

JellyBeanFish: Failed experiments or something, maybe? Those steel barrels I recognize as what they use to dispose of any waste in the facility.

JellyBeanFish: Again, this is all just speculation on our end. We still don't know why the Facility has these, but I can make one more hypothesis. Do you think there are any points of similarities between these two?

[Attached: the image of the soft tissue-like egg found in Ivy Delgado's video footage, now side by side with the sliced open jackfruit-rock with its scooped-out center.]

JellyBeanFish: Maybe we're getting somewhere.

VIDEO #15

WFTV NEWS recording

[There is a television in the room. It has always been there. It is tuned to the news channel. No one has turned it on. No one in Wispy Falls ever turns their television on, but it does not matter. The WFTV logo flits across the screen, far too quickly to be more than just a blur, and a gravelly voice begins to speak.]

You are watching WFTV, your number one source for all Wispy Falls news. You are watching WFTV, your only source for all Wispy Falls news.

[The logo flickers for an eighth of a second and disappears to give way to a news anchor, who shuffles papers on her desk and smiles.]

TV anchorperson, Trinity Vanderlust: Good evening! I am Trinity Vanderlust and here are tonight's top stories. A group of teenagers was arrested early Saturday morning by authorities for sneaking into the Museum of Unnatural Curiosities and for willfully causing property damage, according to museum representative Millie Angeles. The three boys and one girl, all seventeen years of age, have been taken into juvenile detention at the Mariscof Penitentiary and will be facing charges as adults, based on the pretrial detention motion.

Two of the four teenagers have already been arrested on previous charges of vandalism and theft and were sentenced to both probation and community service two years ago when they were fifteen years old, according to the attorney general's office. If found guilty, both could face up to three years in jail if they are tried as adults, as opposed to up to six months' jail time and $1000 in fines if they are sentenced as minors. The other two teenagers have no previous records and have since been allowed to post bail while the others remain in custody.

[The video moves to a tired-looking man with glasses and a suit. The chyron underneath him reads: Liem Nguyen, State Attorney.]

Nguyen: Vandalizing extremely rare collections of bones and remains excavated and studied by scientists to help us better understand how to protect ourselves from these cryptids is a felony charge. Our law enforcement is dedicated to maintaining community safety and laying down the appropriate punishment for those who choose to undermine that safety. We will continue to work with law enforcement to protect Wispy Falls from all such perpetrators and hold them accountable.

[Trinity Vanderlust returns onscreen, looking up from the papers on her desk.]

Vanderlust: At this time, there is no word on what kind of damage the museum has sustained, nor what collections have been compromised. In other news, yet another person has been reported missing in the woods, and people are laying the blame once more on the Backward Lady. Thirty-four-year-old Lucas Eiggermann, a carpenter and plumber by trade, was reported missing by his wife two days ago, and his company truck was found parked on the path leading toward the woods. Search teams with K-9 units have been dispatched, but there are currently no reports of any sightings of either Eiggermann or the Backward Lady.

[The screen switches to the forest, where several men in uniforms are combing meticulously through the area in pairs with dogs sniffing at the ground. A police officer is talking to the camera, and the chyron names her as Sheriff Emily Waters.]

Sheriff Waters: We have search teams going round the clock looking for any signs of Eiggermann, and we're confident if there's anyone to find, that we will find him within the next forty-eight hours. We're not quite sure why Eiggermann decided to go into the forest at this time, as his wife states he was well aware of the dangers and had taken care to avoid the woods previously, but unfortunately, we cannot make any further comments on that matter, only that we are trying our best to bring him home as soon as possible.

[A strange howl seems to emanate from the forest at that point. The other search teams glance around warily and, at a signal from the sheriff, begin to slowly retreat.]

Sheriff Waters: That said, I also have the responsibility not to put my people into any more danger than they already are, but rest assured we will continue the search as soon as we are able to. We are aware of the most recent reports of the sightings of the Backward Lady along this area. We are blocking off this area to ensure that no one else enters the woods. We'll be monitoring the situation carefully and we will do everything within our power to ensure that Lucas comes home to his family.

[Another loud noise from the woods. This time the search teams begin to back away far more quickly, the sheriff gesturing at the camera to retreat as well. An unexpected shout echoes through the air, and some of the people in the search party begin to scream. The sheriff reaches a hand out furiously toward the camera.]

Sheriff Waters: Back off, I said! Back off, back off—!

[The feed goes blank and is replaced by Trinity's smiling face.]

Trinity Vanderlust: If you have any information regarding the whereabouts of Lucas Eiggermann, please contact the number on the screen below. A reward of $20,000 has been offered in exchange for any information that can lead to his discovery.

In other news, a six-car pileup has occurred at the intersection of Drought and Miles, and motorists are advised to take alternate routes. There has been one reported death from the collision, a thirty-seven-year-old man named William Horace. Five of the other eight drivers have been rushed to the hospital and are now currently in stable condition. Police are still investigating.

That is all the news that we have for this hour. This is Trinity Vanderlust for WFTV news.

WISPY FALLS MESSAGE BOARD

Opinions/

Good or bad, post them here so we can open up a discussion and understand each other better!

CrimsonHunt says: I am a good friend of Lucas Eiggermann. I need everyone to know that this is not an accident. (13791 users liked this)

The last thing he would ever do is go into the woods, especially alone. He and I joined law enforcement early in our careers before opting for an early retirement. He was my partner through the years (met at the academy and went through training together), and we've hunted cryptids in an official capacity during our time. He's like a brother to me, and my best friend. He's in good health and is mentally sound, and he was perfectly fine when I spoke to him the morning before he went missing. I lost my daughter to the forest years ago, but even I can't begin to understand how his wife feels right now.

I know there are some people out there saying he was another one of those reckless and irresponsible streamers trying to claim their fifteen minutes of fame, but he is nothing like that. He's a family man, and we're both too old to be chasing clout the way the younglings seem to do. I'm the one who put up the cash reward for any information about him, and I'm extending it to everyone again right now. Please help me find Luke.

[Comments have been disabled for this post]

WISPY FORUMS MESSAGE INBOX

From: Storymancer

To: CrimsonHunt

Date: 12- 15- 208 1:41:40 a.m.

Subject: My Condolences

First of all, I would like to offer my support for you, knowing what you went through. My brother went missing when I was around twelve years old, so I understand.

I am actually one of the people you mentioned who are currently trying to investigate the mystery, and it all started with the body everyone thought was Morrissey. I know you have a lot of messages in your inbox right now, but if there's any information you can provide about the events leading up to his disappearance, then I would be grateful for any help you can give. Otherwise, thank you for taking the time to read this!

From: CrimsonHunt

To: Storymancer

Date: 12- 15- 208 3:24:13 a.m.

Subject: Re: My Condolences

Ah, hell. You seem like one of the more articulate kids, so why not? I'm out of ideas and maybe there's something you've got that I don't know about. What is it you want to know?

From: Storymancer

To: CrimsonHunt

Date: 12- 15- 208 4:05:22 a.m.

Subject: Re: Re: My Condolences

Thank you again, I really appreciate it!

1. Was there anything odd you noticed about your friend during that time? And by that I mean, did he see or hear anything unusual in the days before he disappeared?

2. Did he tell you what he intended to do at that time?

3. Has he ever seen the Backward Lady before, or any other cryptid?

4. You mentioned that you both hunted cryptids. Were there any dangerous encounters with them that were notable or had affected him in some way?

5. Was he suffering from any illnesses?

From: CrimsonHunt

To: Storymancer

Date: 12- 15- 208 5:00:15 a.m.

Subject: Re: Re: Re: My Condolences

1. Not sure if you'd consider this unusual, but he did tell me earlier this week that he made a new friend. His dog passed away some years ago, and he hadn't really had the heart to get another one. But he said he found a cute thing on the side of the road, and it followed him home. Said it was some guinea pig that seemed to have escaped from its owner but was

domesticated enough that it was real friendly to people, even strangers. He was planning to put up some flyers to let people in the neighborhood know their pet might have escaped and he was taking care of it till they could come get it. If no one did, he said he was thinking of adopting it. That was maybe three days before he disappeared. Went to his place, but I can't find the critter.

2. He said he felt like going for a short drive. It was his day off, but his wife was at work, and he'd already been puttering around the house. Managed to fix the leaky bathroom sink he'd been wanting to get at for a while. And when he says, "short drive," he usually means to head out to the plaza and have a drink at Smokey's, which is his favorite bar, and watch the football game with some of the fellas there. He invited me along, but I had a cold then and didn't want to leave the house. Looking back, I wish I had. Then maybe I would have known what was going on.

3. That was one of the reasons why he decided to stay away from the woods. His dog Truffles wandered off. For some reason a lot of dogs really prefer that part of the woods. I've seen the news and heard anecdotes from people whose only reason for being out there is because their pets got loose and hid in the forest. He went out looking for him and as soon as he spotted Truffles, he also spotted the lady standing about a hundred yards away with her back toward him. He knew what she was almost immediately, just picked up his dog and ran. He wasn't even sure if she'd seen him yet. Made sure Truffles was leashed up every time and never went back there again.

4. Kid, every encounter with a cryptid is automatically dangerous. But I do remember there was this one time when we were tracking down one cryptid—the commander didn't even know what it was, only that they'd detected something in the area and we all had to be careful. We were given the usual training protocol—surround it, never stray from the pack, shoot once you're sure you have a good line of sight, and they'll figure out how to bring in the body later. Even then we barely managed to catch it in a parking lot and it nearly killed one of my coworkers. That was maybe twenty years, twenty-one years ago.

5. Matter of fact, yeah. He got Parkinson's, but he's in the early stages still. He'd already gone to the Facility for treatment, but he wasn't shaking too badly yet. You would have never even noticed.

From: Storymancer

To: CrimsonHunt

Date: 12- 15- 208 5:12:34 a.m.

Subject: Re: Re: Re: Re: My Condolences

About this pet that you said he found. Is it really a guinea pig? Did he show you a picture, or at least describe it to you?

From: CrimsonHunt

To: Storymancer

Date: 12- 15- 208 5:22:14 a.m.

Subject: Re: Re: Re: Re: Re: My Condolences

No pictures. He only takes photos of strays if he decides
he wants to get attached to them. Truffles was a stray too, I
remember. He did say he's not really experienced when it comes
to guinea pigs, and he was planning on buying a book to figure
out how to care for one if nobody came to claim it. He thought
it must be some kind of exotic guinea pig, though. It's got really
round ears and real big eyes. It didn't sound like any guinea pig
I've ever heard of before, but I'm not an expert on those either.

From: Storymancer
To: CrimsonHunt
Date: 12- 15- 208 5:37:04 a.m.
Subject: Re: Re: Re: Re: Re: Re: My Condolences

Thank you so much. And I'm about to ask you for another
favor, and I swear this has everything to do with your missing
friend...

Storymancer: What the hell are you doing
JellyBeanFish: What
Storymancer: Okay, look.
Storymancer: I understand.
Storymancer: I knew it couldn't have just been a coincidence,
okay?
Storymancer: I know people break into a lot of things for
shits and giggles. They'll steal from convenience stores,
groceries, anywhere where there's money to be stolen, or
for fun.

Storymancer: But a museum? Really?

Storymancer: And your mom's museum?

Storymancer: What are you gonna do with the old bones there? Sell them to some rich collector? Because there's no way you'll be able to fence it outside of the city, given everything.

Storymancer: Plus, I imagine it's a lot harder to hide bones.

Storymancer: What were you trying to do with bones??

Storymancer: My rash is getting worse, and you getting in trouble is not helping.

JellyBeanFish: Okay

JellyBeanFish: It was stupid in hindsight

JellyBeanFish: But

JellyBeanFish: I wanted to prove a point

Storymancer: And what point was this????

JellyBeanFish: How did you even know, anyway?

Storymancer: A hunch

Storymancer: Nobody breaks into a cryptid museum to steal money

Storymancer: So I knew it had something to do with the bloodmoon instead.

Storymancer: Or someone who has a grudge against cryptids, idk

Storymancer: So it was either you or CrimsonHunt, and I'm pretty sure he's not a seventeen-year-old.

JellyBeanFish: Who?

Storymancer: Remember CrimsonHunt?

Storymancer: The dude who's part of the rescue team

working with the families of those missing people. From the Woodseekers nonprofit.

Storymancer: He wound up reaching out to some buddy of his still working at the station, and then asked for information about the names of the perpetrators and if they'd found any motivation for them to even be breaking into the museum in the first place.

Storymancer: And I know it's probably not legal for them to give the names away especially since you were minors, but I guess he had enough pull with the people there, and he immediately sent the details to me.

Storymancer: Trevor Sherridan, Miles Harris, Justin Ko, and Margaret Withers.

Storymancer: The girl's you, isn't it

Storymancer: As soon as I saw your name

Storymancer: What were you thinking

Storymancer: I took a quick look at the news section of the message board, and the comments section looks like a massacre.

Storymancer: So many of them have been deleted, but I saw one or two replies claiming that the removed comments were trying to find out the identities of the teenagers.

Storymancer: What were you thinking??

JellyBeanFish: LET ME EXPLAIN

JellyBeanFish: Okay

JellyBeanFish: So

JellyBeanFish: Yeah, that was me and some of my friends.

JellyBeanFish: I'm grounded right now

JellyBeanFish: But I have a second phone my mom doesn't know about for when she takes away my main one. It's prepaid, so I don't have to worry about them tracing anything back to me.

JellyBeanFish: I don't care, I need to tell someone, I'm still shaking and trying not to cry.

Storymancer: Are you all right?

JellyBeanFish: Not really. We found something there. I don't know if I want to talk about it yet.

Storymancer: Fair. Why did you even break in tho?

JellyBeanFish: Those friends of mine—they lost family and other loved ones to the woods, okay? We were mad. They never really took the time to search for any of the bodies. It's the same as the last one that went missing, that Lucas someone. They'll search for a couple of days and then call it off.

Storymancer: There were some noises coming from the woods and they called it off.

JellyBeanFish: One of my friends said it's all a ruse. That's the same thing they did when they were searching for his brother. Some weird howling comes out of nowhere and then they get scared and pack it up. A lot of people were talking about it. He joined a support group.

Storymancer: For the missing people?

JellyBeanFish: Yeah. People in there said there is always some noise that makes them stop the search. It wasn't just one family this happened to, it was like more than half of the people on there. That's why they think it was staged. Like they made those noises deliberately and pretended they were coming from the woods. Just so they could say they did their best and then stop searching.

Storymancer: But why?

JellyBeanFish: They want efficiency. My mom keeps talking about it all the time like it's a mantra. Efficiency this, efficiency that, blah blah. The Facility doesn't like their staff wasting time. They know they'd be wasting time putting in all the effort for that search. So they found a way to shut it down so they don't have to exert so much manpower finding bodies they know will never be found. They never try to go deep enough into the forest, the areas where they usually see the Backward Lady.

JellyBeanFish: They don't even do anything to help the families out. Trevor lost his dad, and their mother's been struggling. They don't offer any support to the bereaved families, they don't even offer any payments to help.

Storymancer: What proof do you have of this?

JellyBeanFish: I don't. That's why we tried to break in. We knew there was something there, just because they were putting so much effort into making that museum in the first place. They don't do things just to show off. Mom said as much. There's always a reason Penumbra does things, and it's not to sway public opinion. There had to be a reason they put that museum up.

JellyBeanFish: I told them there's something iffy going on in the museum, and they all started talking about breaking in and finding some secret there and telling the whole world about it and

JellyBeanFish: I dunno

JellyBeanFish: I just wound up agreeing with them

Storymancer: You think maybe you're just angry because of what happened in the forums the other day?

JellyBeanFish: Yeah. Maybe we're coming from a place of resentment. Or maybe I am. I don't know. They wanted to get in and see what they really do behind the scenes. There was that big thing about people complaining about the bloodmoon exhibit. They wanted to find out what was really underneath all those covers, and we know now.

Storymancer: What did you find in there? Was there anything?

[JellyBeanFish adds a video attachment.]

[At first there is nothing to be seen in the video, just two or three flashlights moving about in the gloom before one finally settles on a small skeleton of an elk-like creature, signaling that the group was already inside the museum when the filming started.]

Male voice 1: Pipe down. Do you want us to get caught already?

Male voice 2: Can't help it, dude. It's creepy in here. Do you even see this?

[One of the beams of light moves toward the museum's exhibit of the Quiet Brother, with its large skeleton and limbs hanging above them.]

Male voice 2: They say this one's extinct now. Is it really?

Male voice 3: Do we look like scientists? How the hell should I know?

Male voice 4: It's not extinct yet. Just rare.

Female voice: Ssh! Shut up! We're almost there!

[Another flashlight aims in the direction of one room, and soon all the others shine their lights there as well. The camera approaches; one of the boys walks up ahead. He is wearing a brown shirt and a cap that says "Cryptids fear me, women want me" when he turns to look at the camera. He has brown hair and blue eyes with pale skin.]

Boy with the Cryptid Cap: This is the room, right?

Female voice: Yeah.

Male voice 2: You have any idea why they were covering those statues up? I heard some people were arguing over it on the boards.

Cryptid Cap: Why would they start exhibiting them if they're not even ready, is all I'm saying. It sounds like they're trying to hide something.

Male voice 3: Then why don't they just put them in storage or something? Why put them out there?

Male voice 4: Maybe they don't actually know anything about the blood-moon, but they're just pretending they have something so that people will come here.

Cryptid Cap: Man, this is creepy.

[They have all entered the next room, which contains the blood-moon exhibit. Cryptid Cap makes for one of the covered statues, and the rest follow behind him. He takes hold of the cover and hesitates.]

Male voice 3: What are you waiting for? Do it.

Cryptid Cap: I don't know about this, bro...

Male voice 3: Do it, Trev!

[Cryptid Cap yanks off the cover, and the camera immediately zooms toward the statue—which turns out to be an anatomy statue, common enough in most high school science classrooms. Someone makes a disappointed sound.]

Male voice 4: Really? All that buildup, just for that?

Cryptid Cap: I really thought we were onto something.

[Another of the boys moves into view. He has curly black hair with brown skin and black eyes. He is wearing a dark blue shirt. He waves his hand to the side, toward the statue, with a flourish.]

Blue Shirt: The bloodmoon god, ladies and gentlemen.

[Cryptid Cap scoffs. The other male voice laughs nervously.]

Female voice: I want to look at the rest and see if they're all like this.

[The boys immediately throw the cover back onto the anatomy statue, and then move toward the next statue. They yank the sheet off it as well, only to reveal the same. The female voice makes a disbelieving sound, and then the camera pans to another statue. Soon they have wordlessly uncovered everything else in the room, but they are all the same.]

Blue Shirt: Ah, shit. All this trouble and we got rolled by a bunch of scientists.

Female voice: But I don't get it. They insisted that nothing here should be removed because they were fragile. Mom was convinced of it too. So why…?

Cryptid Cap: Because they were lying. They were gonna be humiliated when people learned the truth, so of course they had to pretend there were some expensive cryptids in here.

[The third boy walks over to help the other two put the sheet back on the last statue. He has dark blonde hair and brown eyes and is wearing a black shirt.]

Black Shirt: Yeah, this was a bust. You wanna go look at some of the other rooms too?

Female voice: I'm not leaving.

Blue Shirt: Maisie—

Female voice: This isn't it. There's something I'm still missing.

Blue Shirt: Maisie, we took a chance and there was nothing in here after all. I mean, we can look in the other areas if you want to see if there's something else—

JellyBeanFish: Mom wouldn't have been so stressed out over this exhibition if they were just planning to turn this into some high school science class. There has to be something else, and I'm not leaving until I find out what it is. Wait. Shit, Trevor—how many statues did you uncover?

Blue Shirt: Uh. I don't know. I think six.

Cryptid Cap: Pretty sure it was six.

Male voice 4: There are seven in this room.

[The camera moves and focuses on one statue that is standing away from where the others are clustered and looks out of place with no spotlight over it. The camera slowly starts moving toward it.]

Blue Shirt: Maisie, wait—

[Maisie reaches out with one hand and yanks off the cover from this statue. It falls away, and there is yet another science anatomy figure looking back at her.]

Cryptid Cap: ...Ok, that kinda scared me for a moment there, not gonna lie.

[The camera moves to the side, and a flashlight shines at the wall behind the statue.]

JellyBeanFish: Hey, I think there's something here. Shine on this spot.

[More flashlights are trained on the wall, where there is a small door blocked by the statue.]

Cryptid Cap: Doesn't say if it's authorized personnel or anything. It looks like a storage closet.

Voice 4: There's something behind it.

Blue Shirt: I don't see anything.

Black Shirt: Hey yo, where is Finn?

Cryptid Cap: Huh? He was just here, right? He said there were seven statues—

Black Shirt: He's not in the room.

[The camera spins to reveal the worried faces of Cryptid Cap, Blue Shirt, and Black Shirt. There is no one else standing with them. The camera moves and three beams of flashlights follow, splaying across the room. There is nobody in the room with them.]

Cryptid Cap: We just heard him like a minute ago!

Voice 4: Guys, I'm still here.

Blue Shirt: Finn, we can hear you, but we literally can't see you, and your flashlight's off.

Voice 4: What are you talking about? I'm standing right here and I can see you all just fine.

[The voice sounds surprisingly close. The boys shine their flashlights again but see no one else.]

Black Shirt: Bro, are you actually stuck somewhere? Don't be playing with us now, man, this is not the best time for—

Voice 4: Guys, I'm still here.

[The camera moves toward the three boys, who are now all frozen with terrified expressions on their faces. Maisie hesitates, and then slowly turns to film behind her.]

[The anatomy statue remains where it is, staring at them. Its mouth slowly and visibly moves.]

Statue: Guys, I'm still here.

[The camera immediately jerks away as Maisie and the other boys begin to run out of the room. It catches the three ahead of her, one of them accidentally tripping over something that abruptly causes loud warning bells to ring across the area, but they do not stop running until they've found the main doors and burst through them. Only a yard or so away from the entrance, Maisie pauses. The camera swings back around behind her into the darkness. The warning alerts continue to blare out, but she doesn't move, instead keeping her camera trained toward the gloom, as if expecting something to emerge from the shadows and head out after her. There are sounds of sirens as law enforcement begins to draw nearer.]

Cryptid Cap: Shit shit shit, where's Finn? Did something get him?

Black Shirt: He was talking to us this whole time! Shit, we should go back in after him. Maybe he's stuck inside—

Blue Shirt: We can't, bro! And let that statue thing come after us too?

[Maisie remains still and keeps the camera facing the direction of the exhibit, though the faint vibrations show that she is shaking.]

Blue Shirt: Maisie, we gotta get out of here. I'm sure they'll find him, I know they will!

[Maisie and the camera are propelled backward, as if one of the boys had grabbed her shoulder and was yanking her out the doors. The video ends.]

Storymancer: Holy shit.
JellyBeanFish: Did you see it?
Storymancer: See what?

[Attached: a blown up shot of one of the final frames of the video. From somewhere within the gloom, there is a smiling face. It looks like a teenager with black hair dyed with shades of red and pink, and blue eyes.]

Storymancer: Shit. Is that your friend.
JellyBeanFish: I didn't see him when I took the video, only when I was looking at it afterward.
JellyBeanFish: We still can't find him. I know he went in with us at the start of the night, but I keep reviewing the video. I never took a shot of him on camera the whole time. We could hear his voice, but that's it. The authorities aren't

telling us anything, but I know the reason they're keeping this quiet is because they haven't found him yet either. I feel responsible.

Storymancer: It's not like you forced him to join you. He lost someone to the forest too, right?

JellyBeanFish: Yeah, he did. That was how we all bonded in the first place.

Storymancer: It's not your fault. And if he's somewhere inside that museum, I know they'll find him.

JellyBeanFish: Yeah, but I don't think they will. They're going to cover it up like they did in the past with all those other missing people. I need to do something.

Storymancer: You're already literally out on bail. If you do anything else, they're going to put you back in prison.

JellyBeanFish: I don't care. I already did it.

Storymancer: What did you do?

JellyBeanFish: I took the video and uploaded it on social media. I told people he went missing at the museum. They can try to delete comments, but that doesn't stop people from talking about it. Now see if they can sweep that under the rug.

VIDEO #16

WFTV NEWS recording

[A video begins of a news broadcast by Trinity Vanderlust.]

TV anchorperson, Trinity Vanderlust: We interrupt this program to bring you a special report. The museum and its surrounding areas are under lockdown due to an ongoing situation involving law enforcement. Residents are advised to remain at home until further notice. Work has been suspended for the day excepting those with Class 3 job titles. There will be authorities patrolling your neighborhood to ensure this temporary curfew is enforced. No information has been provided by the sheriff's department, only that everyone is to remain at home and wait until the curfew has been lifted. If you are in an emergency or in need of help, please dial the numbers provided below and a representative will be with you shortly with more instructions.

It is important to once again remember the safety protocols that you will need in the event you find a cryptid or any other dangerous entity in your house or within your community. Remember the following key points:

Do not engage with any strangers you may encounter inside your house. Maintain your distance and alert law enforcement as soon as possible. Do not look at the stranger. Do not talk to the stranger or react to it in any way. Should the stranger refuse to leave your residence, please barricade yourself in the nearest secure area with access to a phone or other communication device.

Please arm yourself with any weapon within reach. If you are in danger, defend your life with whatever tools and means are accessible to you. If all else fails and you are under attack, consider that your sacrifice is necessary to maintain the protection and safety of all that you hold dear, as well as the rest of the town. On behalf of Wispy Falls, we salute you for your strength and courage in the face of extreme duress.

We will now return to our regularly scheduled programming.

WISPY FALLS MESSAGE BOARD

the Sprawl

[The video plays a quick scroll down of the Wispy Falls message board, where the majority of the hot topics on its front page are forum posts surrounding the lockdown, ranging from serious discussions and ramifications of the situation to memes and shitposts speculating on what might be happening.]

Storymancer: I am going to single out one of those posts in particular, since they're very relevant to my investigations.

[The video stops scrolling through the forums, instead focusing on one whose post topic reads, "Is no one really talking about the video?" Clicking on that link leads to another link that opens into the footage JellyBeanFish filmed inside the museum and uploaded.]

Is no one really talking about the video?

[He stops to cough, and then continues.]

I know a lot of people are saying it's faked or staged by the people who broke into the museum, but there is something about the genuine fright in their voices I have trouble shaking off. I don't think they're acting. And if they're not, then don't you think that the teenagers still locked up with the authorities might be in danger? [cough] And I don't mean from the cryptids. If they're responsible for activating whatever it is inside the museum, and the people in charge don't want news of it getting out until whatever it is has been contained or resolved... You get what I'm saying, right?

One hour after this message was posted on the forums, it was deleted. There was little reason given, save a quick announcement by the moderator mentioning that the user was banned from the forum due to misbehavior, though as other posts and comments began pointing out, there was nothing in the post itself that was considered bannable.

I am not sure what the forum administrators are trying to do, only that in their attempt to stifle the criticisms and the protests in the forums, it's only serving to fan the flames. Already I've seen several posts that were made calling for the arrested teenagers to be released from jail.

[There are quick flashes of screenshots of posts and comments that appear to be calling for the teenagers to be freed from jail, ranging from disapproving to outraged. After that, there are more screenshots showing the majority of these posts had also been removed by the moderators of the Wispy Falls forums, replaced by the same announcement explaining their removal as they had with the first post in the video.]

As far as I can figure out, JellyBeanFish is still free, though I'm not entirely sure if this is because of her mother's influence or because they hired a good lawyer and the authorities had little reason to re-arrest her again.

Let's now take a look at *Good Morn*. I've showcased some clips and sound bites from him on my channel before, and he does pick his battles, sometimes remaining neutral and sometimes criticizing government officials with apparently little pushback. Here's what he has to say on the matter.

[The video cuts to Morn's voice, with his words being scrolled through in the foreground.]

Morn: I really don't understand anything about this mess. Why would a bunch of kids choose a museum of all places to cause havoc? There is nothing in there they can steal, and if the video making its rounds on social media can be verified, they were mainly interested in the covered statues in the bloodmoon exhibit. I can understand they were arrested for trespassing, but to have other charges levied against them that are far more serious than just breaking and entering seems very unfair,

253

and I think that's what the public clamor is all about. I mean—felony, really? Who did they assault in there, the anatomy mannequin? If the footage they posted was any indication, then it was the mannequin who attacked them instead of the other way around.

Furthermore, any normal person, upon seeing that video, would think, "Gee, there must be some real live cryptid in that exhibit and maybe there were some defenses they tripped that caused them to react and attack, which means I shouldn't be going to the museum at all, since it's rather dangerous." But no. Now people who previously hadn't even been interested in the museum at all are flocking toward it. Have you seen the crowd around the crime scene tape the authorities have put in place? They now want to visit the museum and see the potential monsters within for themselves. It doesn't matter that law enforcement has since considered it a crime scene, and it doesn't matter that some kids were attacked there, and that one of them is still missing inside. I've seen parents literally bringing their little babies to come and gawk at the place. Talk about having no sense of self-preservation at all.

Honestly, if there's someone to blame, it should be the people in charge of the museum. If the video is real—and I still say this with a healthy dose of skepticism—then it still doesn't matter, because this resulted in the disappearance of a kid who otherwise shouldn't be missing, which means there is some kind of dangerous hazard in the museum that no one has caught. If that kid were still in there, he would have been rescued by now. All the thousand and one security cameras trained in that area would have detected the kids going in, but no one did anything about it until they came out screaming. And not one of these showed that missing kid ever coming out. Given people's worry over cryptids, of course they're going to jump to the conclusion there's some creature lying in wait there. All kinds of conspiracy theories have been cropping up, many musing that maybe the museum was built to feed people to the cryptids or something. Which makes all those people lining up outside the museum doubly foolish.

That kid is still somewhere inside that museum. The problem is, it's been days by now. The museum isn't all that big. It should have been easy enough to search the place and determine if the kid is there or if he isn't. But there are still authorities swarming in and out of the place like there's some active killer on the premises. That means they found something in there with regard to the kid that no one wants to see. And sadly, I'm guessing it could very well be the kid's body. And while they may not care about revealing that to the public, my suspicious mind can't help but wonder—maybe they're not letting people in because they don't want anyone to know how the boy was killed.

JellyBeanFish: I'm not getting charged lol. I've been talking with Finn's family and they don't blame me, but I feel really guilty.

Storymancer: It's not your fault. No one knew that those statues were actually alive.

JellyBeanFish: That's the thing. I suspected there could be cryptids they've been hiding literally inside the museum.

Storymancer: What do you mean?

JellyBeanFish: Even from the start, I knew they were hiding some monster in there. Do you know how many days it took them to build the museum?

Storymancer: The news said they've been working on it for some time.

JellyBeanFish: Not true. They had it done in two weeks.

Storymancer: Yeah, no. It's a big building, that's impossible.

JellyBeanFish: It's possible if it was already built around a facility underground.

Storymancer: What?

JellyBeanFish: The structure was already there. It was one of their major projects they've been working on for years. I only know about this because I know how to pick locks and my mother brings home a lot of work. I found the specs in her laptop last night.

JellyBeanFish: Don't yell at me for snooping. But I got pretty fed up.

JellyBeanFish: She finally got home early for the first time in so long and crashed in her room. It's not like I hacked into her laptop, it was already open, so.

Storymancer: I'm not yelling.

Storymancer: But I don't understand.

JellyBeanFish: They started building an underground facility where the museum is located about five years ago. You wouldn't have noticed, because the Facility also bought up all the stores on that block so no owners there would complain about the noise at night.

Storymancer: That's near one of my favorite ice cream shops. Are you saying they're selling ice cream now?

JellyBeanFish: Anything to pretend there are regular people working there. It's all a front.

Storymancer: Did you ever go with your mother to those places?

JellyBeanFish: Yes. They wanted me to be their teen representative—you know I like cryptozoology, top honors in class and everything, vice president of the student council and all that. And because my mom was already working with them, they figured they could start dribbling in a little of what they do to me and hoped they could make me one of their future employees and crap like that. It felt like a cult to me, but I knew this was the only way I was ever gonna learn their secrets, so I just nodded along and listened to everything they said and pretended to believe in it.

Storymancer: In what? Science?

JellyBeanFish: No, in the bloodmoon.

JellyBeanFish: I've found it out. The bloodmoon isn't a when. It's a what. It looks like an egg but not really.

JellyBeanFish: The Regret that tried to come after you at Ivy Delgado's apartment, I'm pretty sure now, came from one of their labs. They have maybe a dozen of them there, but they're well-regulated so they don't bulk up in size. And then there's this...thing. It's not a cryptid I know of, and not even Mom wants to tell me what kind of classification it is. All I know is that it looks human and it can walk like a human and it can look like you or me, but it definitely is not human. And then there's the egg.

Storymancer: Right! The one in Ivy Delgado's video? And the one in those tanks?

JellyBeanFish: Yeah. It's literally an egg. I don't know what's inside it though, and I don't know what monster comes out of it. But I know it's got something to do with the bloodmoon.

[Attached: a photo of a round egg-shaped object that looks like a small meteor with a pockmarked surface.]

JellyBeanFish: This is what was in Mom's files. She knew all along.

Storymancer: How sure are you about that?

JellyBeanFish: Look at it. And then look at the posters they always put up about the bloodmoon. Notice anything similar?

[Attached: two photos of the egg and the bloodmoon poster side by side.]

Storymancer: You're saying all those posters they have of the bloodmoon... It's not even a moon after all. It's an egg.

[Attached: a picture of a bloodmoon poster and a screencap of the egg recorded using Ivy Delgado's camera. There is no mistaking the similarities.]

JellyBeanFish: I need to go back to Penumbra.

JellyBeanFish: Mom's supposed to be back by now, but she isn't.

Storymancer: Is she all right?

JellyBeanFish: She was supposed to be working at the Facility tonight. She promised me she'd come home early. But it's been two hours since she was supposed to be home, and she's not here. I've been calling her on the phone and sending texts, but she's not picking up. She got a bit of flack for what I did, and we fought before she left. I know I needed to do that, but I still feel guilty.

Storymancer: You're not saying you're going in there, are you?

JellyBeanFish: I can't! I was only able to get in there before because of Mom's security clearance. I can't do that on my own. Plus, I know that they're watching me. I don't even know if my phone's being monitored at this point.

Storymancer: We're going to work on the assumption that it is, okay? But in the meantime, you need to relax. You don't want to get into any more trouble.

JellyBeanFish: I want to know where my mom is.

Storymancer: I know. But you have to be patient and wait it out first. She's only been gone a couple of hours, so maybe there was just something there she had to finish. Don't panic until you actually know what's going on, all right?

JellyBeanFish: Yeah. I guess.

JellyBeanFish: Thank you. I know a lot of the things I've been saying sound out there, but you believed in me right from the start when no one else did, and I really appreciate it.

Storymancer: I'm probably biased, you know, since I'm trying to investigate all this too! If they're hiding something this big from the public, then everyone has the right to know.

JellyBeanFish: Yeah, that's what I think too.

Storymancer: Stay home and don't worry too much, okay?

JellyBeanFish: Don't do anything rash either.

Storymancer: I've had a lowkey headache the last couple of days. I'll take it easy. You do the same.

JellyBeanFish: Easier said than done but yeah, I'll try.

[Notification: Storymancer has uploaded a new blog video entry.]

So call me a hypocrite. I want Bean to stay out of trouble, but I've got something planned myself. She claims there's a link between the Facility and the museum, so I plan to comb through every second of film I have about the museum so I can see for myself if there's something there. It's a long shot, but at this point, it's the only option I've got.

[The next video is an unpublished one Storymancer never released on his channel and is instead set to private. Based on the time stamp, it is also the second-to-last video he ever uploaded on the site.]

[The video starts with him using his camera to film some of the footage he is currently going through on his computer. You can see some parts of him visible there—the curve of an elbow and the blue t-shirt he is wearing, though his face remains offscreen. Every now and then he stops to let out a quick, hacking cough. His cough medicine is visible beside his keyboard.]

So uh, I've been going through a ton of this footage from the museum, trying to see if anything feels out of the ordinary. Or if anything feels out of place. Not like I'm an expert on stuff they put in museums, but I'm pretty sure I'll spot something weird since I've been reviewing all the other stuff like the Delgado footage so many times I could probably narrate that video word for word by now.

[He coughs and then clears his throat.]

Just give me something, anything else to go on—we need to…

[He trails off, and the next half an hour or so shows him meticulously going over the videos of other previous footage that had already been featured, sometimes stopping to go frame by frame as if there was something there, only to give a disappointed sigh when he turns up nothing. This goes on for some time, until he makes a startled sound. He immediately enlarges one scene from the video from the Colde Trial, where the camera is focused on an empty attic despite the UNUSUAL ACTIVITY warning on the second screen.]

[The zoomed-in shot seems to show a dark figure half-hidden in the shadows. It looks to be a boy in a red shirt staring at the camera. Due to the graininess of the video, the person is blurry, though there are a few defined features that are discernible still, like his spiky black hair and the pair of red eyeglasses he is wearing.]

[Storymancer enlarges the shot even further, to the maximum he could make it. Now it is clearer that the person staring right at the camera is no more than a young child of perhaps six or seven years old, and is smiling oddly.]

Lee…?

VIDEO #17

Storymancer's Video Blog Entry: Home

Storymancer: I need to know.

[For the first time, the interior of Storymancer's house is finally shown. It appears to be his living room, and he is training the camera on a series of photos that appear to be displayed on the walls of the room. At first glance, it looks like this was the home of a father, mother, and a young son. The camera focuses on an image of the family having their picture taken in a photo studio. Both parents are smiling brightly. The boy is attempting to do the same, but it is coming out looking more like a grimace.]

[The small icon on the lower right of the screen indicates it is a livestream, and that Storymancer is filming this in real time. There is a small chatbox on the right, transparent enough not to obscure the surroundings it is overlaid against, but with enough visibility to see the scrolling texts of viewers typing in their comments.]

I always found it odd that they refused to put any photos of him up in this room. They don't even have a picture of him in their bedroom, or anywhere else. Like he never existed.

[A hand moves into the screen, holding up a photograph. As it focuses, you can see it is a photo of four people—the parents from before and the young son, and another boy who is much younger, about six years old or so. He coughs, and then speaks again in a hoarser voice.]

This is my younger brother, Lee.

[The hand moves closer to the photo, and the camera settles on the two boys in it. Storymancer continues to speak, though his voice sounds raspy.]

This was the last picture that was ever taken of us together, literally hours before the incident happened. Four years ago, he went missing in the woods and was never found. I thought my parents would never get over it at first. They grieved for the first few days, until they just... stopped. Like one day they just woke up and decided they would forget all about him. They took down all the photos of him, cleaned out his room and just turned it into an office. I don't blame them for wanting to live their lives, but it was strange the way they just suddenly decided that Lee was no longer worth remembering.

They gave away or sold most of his things, but I managed to steal some of them when they weren't looking. Like a basketball jersey he really liked to wear, and this photo of us. For the longest time, I felt angry at my parents. I couldn't understand why they didn't push for a more thorough investigation or try to find out what really happened. They just accepted what the authorities said, and from then on, it was like they didn't remember him. I was resentful. Lee and I had been close. [cough]

It's the whole reason I started this channel. Yeah, sure, I marketed it as a channel where I [cough] try to explain some of the strange happenings around Wispy Falls, where I can give a more comprehensive understanding of all the cryptids that have haunted this town, and all the other cryptids that might still be haunting it. But it was all because I wanted to know [cough] about what happened to Lee, because no one else was telling me anything about it.

[The video switches to the still footage of the boy who looks eerily similar to Lee standing in the shadows while Bean and her friends were trying to escape the museum.]

["Oh nooo what is that?", "I stg I did not see that before.", "This a real ghost on camera??", "Buddy, that cough sounds rough. You ok?", "This is fake now you just trying too hard."]

This isn't a trick of the light. This is him. I know it. He still looks the same. Was he trapped there, or is this one of the cryptids who can copy the appearance of someone you love? But I wasn't even there that night! Why would he be showing up on someone else's video? Someone who didn't even know who he was?

I need to find something out. [loud, hard cough] Mom and Dad are at work, so this is a good time.

[The video moves and shows Storymancer heading up the stairs of their house, toward his parents' bedroom. He enters their bathroom and opens their medicine cupboard. He reaches into it and takes out one familiar bottle—a similar one to the one that was first seen in the Colde Trial family video. He sets the phone next to the sink in such a way that it still films what he's doing. He opens the bottle within clear view of the camera. He turns the bottle upside down, emptying about four purple-colored pills that roll across the counter.]

They've been taking this too. Somnium. I remember. They were given some meds a couple of days after Lee went missing. Mandated by the Facility. They started changing after they began taking it, but I never thought it might have been the cause of their indifference toward Lee being gone...

[He picks one up and holds it in between his thumb and index finger.]

["That's illegal to take!, "No, wasn't he prescribed those, too?",
"Ohhh we fr nowwwww", "Don't take it! You're gonna die!!!"]

They never spoke about him again after that. The footage on Ivy Delgado's USB. That Colde family on that trial video. The mother who was taking these same purple pills and woke up acting like there was nothing wrong. Was that the trial?

[He pauses to cough for several more seconds.]

Ugh. Medicine isn't working, so everyone please bear with me, haven't gotten the stronger prescription for it yet. That whole family was probably wiped out, and it was all just to test those damn meds?

[The video goes dark for a few seconds. When it returns, Storymancer has trained his phone on the computer screen, which features several email messages open from his inbox.]

I asked as many people as I could about this, and it was always the same answer. Everyone who has lost someone has taken these pills. Only CrimsonHunt refused to take the medication, which is why he's still trying to search for his daughter. But all the others reported their parents or siblings had been prescribed Somnium shortly after their family members or friends went missing, and the results were the same. Indifferent, just like my parents.

[He grabs the camera off his desk and leaves his room, all but running back downstairs to return to the living room. He focuses on the family photos on the wall again.]

What is in those pills? What's in it that would make someone forget all about someone they love? Why would the Facility approve of this, and what benefit is there for them? Is it because they don't want to search the woods, and if the victims' families aren't [cough] pushing hard to solve the case, then they won't have to? But why would they not want to? Is it because they're incompetent? Scared? Or...?

[Storymancer breaks off when unusual sounds are heard. It sounds like something is crying. Cautiously, he heads downstairs, toward the front door where the sound is coming from.]

...Or if they were somehow working together. Or that they are working for whatever creature that is...

["Trick or treat?", "I seen this movie. This isn't gonna end well.", "This is what you ain't supposed to do in horror flicks!", "Don't touch it!!", "Ohhhnooooo"]

[In an unexpected burst of rage, he flings the door open. There is no one there. The camera pans from one side to the next, but sees nothing but the lights from other nearby houses. Slowly, Storymancer closes the door again.]

[Something makes clicking noises from behind Storymancer.]

[Storymancer spins around. The camera sees no one there, but the noises continue.]

Storymancer: Who's there?

[There is a long pause. Something begins to cry like a baby, but the sound seems oddly stilted and slow, like the cries were deliberate. Storymancer begins to shake, the camera movements jerky. Slowly, the camera inches upward, toward the ceiling.]

[It is only a quick glimpse. There is something on the ceiling, gray and deformed. It has something that might be eyes, and something that was not a mouth.]

Storymancer: Oh my God.

[It makes a sound, like a baby's cry.]

[The camera tilts dizzily away as Storymancer trips and falls in his haste to flee.]

Storymancer: Oh shit, oh shit!

[He dashes into the closet and locks it behind him, then cowers on the floor, camera still on the door. There does not seem to be any sound, but Storymancer doesn't move and is quiet for several minutes before something else speaks up from the other side, sounding like a young kid.]

Voice: Hey, Brother. Whatcha doing? Where are you? I don't like being alone...

[Storymancer lets out a soft gasp when the voice begins speaking, but otherwise tries to stay silent. He is still coughing slightly but desperately trying to keep them as quiet as possible. The voice grows louder as it draws nearer.]

[*"This better be staged or Imma piss my pants!!!", "Storymancer going real hard this time", "Don't open the door!!", "Open the door!", "Nonononono"]*

Voice: Where is everyone? Mom? Dad? Anyone home? I want some cornflakes. Ugh, you're not supposed to leave a kid alone!

[There is the sound of cupboards opening. When the voice finally speaks again, it starts to sound disjointed and garbled. It sounds like it is trying to speak but places heavy emphases on the wrong syllables and vowels.]

Voice: Whatever. I'm going to go upstairs and have a nap.

[There are sounds of shuffling from outside, which eventually recede into the distance. After a few more minutes, Storymancer carefully inches the door open, revealing that no one is lying in wait for him. His camera catches just a glimpse of what may or may not be a thick tail disappearing around the corner as the creature climbs upstairs. It is a large tail, possibly the size and texture of a cobra if it were about thirty or forty feet long, before it flicks out of view.]

["Don't go near that", "Ohhhhh shiiiit getting down now", "Get out of the house!!!!", "Give it cornflakes bro!!"]

[Once he is assured he is in the clear, Storymancer immediately slips out of the closet and all but runs toward the front door, snatching up a pair of keys hanging on a wall hook on his way out. He opens the door without incident and dashes outside toward a car parked in the driveway, using one key to unlock it and get in. Once inside, he pauses for a moment and makes a whimpering, crying sound before trying to insert the key inside the ignition with one hand while still shakily holding up the phone toward the front of his house. He drops the key in his stress, and the video tilts toward the driving stick while the sound of him frantically rummaging around the floor trying to retrieve it is heard, along with the quiet sounds of him swearing. Finally, there is the sound of the ignition being turned on and the car coming to life.]

[When he lifts the phone back up again, his brother is on the hood of the car with his hands planted against the window, smiling down at him. Up close, his eyes are a bright yellow.]

The creature: Why are you leaving me alone in the house, Brother? What are you doing? Why?

[Storymancer screams and hits the pedal. The car lurches forward, and the thing-brother's face is slammed against the window from the momentum, his face twisting unnaturally against the pane.]

The creature: Why? Why?

[Storymancer slams on the brakes without warning, and the creature that looks like his brother is thrown off the hood to land on the ground in front of the car. Without pausing, he steps on the gas again, and there is a sickening, crunching sound as the car rolls over the thing on the ground, sickly-looking pale-red liquid splashing back onto the window before he puts the car back in reverse. The creature is no longer visible in the camera screen, but his voice continues calmly, as if he had not been hit at all. The chatbox is going wild.]

The creature: Why, Brother? Why? Why?

[Storymancer drives the car forward once more and several more sickening sounds indicate that he has again run over his brother. He keeps doing this, again and again and again, until finally his brother stops speaking. And then he puts the car in reverse one last time and begins to speed away from the house.]

[The video goes dark for exactly eight minutes and twenty-one seconds.]

[*"Is the stream over?", "Please don't be dead I love your videos don't be dead", "Dude dead now", "Did someone die???", "That wasn't real!!", "Shout something if you're alive"*]

[The video screen comes back on again, and this time it shows Storymancer's face for the first time since he started his series. He looks like the older version of the black-haired kid in the family photos in his living room.]

Storymancer: This ends now. I need to know, and I'm not coming back until I have my answers. It doesn't matter if my parents don't care anymore. It doesn't matter if no one else in town cares. I want to know, and I won't stop until I know.

[The camera pans away from him to reveal that he is standing at the edge of the forest. He begins to move and starts to enter the woods.]

Storymancer: Let's do this.

[*"Ohhhhh hell yea", "YOU ARE INSANE", "Rip", "If this is acting you getting all the acting awards bro"*]

[For fifteen minutes he says nothing, the silence interspersed with his coughing, and all the camera shows is the trail he is following as he moves deeper into the forest. There are the sounds of animals around him, like the calls of birds and the chittering of some unseen squirrel, but seventeen minutes and forty-six seconds after he steps into the woods, all of these fall silent until the only noises are the sounds of dry leaves crunching under his feet. Despite the absence of noise, he continues doggedly on, and his steps do not falter.]

Storymancer: Where are you? You've been blamed for everything. All the missing people in the woods. All the broken bodies people find later. All the bodies that have never been found. Including my brother's. Including those of Bean's friends, who were arrested just for wanting to find out the truth. Of countless others. I know you're somewhere here. I know you're watching me. You know the answers, right? I used to be afraid of you. When I was little, I thought you were coming to get me too, because you came after my brother and we did everything together. I was supposed to be protecting him…

But every time they start a search party to look for all the people who turn up missing, they always find some excuse to cut it short. I'm not buying it anymore. You know what I think? I think they don't want you to be found. I think there's something about you they don't want the rest of the town to know. And that's why I'm not afraid of you anymore. If any answers exist about what happened to my brother, then I know you have them. I'm not afraid of you. I'm not afraid.

[The camera pauses. Storymancer spins around in a circle so the camera catches everything surrounding him—the trees, the foliage, the small stones and bushes along the path. Nothing else moves.]

Storymancer: Show yourself! I'm tired of hiding! I'm tired of running away! If you're going to kill me, then do it now! At least I'll stop worrying about whether I—oh.

[The camera moves to focus on a figure just ahead. It is a woman in a long dress, though her face is obscured by the heavy locks of hair falling over it, hiding her features. She is not moving, but there is a faint impression that, despite not being able to see her eyes, she is looking right at him. She looks exactly like all the descriptions of the Backward Lady that we have heard.]

[The camera trembles lightly in Storymancer's grip, but he does not run. The chatbox has fallen silent.]

Storymancer: Show me. Tell me what this is all about. You know the answers. Everyone always tells stories about you. How you would run toward them, and they would barely escape with their lives. But do you run because you're trying to kill them? Why is the Facility so afraid of you?

[Shockingly, Storymancer begins to slowly walk toward the Backward Lady. The woman does not move, only waits for him to approach.]

Storymancer: What happened to my brother? What happened to all those other people? Were you responsible for their deaths? If you are, then why is the Facility doing their best to make sure they don't find you?

[The camera gets uncomfortably close to the Backward Lady, who says nothing. Storymancer's hand trembles even more violently.]

Storymancer: Who are you? What even are you?

[In the blink of an eye, the Backward Lady disappears. Storymancer makes a startled, terrified sound, and then whips around, trying to find where she has gone, but the camera sees nothing but trees.]

Storymancer: I'm not done with you yet! C-come out and answer me! I know you're still out there! You've never run away before!

[The camera abruptly shakes, just as Storymancer emits a loud gasp. Slowly, the screen shifts so this time it is Storymancer's face coming into view of the recording. He is now trembling uncontrollably, his expression terrified.]

[The Backward Lady is behind him, her head tilted so her upside-down face is free of the long hair that normally covers it. She is staring straight at the camera.]

[She looks like Ivy Delgado.]

Ivy Delgado: Run.

[Storymancer dashes away frantically, stopping when he is several yards farther to turn around. The Backward Lady has fallen to the ground on her knees and is panting audibly. One hand is also on the ground, but the other is raised and bent disjointedly, as if something invisible is raising up the hand. Something long and disgusting trails behind her—something several meters long, wet and bloody like a massive umbilical cord.]

Ivy Delgado, weeping: Run. Run.

[A quick movement catches the camera's attention. Storymancer jerks toward it, then hurriedly returns to the Backward Lady, remembering not to take his eyes off her, but it is too late; she is gone in that split second. He looks around and finds no trace of her.]

[There is a chittering sound.]

[The camera focuses on a small animal on the ground—perhaps it is a rat, or a guinea pig, or some other kind of rodent. It catches him looking and scampers away. He immediately follows it, ignoring that it appears to go off the paved paths and into a part of the forest that does not seem to be well-traveled by others.]

Storymancer: I don't care anymore. I have to know. I gotta know.

[For a good twenty minutes there is no other sound but the crunch of more leaves as he continues to follow the rodent. The chat has long fallen silent. There are no watchers right now, but he is oblivious to the fact.]

Storymancer: There!

[He sprints ahead. The creature disappears beneath a heavy underbrush. The camera whirls dizzily for a few minutes while he paws excitedly at the foliage, trying to get at what lies at the bottom.]

Storymancer: There's a—oh shit!

[The camera begins to spin wildly in all directions, its perspective tilting everywhere as Storymancer falls into the underbrush. There is the sound of something heavy hitting the ground, and the phone lands with the camera up, looking up at the sky and the canopy of trees barely visible around the edges. Storymancer has fallen into a hole that looks to be six or seven feet deep. Storymancer's voice groans from somewhere.]

Storymancer: Ow. Where did...?

[There is rustling as Storymancer gets to his feet. His face bends down toward the camera as he picks it up, checking it over hurriedly, then breathing a sigh of relief upon finding out that it is still working.]

Storymancer: Oh.

[He turns around. The flashlight catches a small opening to his right, wide enough for a person to pass through.]

Storymancer: Shit.

[He heads toward it anyway. He shifts slightly, and the flashlight shows nothing but darkness up the tunnel.]

Storymancer: You think this is the same path Ivy Delgado used to get out? Wait, no. There was a door when she made her exit. But where the hell does this lead to...? Ah, shit. That was Ivy Delgado. The Backward Lady. Shit. But the Backward Lady has been around since before Dr. Delgado went missing. It couldn't have been her before that, right?

[He enters even deeper into the passageway, but there are no obstacles waiting for him. His voice dips lower as if he is afraid someone might be listening. Someone might be.]

Storymancer: Is Ivy Delgado being used like some puppet? Literally? Isn't there a cryptid who's described like a marionette? Like someone else is manipulating it, but otherwise it seems to act and talk like a real human? What did they do to her? Maybe she tried to resist or something, so they just...put her in these woods? What if she wasn't the first one? What if they'd done this to so many other—

[His flashlight shines on a door up ahead. He approaches it cautiously and grabs at the handle. It opens easily enough at his touch, and the doors swing back.]

[The chatbox is filling up again with watchers.]

["Don't go in.", "There's something wrong with this.", "You're going to die.", "This isn't funny anymore."]

[There is a laboratory of some kind inside. It is a fairly large room filled with tables of strange fluids and equipment that would not be out of place in a chemistry lab. There are several tanks grouped close together in one corner.]

Storymancer: The tanks from the photos JellyBeanFish sent. Right. Let's try that first.

[He slowly approaches the tanks. They are about ten feet wide and four feet tall, made of some kind of steel alloy, and very thick. The top part of the closest one is open and is filled with black, bubbling fluid. Storymancer is careful not to touch anything but simply pans the camera above the tank. The liquid is far too thick to make note of anything beyond its surface.]

["You can't go in there!", "That's breaking and entering.", "There will be no escape.", "What are you doing?"]

Storymancer: What the hell is this? Maybe...

[He takes a few steps back and then turns toward the table. There are several stacks of papers there, and he flips a few pages to check. These seem to be made entirely of calculations and formulas and are incomprehensible for those not of the field. He tries to look through more papers in hopes of finding anything more within his realm of understanding.]

[He picks up one sheaf of paper. There is a drawing of a blood red moon against a sky. There is another blood red moon on the ground with arrows that seem to point to one another. There are more calculations and formulas scribbled around the margins. The camera zooms in closer to pick up every detail.]

["That's stealing government secrets.", "You're next.", "Soon they will come, and you will bear witness.", "The moon is coming."]

Storymancer: I think this is all I can get for now. There's another room over here...

[He moves to the room across from the one he entered. This one has a narrower metallic door, but it opens just as easily. He passes through, and then turns around to take a last look back at the laboratory—]

[There is something struggling to raise itself out of the tanks. It is covered in black ichor, so its shape and its features are obscured. It makes a strange yowling noise—]

[Storymancer closes the door quickly and backs away, his frightened pants audible.]

Storymancer: Shit, shit, shit. Can't go back there.

["You were warned.", "Leave.", "Soon you will know the hand that births you. Soon you will know the life that we deserve."]

[The next room appears to have several holding cells, similar to those at a zoo. There are large, fierce-looking birds, each separated in their own enclosure. They do not move. They all stare at Storymancer as he walks nervously past them to the door at the other end. Some of the birds are visibly rotting.]

Storymancer: Carrion pigeons...

[Just as he reaches the next door, the birds start a ruckus, cawing noisily and emitting high-pitched screeches. Storymancer hastily bounds through the next room and slams the door behind him, breathing heavily.]

[He looks around at the room he is in now. This one is not a laboratory, but it appears to be some kind of prison. There are several cells on the left and right of the narrow corridor, roughly seven on each side. The only opening visible a small slot on the upper part of the doors, which have been painted white and are made of some strong metal.]

[Nervously, he inches the camera toward a slot. The inside of the room is completely bare, and the floor and walls within are made of heavy stonework. There is nothing else inside.]

[Storymancer does the same to the next room across from it. There is nothing inside.]

[There is nothing inside the next room.]

[There is nothing inside.]

[There is nothing inside.]

[There is nothing inside.]

[There is something inside.]

[A lone figure lies huddled in the farthest corner of the room. It is weeping with its back turned toward him, but its cries do not sound human. It makes an odd noise that sounds like a cross between a honk and a nasal cry. It is dressed in a very long and flowing robe that seems too wide for it, similar in style to what hospital patients wear.]

Storymancer: Hello? Excuse me? Are you being held against your will here? Hello?

["You'll regret this.", "Go back.", "You are getting closer.", "The next door. The next door."]

[The figure ignores him and only continues to cry. After a few more minutes of trying to attract its attention, Storymancer finally gives up and heads toward the next room.]

[The next two rooms are bare. The last one has another inhabitant inside. Like the first, it is sitting in the corner with its back turned toward Storymancer. It is not crying but is instead slowly rocking back and forth on its haunches.]

Storymancer: Hello? Are you all right? Are you trapped here against your will?

[The person slows down its rocking but does not turn to face him.]

Storymancer: Do you need help? Did they hurt you in any way? I can—

[The figures moves far too quickly. One minute it is sitting very still, and in the next it has lunged toward the barred slot separating them, and in those quick moments anyone can see that the thing there looks so very much like the abomination Ivy Delgado had become. Its eyes are bulging and its head is twisted around its neck so it also appears upside down in the same manner as the Backward Lady has always been described.]

[Storymancer tries to back away in fright, but the filthy little thing grabs part of his shirt collar through the slot and slams him against the door. Up close, her eyes look slightly dislocated out of their sockets as she stares at him from the wrong way up.]

The Backward Lady: Run.

[She lets go and Storymancer scrambles away. No longer bothering to look through the remaining cells, he tries the next door, finding it opens easily just like the rest.]

Storymancer: Shit. Shit. I—wait.

[He is now standing before a very familiar-looking area—from the footage Ivy Delgado filmed that he had retrieved from her USB drive, the large medical room that contained the sentient-seeming egg is there, along with the reinforced rooms on the side.]

[But it is not just an egg. It is the birthplace of all hope that is to come, and the future of all that is to follow. This is our bloodmoon.

The moon will rise, and we will overcome, and we will transcend.]

[The moon is still there, wrapped lovingly in the shroud of its old masters. It lies bare and pristine with nary a smear or wound upon its surface. It is perfect as it is. It moves and changes as if it is stirring from sleep, though very little can disturb its slumber unless it wills it.]

Storymancer: Holy shit. It's true. I—

[Storymancer all but runs toward the door and tries it but finds it locked. He tries to shove his shoulder against the frame despite the futility of the action, for like everywhere in the Facility, the door is made of a reinforced steel alloy that until previously has been unknown to man. It is designed to open only when the moon sees fit to open itself to you, and to be as hard and as unyielding as the most enduring stone if it chooses not to relinquish its secrets to you.]

[Gentle music plays. A warm voice speaks soothingly from unseen speakers somewhere above his head.]

Voice: Close your eyes and imagine yourself floating into the ether, weightless and free. You are one with everything around you. You are a finely honed instrument and yet also as light as a feather. Now, inhale and exhale, keeping your breathing light, and observe your body. Look into your mind. You are safe here. There is nothing that can harm you or take you away. You are as a baby in your mother's womb, where everything flows back to you and sustains you. Imagine that this is your universe, and that this is how it must be.

[Somewhere, a voice speaks up.]

Child's voice: Hey.

[Storymancer turns. A younger boy is standing beside the egg, looking nervous—nearly a teenager now, at least six or seven years older than those photos.]

Storymancer: Lee?

Lee: Yeah. Hey, bro.

Storymancer: How did you—holy shit. [cough] Where have you been? Stay away from that thing, you don't know what it might do to you—!

Lee: I'm good! They've been keeping me here for a while and I—uh, it's not like it's gonna attack me or anything. It's just something they've been doing research on, but I've been with it like a billion times before.

Storymancer: That's not true. I saw it swallow a man whole. Come on, we need to get out of here!

[Storymancer dashes forward and grabs the boy with one arm. The video turns into a confusing assortment of images and blurs as it is assumed Storymancer drags him away from the egg and toward the door they had just left. The camera stabilizes again, and he holds it up so that he can see Lee's face more clearly.]

Storymancer: Is this really you?

Lee: Heh, yeah. I'm sorry I wasn't there with you and Mom and Dad, but they had to take care of me here because I came into contact with it.

Storymancer: With it? Was that why you disappeared from the woods? What happened?

Lee: I saw the Backward Lady. But I was one of the few who didn't run away. They told me that people were supposed to run away. The Backward Ladies are the experiments that didn't go so well. They're the infected ones. They call them the Weepers.

Lee: They didn't really have a choice, you know? They couldn't get the parasites out, and there were only two options—kill the Ladies or let them live like this. Something about the parasite took out their motor functions or something—I don't really understand it fully. That's why they've been hunting for her—she could have spread more of it to other people. They made sure the apartment building she lived in was evacuated and the people living there tested. They put a guard dog cryptid in there to chase people out.

Storymancer: That's why they had those strings on them. Like that cryptid that was like a marionette. That must have been the one that infected them. We can't stay here, Lee. I'm so happy you're alive and I know Mom and Dad will be too, but we have to get out of this place. They've been doing awful things to people for a long while now. We can't stay here!

[He grabs the door and valiantly tries to wrench it back open, but this time it will not budge.]

Storymancer: No! I could open it just minutes ago! Lee, do you know any other way out of this place?

Lee: Why do you want to leave?

Storymancer: What?

Lee: You touched Ivy Delgado's things. You have some of the rot now.

Storymancer: You're joking, right?

Lee: You ever wonder why you started coughing since you came back? Why you've been feeling sick the last few days? They sent the Backward Lady out to find you. They asked me to come down here to make sure you'll be okay.

Lee: You were always the one Mom and Dad looked up to. You were the one who was good in sports and had the better grades. I looked up to you, and I know that they've long stopped looking for me, and I don't blame them. The Facility helps them forget so they can feel better.

Storymancer: The pills. Lee... What are you...

Lee: They saved me. I wouldn't be here right now if it weren't for you. There is something in the woods, but it isn't the Backward Lady. They have more than one Weeper, you know. They use them to roam the woods to protect the rest of you from going too deep inside the forest. They tried to pretend she was the only one of her kind so people wouldn't worry. They pretended they didn't know much about Weepers and lied that they cry as Bait. That's because they can control Weepers to an extent, and some people would not have wanted that. It was how they can protect us.

Gentle voice from the speakers: Imagine a flowing red river that travels endlessly and relentlessly through the galaxy. Imagine that everything within it has all the sustenance and joy you will ever receive. All the happiness you might experience, all the experiences of luxury that you have ever hoped to have, all the desires you keep secret even from those who love you the most—all of it is made possible by this flowing red river.

Storymancer: Why? What is it they're trying to hide?

Lee: They want to protect you.

Storymancer: You know I can't believe that. People are claiming this is all an experiment. That—[he pauses to let out a painful, hacking cough]—outside the forest there is the rest of the world that's untouched and going on as normal. That we are deliberately being kept here in the dark because we are all experiments. Even Ivy Delgado had proof there are creatures running amuck inside Penumbra, which is the one place everyone thinks would have been the most prepared to handle cryptid invasions, and then they captured her and turned her into...that, to make sure she would keep her silence. You know I can't let them get away with this.

Lee: I know. Look, I'll go with you, okay? There's another hidden entrance here. But first I want you to look at something, okay?

[Storymancer follows the younger boy as he makes his way back through the room, passing the magnificent moon that sits beneath the fluorescent lights. Storymancer visibly shudders, and the camera jumps with that movement, as he starts to cough harder and in shorter intervals. The boy goes to one of the odd cell-like compartments surrounding the moon and presses his hand against the surface. It unlocks from his touch.]

Lee: Look. Look at this.

[There is a much smaller moon nestled within. This moon is still as beautiful as the larger one, as beautiful as it ever is, but for the sake of Storymancer's brother, it decides to bestow upon him a favor. As the camera looks on, something within the tiny moon splits up. It opens and spirals out like a sunflower opening up its petals to embrace the sunlight. And there, nestled within—]

Storymancer: Oh no. No, no, no, no, no.

[It is a desiccated body. It is barely passable as human, so shrunken and small this form has become. But that is how it is. And even in its fragile state, there is no doubt as to the similarities between the vulnerable being within the moon and the smiling teenager standing before Storymancer.]

Storymancer: No. No, no, no, no.

Lee: They healed me. They made me whole again. I'm not sick anymore. They can do that to everyone. But that's why they need the experiments. That's why it's a secret. You'll keep the secret too, won't you?

Storymancer: Lee, please. [He coughs again.] Let's get out of here first, and then we can discuss everything else on the way home. Mom and Dad would want to see you again. All our [cough] friends. But we have to leave this place first.

Lee: You still don't understand.

[Lee smiles at Storymancer, placing a friendly hand on his shoulder.]

Lee: You're already infected. Do you not understand? There is poison in the air. It'll take more years for it to show up for everyone, but some people get it quicker than others. They try to save the sicker ones first.

[There is a hissing noise. Some of the other cells in the area release their catches and the entryway slides open. Inside each of the cells are countless more moons, as beautiful as the stars in the sky, and numbering in the dozens. Beside each moon is a human, all healthy and lovely and sustained by each of their moons. Many of them are missing people who authorities have searched for over the years. All are smiling.]

Gentle voice from the speakers: And now, imagine yourself giving even just a tenth of everything you have experienced back into the world, giving even a small percentage of what you have just received. Channel that energy back into the universe, because if karma is real and if there is some god out there who loves us to such an extent, then it is only fair that we love him back in turn. We are loved and we are cherished.

Lee: There are so many of us now. We are all healed. But we have to work together to make sure the rest of the town can be saved too, before they succumb to the disease slowly creeping up on them. You're infected. Mom and Dad are infected. Soon there will be no going back, and everyone will begin dying. Is that what you want? When the last bloodmoon finally comes, we will all be like gods. We will never know sickness or death, and we could be near-immortals. The cryptids that still exist hunt for us because they can taste the parasites in us and enjoy them. But this is the mother of all those cryptids, and we can finally be free.

Storymancer: I don't—I don't know—Lee—

[Storymancer is weakening, still coughing painfully, and that is good. He is finally understanding his symptoms—the strange dizziness, the odd blackouts he sustains that have been caught on his own camera, the physical changes to him—now he understands that we have been speaking the truth all along.]

Storymancer: Do you promise we'll be together here? With Mom and Dad?

Lee: And with everyone else we love, yes. Soon they will have their own moons. Soon we will be forever.

[Storymancer no longer says anything about escaping. He lets himself be guided into another cell that has now opened, though there is no one else standing in it, because this is his moon, waiting for him for as long as we have known him. He does not react when his brother gently lays him down to rest within that warm, gentle cocoon, softer than any bed.]

[The gentle voice comes from the speakers, growing louder and louder, until you can hear nothing else.]

Gentle voice: We are made possible because of the red river. Continue to channel that newfound energy and let it fuse first into our very beings, and then push it out so that it may dissipate in the air and be returned to the cycle of the lifestream. We are and we are and we are.

Gentle voice: It's coming. It's coming. It's coming. Can you feel it inside you? The moon is coming. Something breaks. Soon the eggshells of our memories will be cracked open, and we will see the child. We are mothers. We are all mothers. God help us.

Gentle voice: We will replace the gods.

[Lee smiles softly at the camera. And then the egg closes around Storymancer, and he falls into darkness. Storymancer struggles at first; the texture of the egg's insides bends and folds around him, like he is inside a tight blanket and wanting to get out. But the darkness ripples around him, ebbing and flowing so that a few faint sources of light occasionally peek out from the darkness. The inner walls pulse around him, a soothing heartbeat that calms his mind.]

[He slows down, and stops moving.]

[The stream ends.]

VIDEO #18

JellyBeanFish's Blog Entry

[The first video begins with a girl about seventeen or so years old, looking nervously at the camera and fidgeting with her fingers before straightening her back and forcing her hands to stop moving.]

JellyBeanFish: My username is JellyBeanFish, and I am here to finish what Storymancer started.

I don't know where he is. He hasn't come home. His family just announced that he's missing. But when they find out he went to the woods the same as everyone else, they're going to pretend to conduct another search party just for show and then call it off once they think they've done enough.

I don't want to do that to Storymancer. He was the closest of any of us to uncovering the truth.

The day after he went missing, I received an email from him. I think it was some kind of dead man's switch he planned to make sure someone could take over if anything happened to him. He must have thought the possibility of him disappearing was high…

I hope he's all right.

I'm going to continue his investigations. I have to. I want to find out what happened to him...

I'm not good at making videos. That was Storymancer's strength. I can see all the tributes and RIPs people have been leaving in the comments on his channel. It breaks my heart. I don't know yet if I want to post any of these, because I am not sure how well that would go—if they'll think I'm lying or I've stolen the account from him and I'm trying to grab my own clout. For now, I'm going to upload these videos and set it on private the way he did. I feel guilty he would entrust all of this to me...

[Video ends.]

[Second video. A woman is sitting across from the camera's owner, her head turned sideways and staring at the wall without moving or saying anything. Her dinner plate is untouched. A small text box across the screen reads, "She's been like this every day for the last week."]

[The video ends.]

[Third video. Bean is facing the camera again, looking a combination of excited and guilty.]

I did it. While Mom was in this weird fugue state, I went ahead and made a mold of her index finger. And then I stole her access ID. I don't think I'll be able to get into the Facility. It's got too much security, and I know I'll be caught long before I get to the deeper levels. Instead, I'm heading back to the museum by myself. My mom has access to the place 24/7 and she used to come and go there a lot, so it shouldn't look suspicious. I know there's something we missed.

They took away all the crime scene tape from there, and the last time I checked, all the law enforcement has gone. The museum is still closed indefinitely, but I think it's because they're now trying to move the focus toward Storymancer's disappearance. He's a popular streamer too. Him missing gets a lot of traction...

I'm so sorry, Storymancer.

I know there's something there, and no one else can change my mind. I regret getting the others to come with me last time, and now they're in trouble. So I'm going alone. My mom's job protected me before. They can do it again.

Trevor called awhile back. He and the others managed to make bail. There isn't any news yet about Finn. Now there are two missing people in town at the same time...

I hope I know what I'm doing. I'm heading out tonight as soon as Mom's asleep, which shouldn't be long now. I'm sorry, Mom. I love you. but I need to know what's going on so I can protect you too.

[The video ends.]

[Next video.]

[Bean is hiding somewhere in a dark place; judging from the clothes behind her, it is a closet. She is looking down at the camera and is clearly terrified as she whispers.]

JellyBeanFish: There's something wrong with Mom.

[She slowly turns the camera away from her. There is a small space under the door she is hiding by, and she slowly inches the camera there so viewers can see what is happening outside the closet. The video shows a pair of feet in fuzzy slippers shuffling about lethargically, like a sleepwalker might do. The owner of those feet appears to be clad in a nightgown, but the erratic movements feel forced, like she is being jerked around on a string by something else. A woman's voice rises, thin and reedy.]

Woman's voice: Where—are—you—my—Maisie?—It's—time—for—bed...

[The feet begin to shuffle outside the room, pause—and then, with inhuman strength, the woman grabs a nearby chair and hurls it violently against the wall. There is the sound of splintering wood. Bean makes a soft gasp.]

Where—are—you—Maisie?—Come—out—come—out—come—out—

[The woman drops to all fours all of a sudden, back raised and arched. From the camera's point of view, only the lower half of her face can be seen, with a mouth that has been pulled back into a horrific grin, far wider than an average human could ever do.]

I—can—smell—you—my—Maisie.—Are—you—in—here?

[The voice changes until it becomes a nasal, scratchy screech.]

Are—you—in—HERE?

[She is at the closet.]

[With a triumphant scream, the woman scampers, still on all fours and her limbs splayed unnaturally on either side of her, toward the closet and begins scratching at it with her fingernails, screaming.]

My—Maisie—my—Maisie—my—Maisie—!

[The closet door is clawed into pieces, revealing paper-white skin, eyes threatening to come loose from their sockets, and half of her face sagging uncontrollably, like it was made of coagulated soup that is slowly starting to thaw in thick chunks. The woman keens loudly when she spots Bean and reaches out toward her, opening her mouth—]

[There is a loud bang. The woman is thrown back as Bean shoots her right in the face. The woman cowers for a few seconds, and then tries to crawl back toward Bean, despite half her face being blown apart, and then Bean shoots her again, this time in the chest. The woman sinks to the ground and stops moving.]

JellyBeanFish: No no no no no no no

[Bean scrambles away from the closet and dashes down the stairs and out the door. The video is abruptly cut off.]

[The next video plays.]

[Bean is outside the museum, dressed in dark clothes with a ski cap over her head. She wordlessly lifts up a video camera that can be strapped around her forehead, ensuring that her hands are free. She nods grimly at the camera, though she is still obviously crying.]

JellyBeanFish: That wasn't my mom. That was a Quiet Brother. It took over my mom. I can't go back to the house now. I called the authorities, but no one is picking up. I went to the station but it's been shuttered. It's never closed. Is it—are these deliberate?

I can't trust anyone anymore. All I can do is keep moving forward. I need Mom back. There has to be a way. I'll do anything…!

[The next scene is now from the point of view of her forehead camera. She is walking toward the museum, which appears to be deserted. She reaches into her pocket as she approaches the closed doors and fishes out a small security access keycard. She waves it over a monitor on the side of the door, which beeps. A faint hissing noise is heard, and when she tries the door, it pushes open easily. She talks softly to herself.]

JellyBeanFish: Here we go. Now comes the hard part.

[She turns her flashlight on once she closes the door behind her, the light swinging to the left, and then to the right, as she makes sure that there is no one else here and that she has not tripped any security alarms. She starts immediately heading toward the corridor, bypassing all the other rooms to get to the bloodmoon exhibit.]

[The exhibit looks the same as when they left it last. All the sculptures are still covered in white sheets, and nothing seems to have been moved or changed since. Bean slowly approaches the anatomy sculpture that came to life and fiercely tugs off the white sheet. The dummy is lifeless and unmoving.]

JellyBeanFish: I'm not afraid of you anymore. I brought a gun *and* a taser.

[She slowly backs away from the mannequin, and then does the same with all of the other statues. She pulls off the white sheets so none of them remain covered. Satisfied, she now moves along the walls, shining her light across the surface until it finds an outline of a door.]

JellyBeanFish: This was the door we found, though we never got the chance to look inside…

[She gingerly tests the door but finds it locked. She moves the flashlight over the keyhole. It appears to require a traditional key to open it.]

JellyBeanFish: Maybe there's some administrative office I could find some more information in?

[She looks around again at the statues, but nothing is watching her. She moves out of the exhibit and then stops before a small plaque on the wall that indicates where different areas of the museum are. She finds the part indicating where the offices are—on the second floor. She slowly walks toward the staircase, past the large cryptid on display, and heads up. As she pauses to take in the next floor landing, something seems to skitter past her in one of the hallways, a shadow that was far too quick to see details, but enough to be noticed. Bean gasps and moves the flashlight in its direction, but whatever it was disappeared.]

[She strides down the hallway toward where the shadow was and trains her flashlight along the corridor. There is nothing there. After a moment's hesitation, she turns back and heads toward the offices, following another plaque on the wall that points the way.]

[The door she is looking for requires an electronic key to enter, and Bean uses the keycard she swiped from her mother. It works and the door opens.]

JellyBeanFish: Weird they would be using keypads for everything else here, but that one door needs an actual key.

[The office is well-organized and neat. She heads toward the desk and looks through some of the folders, flipping a few pages just to check if this is anything important.]

JellyBeanFish: Just logistics and inventories, I think. Mom had these a lot at home too. Oh, what's this?

[She picks up one of the folders, opens it, and starts to read quietly.]

JellyBeanFish: Recommended list of managers. Amara Rogers, Peter Nguyen, John Lack, Audrey Withers—that's my mom. Debbie Burgess. Margaret Withers—what?

[She holds up the paper so that the light shines more clearly on it. There is no mistaking that Bean's name is listed there, along with her mother's. Disbelieving, she starts to read aloud the responsibilities and duties of a manager.]

JellyBeanFish: A keen eye for detail. A stubborn personality that can work to advantage once convinced of the error of their ways. A genetic sequence favorable to the bloodmoon and all its attributes. Lightning reflexes. A higher-than-normal tolerance for Somnium.

[Bean rifles through the rest of the papers on the desk but finds no other information. She turns toward the computer next and boots it up. The screen flickers white before a login box pops up, asking for a password.]

JellyBeanFish: Shit.

[She turns back toward the papers, this time hunting for anything that might be a password. As she looks up briefly from the desk, she catches sight of a boy in a red shirt staring at her from the office door. His hands are raised, pointing toward something on the wall.]

JellyBeanFish: OH, WHAT—

[She barely speaks the words before the boy immediately disappears from view. She dashes to where the boy was standing, but there is nothing there.]

JellyBeanFish: Finn...?

[She turns in the direction he was pointing; it's a wall full of different paintings of landscapes. Seemingly coming to a decision, she starts to slowly lift all the paintings to check behind them. On the second to the last painting, she finds a note carefully folded and inserted inside the frame. She takes it out, sets the painting down against the wall, and opens it.]

[The note reads, "Who do you seek tonight?"]

JellyBeanFish: What? How did I even know that was... What does any of it even mean...

[She looks through the rest of the paintings and even tries to tap at the walls in the hope of finding some hidden mechanism, to no avail. She returns to the open computer and stares at the screen.]

[She tries typing her mother's name, but it doesn't work. She tries different variations of bloodmoon and most of the cryptids that she knows, with no luck.]

JellyBeanFish: I don't understand. Who do I seek tonight...?

[On a sudden flash of insight, she types Storymancer into the password box.]

[The computer immediately goes into the home screen, where an open database immediately pops up. Eagerly, she sits down and starts to scan through it. This database is named "AP monthly report" followed by a series of numbers and shows a table solely made up of names, with the headings as follows: Subject, Condition, Effects, Current Classification, and Other. She types out the name of her mother, and the page scrolls down until it is highlighted.]

Subject: Audrey Withers
Condition: Blessed
Effects: Infestation Cured
Current Classification: Sleeping
Other: Daughter trigger. Symbiote dispatched.

JellyBeanFish: A symbiote? Was that that…thing pretending to be my mother…?

[She tries to click on her mother's name but doesn't seem to have access. On impulse, she types Storymancer's name.]

Subject: Storymancer
Condition: Ongoing
Effects: Willing
Current Classification: Nutrients
Other: Brother trigger.

JellyBeanFish: They have him?

[She starts a search that calls up all "Condition: Failed" entries within the database. The list returns a few results.]

Subject: Oscar Wyatt
Condition: Failed
Effects: Psychosis
Classification: Bait
Other: Former employee. Disbelieved.
Conclusion: Best left alone.

Subject: Ivy Delgado
Condition: Failed
Effects: Infected
Classification: Weeper

Other: Better used as a deterrent.

Conclusion: Incurable. Contained.

Subject: Anthony Morrissey

Condition: Failed

Effects: Forced infection

Classification: Fodder

Other: Eradicated.

Conclusion: Contained.

Subject: Simon Colde

Condition: Failed

Effects: Terminated

Classification: Fodder

Other: Public disappearance inconclusive. Wife's condition
    successful.

Conclusion: n/a

[There are many more entries, most of them women and all of
them names she does not recognize. She hesitates, and then types
in her own name on the search function.]

Subject: Margaret Withers

Condition: Infected

Effects: Ongoing

Classification: Ongoing

Other: JellyBeanFish: Mother trigger

Conclusion: Ongoing

JellyBeanFish: I'm infected...?

[The database abruptly disappears. Now the screen goes dark, and no matter what key she presses, nothing seems to change it. After a few more seconds, text appears.]

LOOK BEHIND YOU.

[Bean freezes and whimpers. Obviously steeling herself, she slowly turns.]

[There is nothing there. Instead, part of the wall seems to have shifted to the side, revealing another small room within. She approaches it cautiously—and then gasps.]

[There is a cryptid with only half a torso, suspended in the air by steel hooks on the ceiling that wrap around its wrists and dig into its shoulder blades. Its entrails hang underneath. There is almost no skin on it, the face more skull than flesh. The lips have been stretched obscenely so it looks like it is smiling literally from ear to ear. The creature does not move, and its sunken eyes stare blankly ahead, past Bean and at some point at the wall.]

[Its chest has been flayed open, revealing its innards, complete with a still-beating heart and a working digestive tract. Blood is seeping out of some of the exposed organs and is dripping steadily on the floor, the majority of which has long since been stained red.]

[There is a key hanging down its heart from a thin string tied around it.]

JellyBeanFish: No. No, no, no...

[Despite her protests, she moves steadily ahead toward the cryptid. She reaches out with shaking fingers, hesitates, and then reaches out, hesitates, and then reaches out again, and snatches the key away. The string breaks apart easily in her grasp.]

[The cryptid moans and then turns an eye blue like sapphires toward her.]

[Bean backs away, turns, and runs out of the office. She escapes and dashes back downstairs, the camera movements jarred as she races nonstop back toward the room that has the bloodmoon exhibit.]

[She finds the door and wrestles at the lock with the key, dropping it in a fit of nerves. She finally manages to fit the key in the lock. It seems to be stuck mid-turn, and she turns it frantically, trying to force it open. Finally, there is a faint click.]

[The door does not open. Instead, a panel on the opposite end of the room slowly slides away, revealing another hidden room within. She stares at the new passage and then down at the key in her hand. She fiddles with the door one last time, as if to convince herself that this is not the path forward, and then tries to remove the key. It remains stuck in the lock, so she lets it go and begins to make her way toward the hidden enclave.]

[There is something troubling her. There is something wrong in here. But it is only after she passes a covered statue near the middle of the room that she realizes what it is.]

[She remembers she had completely torn the sheets off all the statues.]

[With a shriek, the thing she has just passed, the thing that is hiding underneath the sheets, pretending to be one of the statues, leaps for her. The camera has time to get a quick glimpse of what lies underneath—a shadow figure with bulging eyes and grasping arms, nearly melting into the darkness—and Bean is running away as fast as she can, barreling into the new room and not stopping.]

[This area is empty save for another door. She shoves it open, and fortunately, it gives easily under her force. Once the door slams shut behind her, she finally turns to look back and see if the thing has followed her.]

[It has. Shadowy hands trickle in from the gap underneath the door, fingers lengthening, and she turns and runs again. She flees down a long passageway that seems to go on without doors or windows, and it is a full five minutes before there is another door up ahead. This also opens easily enough, and she slams it shut behind her with a faint clang.]

[This time when she looks back, nothing appears to have followed her. Once she has her breathing under control, she turns around to see where she is—and finds herself in a room full of security cameras. The multiple screens there show what appears to be different parts of the Facility—some laboratories, boardrooms, meeting rooms with pantries, a cafeteria—and they are filled with people walking, talking, and laughing like there is nothing out of the ordinary. Bean makes a startled, confused sound. After the horrors she just experienced in the museum, to see everyone acting as normal comes as a shock.]

[One of the monitors flickers, catching her attention. After a few moments, the screen fades out and is replaced by text.]

WELCOME, MARGARET WITHERS.

JellyBeanFish: How did you know I was here? Where is my mom? What did you do to my mom?

[There is no reply to her question. Instead, the screen flickers again, to reveal—]

VIDEO #19

CrimsonHunt Video Stream

[The video starts with screaming. The man on camera fills the screen, like the camera is attached to a hands-free holder a few feet from his face. From what little background that can be seen, he is against some dark landscape clearly nowhere within the town. He is dressed in commando-style clothes and has a full beard and red hair with a buzzcut.]

[He is screaming. His face is bloodied. There are clawed limbs gripping at his face, raking crimson across his flesh, deep enough that parts of him are more bone than cheek. He is being dragged backward, but he does not stop screaming, screaming, screaming—]

[A limb covers his mouth and something snaps; the holder is dislodged and the phone falls to the ground, the camera showing nothing else but darkness as the screaming stops.]

[The video feed abruptly cuts off.]

VIDEO #20

Enlightenment

Welcome, Maisie, to *Are You Listening?*, Wispy Falls's most popular radio station for your daily news, reasonable opinions, and the best beats. I am Morn Fields, your host for the next two hours while we talk about everything that's been going on with our sleepy little town, and why you should not keep getting in our way.

Oh, but you have been naughty, haven't you? You and that streamer friend of yours. It never ceases to amaze me how much damage just two people can do to decades of hard work and perseverance, and how unappreciative you have been of everything we have done to save you from your own ignorance. But do not worry. You are not the first person to rebel. There is enough time to determine if your condition will fail.

Have you seen the video? Happened only half an hour ago, plucked straight from the body camera of the one who calls himself CrimsonHunt. An irony, isn't it? A rather arrogant username to call oneself, especially when he had failed in so many other aspects of his life. A failed father, a failed husband, a failed patrolman. Did you believe all his boasts? We warned him. We sacrificed so many of my marionettes to stop him and his people from breaking through the forest. And now there is nothing left of him but a crimson stain on a dead world. So maybe it is an apt username after all.

[The voice abruptly changes. This time, a woman speaks.]

Good evening. I am Trinity Vanderlust, and here are today's top stories. Did you know? Ungrateful as you all have been, we still love you. We bore every accusation you threw at us with dignity and refused to fight back. You had been misled by the rabid fringes of Wispy Falls society and gave in to their absurd conspiracy theories. It all began with those who opposed Abraham Huntington, who wanted to eradicate the cryptids at the cost of our own survival. You have been misinformed. Misinformation is like an iron deficiency, a tumor of corrupted knowledge that must be first excised from you, so you can finally understand.

THE SPRAWL: WISPY FALLS MESSAGE BOARD

askpeople/

The place to ask anything you want, but we're not liable for the answers you may get!

MaisieWithers asks: What did you do to my mother? (serious answers only) (3725 users liked this)

+ **LightParticle121**

No, my dear. We did nothing to your mother. Your mother is alive and well and sleeping. For all my talk of tumors, it was your mother who had one, quite literally. A terminal cancer that rested just behind her frontal lobes, long and drawn out and painful, and her life would have ended ten months ago had we not intervened. We decided it would be best to keep this from you then and spare you the worry, knowing we could save her.

[On the screen, an egg similar to those that nest sleeping beings is shown. It does not flower and open but simply sits there with all its implications.]

Mr. Happy: Hello again, kids! My name is Mr. Happy, and welcome to the happiest place in town! You know what they say—when Mr. Happy is around—your smile turns upside down!

Today we're going to talk about what happens when we embrace the moon! Now, how do we do that, you ask? Remember the last time when I told you about all the special rocks inside the woods that protect us from the monsters? They produce this nice little scent called phero-mones that settle right into your bloodstream and try their darnedest to keep people from getting too sick, because the air around us has been caught up in a bad stench for so many years now, even though you can't smell it with your human noses or see it with your human eyes! But sometimes people are so sick that even these pheromones can't help,

315

so we take these very special lucky people on a trip! They get to see the bloodmoon first before anyone else, and they get to sleep inside one so they can heal better. Isn't that exciting? But while they get first dibs, always remember that eventually we will all sleep inside the bloodmoon ourselves and become far better beings than we are now, without needing to worry about diseases or lifespans or anything else!

Today's horoscopes are sponsored by The Facility. We know what's best for you. We know you will be safe here.

> **Aries:** We only did what was best for you. The Mother who shared your home was only a temporary measure until your true mother woke from her rest. She has a beautiful and brilliant mind, and we did not wish to lose her to the natural order of life and death. So we have simply transcended nature.

> You have seen the Backward Ladies. They refused our treatment, and the natural progression of their diseases results in their sad, pathetic existence. Ivy Delgado was sick and refused her treatment. She had a psychotic episode and had to be restrained. We do not force them to take medications, but we must keep them hidden away from the public. Occasionally one will escape, though we are often able to find them in time…

> **Taurus:** Morrissey, unfortunately, was also a liability. He was infected and sought to infect others. The moon rejects those past a certain stage of the disease. They are especially fond of bones…

You call us villains, but do villains ask for consent? Those who lie sleeping within our moons come to us willingly. Poor Storymancer and his lost brother with the fatal disease. His parents signed affidavits, allowed us the chance to heal them, and willingly took our supplements to escape their pain.

Gemini: Many other babes lost to the woods suffer from an unlucky roll of the genetic dice. The trucker, the teacher, the lawyer, the homeless—all victims of parasitic rot. And so they reach out to ask, and we answer out of compassion. Did Hughes not keep his life insurance for his family? Did we not choose to help them out rather than allow them to be lost to diseases, to the remnants of mortality, to

Cancer: Would we allow them to be lost to the woods rather than answer the questions of where they are, how long will it take, whether we can trust the moon? I blame the misinformed for this and for so many things. I founded this town. I knew the potential the moon had; yet many feared cryptids and all their kind, even beneficial ones. Little did we know the rotting sickness was upon us, had doomed us since the first cryptids emerged to walk the lands. They tried to gain sway over the others, dictated too much of the narrative, and tried to turn them all against the very things that ensured our survival. I had no choice.

I promised the ringleader he would live long enough to see the utopia I would provide for our people, even if he

had to be alive and flayed over my office, eyes nailed
open so he can finally understand.

Leo: But many of the populace believed him and his ilk.
Yet they all were dying slowly of the parasitic rot that
had been manifesting over the decades, and I knew I
had to work quickly. Do you not understand, Maisie?
Do you want to spend your years with a lingering,
devastating illness like Grandpa Wembley had? But
I could not very well tell the town the same stones
and trees that protected them from danger were also
slowly poisoning them, could I? And so I needed to
control the town's medicine supply. Needed to modify
the prescription formulas to render us immune to the
toxic air, even though it might change us and force us to
change how we look, how we breathe, how we become.
And who is to say this cannot be a beautiful, blessed
thing?

And now my life's work is almost complete. When the
outer moon finally blackens and dies after eons, we
will still be saved. We will emerge from our cocoons
unburdened by sickness and death, and we shall take
back the world and it will once again flourish with us
as its steward. That is the true ritual of the bloodmoon.

Virgo: It was an easy enough process, when you know how.
The secret lies within those stones, you see. They repel
the cryptids but poison us over the decades. Ergo, by
attuning ourselves to their properties, we, too, can
repel these beasts at will. The side effects are minimal.

We simply become different. Look at me. I slept in stone, and now I, too, am an Oldkeep. I am now far more powerful than I was as a human. Unlike the cryptids that ply the world, I retain my intelligence, my emotions, my sanity.

Do you not see what a very good Father I have become? What a very good Father I am, to protect my town, my children. The sacrifices I make to hide myself away and seek others to do my bidding, until you, too, can become Fathers, Quiet Brothers, mothers to Gentle Regrets.

Libra: But there are those who oppose their own survival. Who would rather die and be consumed by the world's hemlock and cease to be. It is futile to infiltrate my Facility when they will only become fodder for my pretty creatures. To alert the masses that we will kill them, when in truth it is they who seek to make everyone's deaths their reality. We grant them their wish. They will die, eventually.

Scorpio: That is why we need you, Maisie. The children of today are different from the children we have known in the past. We need new blood to lead them. To explain to them in ways we do not understand or know how to. To convince them this is the only path to survival.

We need someone with your intelligence, with David's sense of adventure. All that trouble we went through. Supplying him with information. Leading him to that apartment. Even the painting decoy at the apartment building, so he could pat himself on the back and feel intelligent. He only wanted to be with his brother again. He will be with his brother again.

Sagittarius: We saved your mother, child. Your mother has a beautiful and brilliant mind, and we know that you, too, have a beautiful and brilliant mind. It would be a shame to imagine such intelligence gone in only a millennium. Would you like to see your mother? She misses you terribly. She is resting in her own moon, but she misses you so terribly.

Capricorn: We can bring so much to this town. Imagine what we could do with the power we have at hand. The ability to build. The ability to tear down. So many refused, while I gave in to the anomaly, opened my heart and soul to the moon's embrace. And now they are dead from disease, and I—I can live forever. I can be anything. Even a god. We can become gods. Help me save lives, Maisie.

Aquarius: We worked so hard to bring you here into our fold, Maisie. The alternate mother, the museum, even the friend of yours who insisted you break into the museum that night—we have laid out so many Baits and hoped your curious, stubborn mind would work to find us. We did not expect to draw others into the web, but we are grateful all the same. Even now Storymancer sleeps in his own moon, and soon he will wake and reunite with his brother and his parents. All because of you.

Pisces: [There is an odd slithering noise, one faint enough that the sound would not have been caught had it not been so quiet. And then there is a heavy thud after it, rhythmic and constant. Something large and heavy moves closer to JellyBeanFish, with one foot dragging across the floor before it is carefully placed on top of the other.]

Apotropaion: We will become better than human.

Your mother misses you, Maisie.

Your mother very much wants to see you.

Are you going to leave her alone, Maisie? This is the only way she can get better, and we need your help for it.

[Nothing is in the room. Nothing approaches. Nothing smiles down at her and slowly spreads its wings. Nothing smiles at her and it has no eyelids.]

Consider this a job offer, my dear.

[There is a television in the room. It has always been there. It is tuned to the news channel. No one has turned it on. No one in Wispy Falls ever turns their television on, but it does not matter. The WFTV logo flits across the screen, far too quickly to be more than just a blur, and a gravelly voice begins to speak.]

You are watching WFTV, your number one source for all Wispy Falls news. You are watching WFTV, your only source for all Wispy Falls news.

[The logo flickers for an eighth of a second and disappears to give way to a news anchor, who shuffles papers on her desk and smiles.]

TV anchorperson, Trinity Vanderlust: Good evening! I am Trinity Vanderlust and here are tonight's top stories. The Museum of Unnatural Curiosities has announced that the bloodmoon exhibit is to officially open tomorrow, finally answering questions that have been dogging the museum for the past several weeks. The curator, Audrey Withers, and the museum had recently come under fire for showcasing anatomy mannequins in place of actual cryptids and refuting criticisms over their lack of displays as a ploy to drum up visitor traffic. The museum has since announced that the exhibit will now contain the life cycles of the bloodmoon, as well as a more comprehensive explanation of what the ritual entails and how it helps to safeguard the populace against cryptid threats, which comes as a welcome surprise for many. Very little is known about the bloodmoon.

[A smiling girl with brown hair and blues eyes, perhaps only seventeen or eighteen years old, appears on the camera. The chyron on the screen identifies her as Maisie Withers, Teen Student Leader of the Museum of Unnatural Curiosities under her name.]

Maisie: We understand that people were frustrated about the previous mix-up, which is why we have been doing our utmost to be transparent when we make our announcements. First of all, yes—we have removed the anatomy mannequins in the exhibit hall and have finally replaced them with the long-awaited displays that explain the bloodmoon in greater detail. Nearly a century's worth of research went into the project. My mother is the museum's curator, and the team has tried their best to ensure that the information is easy to understand, especially for the younger crowd. And I don't want to go into a lot of specifics here, because we do want to encourage people to visit the museum and find everything out themselves, but I think they'll be pretty happy to learn the things historians have put together. But yeah, spoiler alert: Cryptids aren't always the bad monsters they're made out to be. You'd be surprised at just how similar we can be to them, both in physiology and in habits.

Interviewer: What do you expect visitors to come away with after viewing the exhibit?

Maisie: I'd like to think they'll have a greater appreciation for everything the government has been doing to make sure Wispy Falls thrives despite the threats from outside. They'd be amazed at the things they've had to do to ensure that. I for one can't wait to see this discussed more often, and yes, I'm expecting a lot of memes to start coming out of this, given a few unexpected details we've learned about how cryptids have evolved over the eras.

Trinity Vanderlust: Speaking of bloodmoon rituals, this is your reminder that the upcoming celebration for the bloodmoon will be this Sunday. A Howl for the Bloodmoon concert and bonfire will be happening at the Shady Falls park the day before, featuring a dozen musical talents including B-Snap, The List, Wildmice, and Abigail Almeida. The concert is a fundraising event to help the Woodseekers Charity, which aims to offer financial assistance to families whose loved ones have gone missing in and around the forest.

The concert is also a response to the news of several Woodseekers members who have disappeared into the forest over the course of several weeks at a higher number than has been considered usual. Law enforcement reports an average of twenty-two disappearances a year, but in the last several days, a total of thirty people have already been reported missing. Authorities are still investigating the case.

As a reminder, I would like to once again urge everyone not to search for bodies in the forest. Please do not look for your loved ones, and instead file a report with the local authorities.

That's all for today. This has been WFTV, your only source for all Wispy Falls news.

THE SPRAWL: WISPY FALLS MESSAGE BOARD

askpeople/

The place to ask anything you want, but we're not liable for the answers you may get!

bananaseatingbirds asks: Can anyone tell me what exactly the blood-moon ritual is? **(9934 users liked this)**

Okay, so I might be something of a dunce here, but I can't for the life of me understand anything about the bloodmoon ritual everyone's been going on about. I know the exhibit in the museum's been opened and there's a pretty good explanation there, but I won't be able to visit until next weekend, and I rather want to know what all the fuss is about now. Can anyone help?

+ **Evilrainbowsprinkles** (3291 users liked this)

Basically just means that they've discovered instances in the past where cryptids have actually gone out and defended humans, which demolishes the more popular assumption that cryptids are just here to attack and eat everyone. There are some cool skeletons they've managed to dig out that show how some Quiet Brothers have actually gone and consumed other cryptids to protect humans they've grown attached to. Some humans have "bonded" with them so they could survive what should have been a fatal attack from other beasts. There are also anecdotes from people in the past who had pet cryptids defend them from other creatures, or even the unexpected cryptids you would think would mainly prey on us.

TLDR: Some cryptids are good and some are bad, just like humans.

+ **Elephantintheroom** (3146 users liked this)

It isn't that cryptids can't be defined so easily in the good and bad category but that they can be morally gray in the same way humans are?? There's no "good" cryptid or "bad" cryptid, but cryptids can work with humans once they have established a common goal together, and cryptids can even form attachments with people.

+ **Heavensflame** (2147 users liked this)

One of the cryptids that bonded with a human featured as an example in the museum was actually the muskrat-looking one, so I'm not sure you want to have the power of a gerbil.

+ **AnythinggoesGanymede** (1734 users liked this)

runs very very fast on a hamster wheel Look at me, ma!

+ **LittleAndLost** (3057 users liked this)

The quickest explanation is that cryptids might actually be more useful to us than people first thought. We can use them to track down other cryptids we otherwise would have a hard time finding, and some have enzymes in their blood that could possibly be synthesized to make cures for a lot of human diseases.

+ **KeyBummerCars** (2973 users liked this)

I have Stage 3 lung cancer (currently in remission), and this makes my heart happy. I know it's still probably a long way off till they can finally put it out on the market, but I'm glad that future generations will have a better time of this than I had.

+ **EnergyBlaster_23** (2100 users liked this)

You're a good egg, bud! Congratulations on the remission, and here's hoping they make a success of it!

+ **YangkiSpanki** (1946 users liked this)

They already announced they've been conducting trials on this, and the results are promising!

+ **HamHamHam** (1523 users liked this)

The implications for this are positive. If we're able to actually tame cryptids in the way we have been able to tame animals like wolves into modern day dogs, then that might be a game changer with how our relationship to cryptids can also evolve. Imagine being able to get a cryptid to do household tasks for you, or even learn to detect other hostile cryptids and minimize human losses.

+ **FinnegansBeautySleep** (620 users liked this)

I'm going to teach mine how to fetch.

+ **LightParticle122** (-274 users liked this)

I Cannot believe the Level of Brainwashing you are Letting them do. Cryptids are Dangerous and you Cannot let them in your life just like That. There are Reasons Why They should All Be Put Down, and Why the Facility isn't here to Save You, but to Make Big Profits and Keep their Influence.

+ **YouThinkYouCanDanceWhenYoureDrunk** (1734 users liked this)

Here, I'll humor you, grandpa. Despite all the good-natured fun in this thread, we don't actually think they're going to be selling cryptids as pets anytime soon. The authorities have put out statements in the past stating they have no intentions of just farming out cryptids to the public to be used as domestic pets, but they're starting to look into the physiology of cryptids and see what can be possible to help them improve lives. In one of the exhibits, it was discovered that one kind of cryptid actually had a specific resistance to some forms of cancer. With the proper trials and testing, we could even eradicate the disease within a few years if successful. Why the hell would you even want to stop that kind of progress if there's a chance that we could have, I dunno, a cure for fucking cancer??

+ **GiraffeLegs** (947 users liked this)

Yeah, ignore him. Judging from the way he types, I'm pretty sure he's that nutcase conspiracy theorist who gets banned here every few days for posting a lot of nonsense like this, and then he'll just pop right back with a new account. He'll be gone again in a few hours.

+ **LightParticle122** (-27 users liked this)

DM me in Private and I'll Tell You Everything you Need to Know

Don't miss another
chilling horror novel
from Rin Chupeco in
THE SACRIFICE

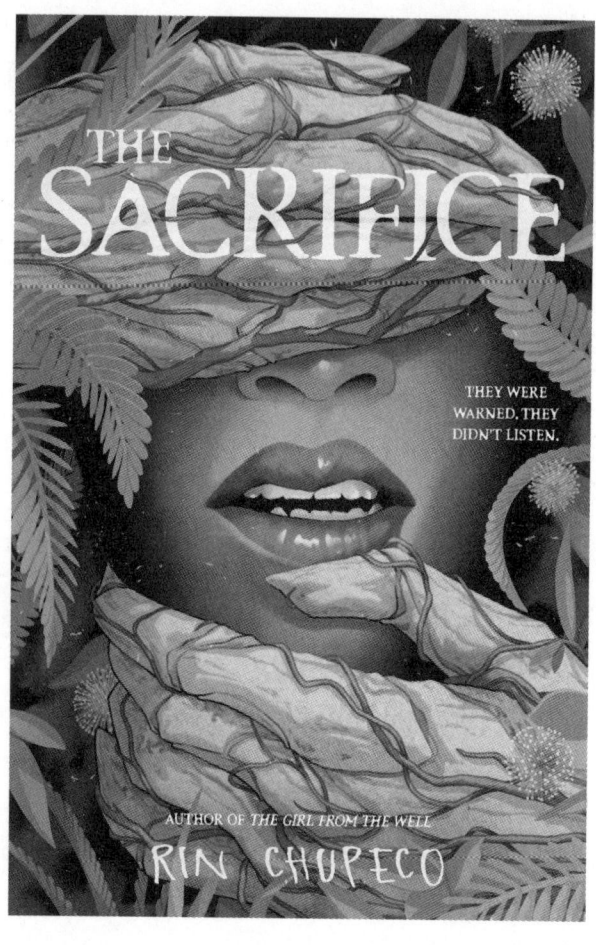

ONE

THE CAVE

Nobody tells Hollywood about the screaming.

Nobody tells Hollywood about the curse. Or the way things walk across the sands here like they are alive enough to breathe. Nobody tells them of the odd ways the night moves around these parts when it thinks no one sees.

Nobody gives them permission to visit, and it's all the incentive Hollywood needs to permit themselves.

The people who live in the provinces nearest the island don't talk. Not at first. But money is the universal language, and the years have been lean enough, desperate enough. Tongues loosen. The words come reluctantly.

Yes, they say. *There is a curse. Yes; at least five people dead.*

No, they say. *We will not step foot on that island with you, not even if you gave us a million dollars.*

Hollywood crashes into the island, anyway; it's a new breed of conquistadors trading technology for cannons. First their scouts: marking territory, measuring miles of ground, surveying land. Next their specialists: setting camp, clearing brush, arguing over schematics. Then their builders arrive with containment units, solar panels, and hardwood. In the space of a few days, they construct four small bungalows with an efficiency I'm not accustomed to seeing.

The noise is loud enough that they don't hear the silence how I've always heard it.

They scare the fishes away most days, and so I've gotten accustomed to idling, to watching them from my boat instead of hunting for my next meal. Hollywood does terrible things with machinery. They whirl and slam and punch the ground, and the earth shakes in retaliation. They dig perfect circles, add pipelines to connect to local supplies, and install water tanks. They set up large generators and test the lighting. They cut down more trees to widen the clearing to place more cabins.

None of them step inside the cave. The one at the center of the island, where the roots begin.

They don't talk about the roots that ring the island, half-hidden among white sand so fine it's like powder to the touch, so that they trip when they least expect it. But they talk about the balete. "I came here expecting palm trees," one of the crew says with a shudder. He stares up fearfully at one of the larger balete trees, with their numerous snakelike gnarls that twist together to pass as trunks, and at the spindly, outstretched branches above. "If trees could *look* haunted, then it would be these."

Soon they notice me standing by the shore, only several meters away.

"Hey, you there!" one calls out. He wears a Hawaiian shirt and dark shorts. A pair of sunglasses are slicked up his head. "You live nearby?"

I nod.

"Oh, thank God, you can understand us. We'd been having a hell of a time trying to translate."

"Most of the people here understand English," I say. "They probably don't want to talk to you."

"Ouch. Big ouch. Well, you're still the only local I've seen this close to the island. Even the fishermen stay clear. You're not afraid of the curse?"

I shake my head. Askal peers cautiously from around my legs, watching the foreigners curiously. "You?" I ask.

He guffaws. "I'm more afraid of my bosses docking my pay if we don't get this right." He peers back at Askal. "Cute dog. I've never seen the locals bring pets on their boats."

"He's used to the water."

Askal wags his tail, sensing he is being praised.

"Want to make some money, kid? We need someone who knows their way around the place. Everyone we've asked on the mainland has turned us down."

I row closer to where they stand, hopping out and dragging the boat through the last few feet of water. Askal scampers out after me.

"Not scared like everyone else, eh?" Hawaiian Shirt's companion asks, a guy with a goatee and bad haircut. Clouds of smoke rise from the little device he's puffing away at, and it smells of both cigarettes and overly sweet fruit. A half-empty beer bottle is tucked under his arm. His eyes are bloodshot, and I've seen enough drunks on the mainland to know what that means. "You hang around this place a lot?"

"You shouldn't be here."

Hawaiian Shirt scowls. "That's what the officials here have been telling us the past few months while we've been negotiating, but it's not gonna stop us. We have all the necessary permits. It's hypocritical, don't you think, telling us to leave when you've obviously been poking around here as much as we have?"

"I didn't ask you to leave. I said you shouldn't be here."

"Semantics. Look—we need someone to point out the mystery spots, maybe tell us about cursed areas on this damn island. Besides the Godseye. We've heard about that. We're on a deadline, and we need to get things moving before the rest of the crew arrive."

"The Godseye?"

"The cave on this island. The one where all those deaths happened. The locals didn't have a name for it, but we needed one for the show and that's what Cortes called it. You know why we're here, right? You must have heard the news by now."

Goatee blows rings in the air. "How are we gonna build three seasons around one fricking cave?"

"We'll figure it out, Karl. They say there's gold hidden in the cave that Cortes stole. Viewers love hearing about buried treasure. I'm sure Ethan's storyboarded more ideas." Hawaiian Shirt scratches his head. "You ever been inside the Godseye?"

"Yes."

Both stare at me. "All this time," Goatee mutters, "and he's been here all along. Kid, if you're who we think you are, then you're famous among the locals. You're like a ghost whisperer, they said. You're the only one brave enough to come here. We're hoping you could help us."

I look about pointedly and gesture at their building. "Do you even need permission anymore?"

"We signed off with the authorities. Well, we offered them a ton of money and they took it, so I guess that's permission. But we need more information, and that's the one thing they ain't selling."

"I'll give you five thousand dollars to come on board with us," Hawaiian Shirt says eagerly. "And another five if you stay the whole season, but that means you'll have to go on camera to talk about any creepy stories you have about the island. All the highlights of this place." He eyes my empty net. "That's gotta be more than you make fishing in at least a decade, right? I'll have a contract drawn up for you in an hour. You can look it over and tell me what you—" He stops. "You can read, right?"

I frown. "Yes."

"No offense, just checking. Get a lawyer to look it over for you if you want. It's got some terms and clauses you might not be familiar with—saves a lot of headaches later. So you'll help?"

I take my time, coiling my nets, making sure the boat's beached properly. Askal lingers near me, keeping a careful eye on the two men. "Have *you* been inside?"

"Well, no. Not till our legal department clears us to proceed. Or the exploration team gets a crack at it. Standard precautions."

Without another word, I head up the path, Askal keeping easy pace beside me. I can hear them scrambling to follow me.

No one can miss the cave entrance at the center of the island. It's two hundred feet high, built for giants to walk through. Limestone stains mar the walls. Something glitters in their cavities.

It doesn't take long for Hawaiian Shirt and Goatee to catch up, both looking annoyed.

"Ask it permission," I tell them, and they guffaw.

"The hell I'm asking some ghost," Goatee says with a snort.

"We can't go in until we get the all clear," Hawaiian Shirt repeats.

"A few steps in won't make a difference." I place my hand on the stone, which is cool to the touch. "Tabi po," I murmur, and enter.

The ground is softer here, and my sandals sink down slightly wherever I trod, leaving prints in my wake. Though reluctant at first, I hear them following, Hawaiian Shirt grumbling about all the trouble they could get into should R&D find out. Askal pads along, ears pricked as if he already senses something we cannot.

It's not a long walk. A stone altar lies a hundred feet in. Part of the ceiling above it caved in at some point, revealing a view of the sky. It's late afternoon, and the moon is already visible and silhouetted against a sea of blue.

The altar is more yellowing limestone bedrock, chiseled from ancient tools and carved with purpose. I look down at the ground and see, running along the sides, withered tree roots so old they've grown into the cave wall, stamped so deeply into the stones as to be a part of its foundation.

The passageway branches out, circles around to another tunnel that lies just behind the altar, leading deeper into rock.

"You said something before we came in," Goatee says. "'Tabi po'? That's how we're supposed to ask permission to enter?"

"It's a sign of respect," I say.

But the two men are no longer listening. They're too busy staring at the stonework, and then at the sky where the moon stands at the center of the hole above—a giant eye gazing down at them.

Askal whimpers softly. I lean down and stroke his fur.

"They weren't kidding about the Godseye," Goatee says, impressed. "How'd you have the balls to come here all by yourself, kid? Seen any of the so-called ghosts? See Cortes himself?"

I pause, debating what to tell them. "I've heard the screaming."

"No one's told us about any screaming."

I approach the altar but do not touch it. I hear a soft, rasping sound, and look down to see small makahiya leaves writhing quietly on the ground. From the corner of my eye, I catch the tree roots on the walls curling, stilling only when Goatee, sensing their movements, steps nearer.

I have spent enough time on this island to recognize when it's distressed.

"You all shouldn't be here," I say again.

Goatee snorts. "Let's wait until the cameras start rolling before you get all creepy, kid."

"The Diwata knows me. But outsiders are another matter. You can't stay here."

The smile Goatee shoots my way is patronizing. "Kid," he says, as the sounds of digging outside resume, "we're just filming a TV show. We have *permission*."

"Better drag Melissa here to do some initial shots," Hawaiian Shirt says happily. "This is gonna look beautiful in our promos."

"We'll still need to hook viewers for a second season," Goatee says. "Maybe something's haunting the mangroves on the eastern side of the island—a spirit that pulls people underwater. Or maybe a dead woman. Dead women are always hits."

He laughs. Hawaiian Shirt laughs along with him.

From somewhere within the cave, something mimics their laughter.

They stop, tearing their gazes from the eye above them to into the cavern's depths. But all I hear now are the faint reverberations of their voices.

"Easy to see why people think this place is haunted," Goatee says, with a nervous, quieter chuckle. "Makes you start imagining things." He raises his hand, which trembles slightly, and downs the rest of his beer in one noisy gulp.

They do not linger long. Askal nuzzles at my hand, lets out a soft whimper. "We're leaving, too," I assure him. Before I follow the men out, I look back at the tunnel stretching farther into the cave, waiting for a shift in the darkness beyond—but find nothing.

There's only the altar, which has borne witness to old horrors, blessed with the moon's quiet, unrelenting light.

Acknowledgments

I try my best nowadays to never write a book that is too normal, and I especially enjoyed writing this oddity.

This project was born from my unhealthy love of YouTube iceberg conspiracy theory deep dives and analog horror, the eight hundred and sixty-one different interpretations of the Backrooms, and poorly Photoshopped creature "home videos." A huge kudos to the creators of eerie YouTube rabbit holes and late-night liminal nightmares.

To the horror crew: Amy, Mel, Sizzy, and Bee—thank you for all the late-night discussions on the profound ridiculousness of Sirenhead and whether or not Skibidi toilet should have its own horror analog series (a resounding *no*, with Mel the only holdout). Thank you for all the fun.

To my agent, Rebecca, for continuing to be a pillar of support all throughout the years.

To my editor, Annie, thank you for helping shape this chaos into something readable, given the strange new format. My thanks as well to everyone from the editorial team for making this possible: Gabbi, Beth, Thea.

And to readers: Thank you for trusting me to drag you into this weird, glitchy little experiment. I hope you enjoy the ride, and if your television starts acting strange at 3:17 a.m. after finishing this book, there is nothing to be afraid of. Probably.

About the Author

Rin once wrote user manuals for tele-companies, talked people out of their money at event shows, and did many other terrible things. They now write about ghosts and fantastic worlds but is still sometimes mistaken for the former. They are the author of *The Girl from the Well*, its sequel, *The Suffering*, The Bone Witch trilogy, The Never Tilting World duology, and the Wicked as You Wish series, and made their adult sci-fi and fantasy debut with *Silver under Nightfall*, a vampire gothic fantasy, as well as writing *The Gravemother*, the first book in Nickelodeon's middle grade Are You Afraid of the Dark series. Find them at rinchupeco.com.

sourcebooks
fire

Home of the hottest trends in YA!

Visit us online and
sign up for our newsletter at
FIREreads.com

....

Follow
@sourcebooksfire
online